THE
REVENGE
YOU
SEEK

USA TODAY & WALL STREET JOURNAL BESTSELLING AUTHOR

TRACY
LORRAINE

THE MISTAKES YOU MAKE

CHAPTER ONE

Letty

"For the record, I think this is a really bad idea," Harley, my little sister, moans from my passenger seat.

"It'll be fine," I grit out through clenched teeth. It's not the first time she's said similar words to me today, and I'm fed up with hearing them.

She scoffs at my response and folds her arms over her chest.

I know she doesn't want to be here. I know she doesn't want to go to this party.

"I told you, you could have stayed at Dad's."

"And leave you alone? Nah, I don't think so."

"I don't need my kid sister tagging along for support."

She turns her narrowed eyes on me.

"He's not going to be there," I assure her for the millionth time.

"It's a Harrow Creek party. They will be there," she warns.

My stomach flips and I fight to keep my expression neutral.

"I've been assured they won't. And if they show up, then we'll just slip out unnoticed."

Harley's eyes burn into the side of my face, but I refuse to look at her and keep my eyes on the road as we make our way to Skylar's house.

It's her birthday weekend and her parents have stupidly left her the house. They think she's having a quiet night with some girlfriends. They have no idea that almost every teenager in Harrow Creek is about to descend on their home.

I haven't been back here to see our dad or my old friends in months, and I'm desperate to rediscover the old me.

It's no great secret that I hate the place, but unfortunately, when Mom found us a new life in the neighboring town of Rosewood, we were forced to leave some of those we love behind—mainly our dad, who for some crazy reason didn't want to leave his beloved trailer and shithole of a place behind.

Harley's knee continues to jiggle nervously in the passenger seat as we drive down the street lined with cars, indicating that tonight's party is well underway.

I eventually find a parking space and kill the engine, but I don't rush to get out.

Butterflies flutter in my belly as all of her concerns about tonight race to the surface.

I need to believe what my friends are telling me and that I'll be able to enjoy my night without looking over my shoulder and being ready to run at any moment. But

Harley is right, the chances of him being here are high, and my decision to try to have a normal night with my old friends could be one of the biggest mistakes I've ever made.

"It's not too late to turn around. We could order a pizza, watch a movie," she offers.

I know she doesn't have a lot of interest in this party. She was only thirteen when we left this place, it was easier for her to leave her friends behind and start over. But at sixteen, I was turning my back on possible lifelong friends. Friends I didn't want to leave behind.

I glance down at my little black dress and suck in a deep breath.

"No. We're going to enjoy our night."

He has ruined enough of my life in the past. I am an adult now. I'm a college student. I should not be running scared from the boy who tried to make my life a living hell.

"Okay," Harley concedes, pulling the handle and shouldering the door open.

A second later, I follow. Locking the car behind me and smoothing down the front of my dress.

I felt good, and I didn't need the looks from a few of the guys loitering outside of Skylar's house to tell me that I looked good. The dress I'm wearing clings to my curves like a second skin, my hair is sleek, hanging down past my shoulder blades, and my makeup is dark, accentuating my gold-flecked dark eyes.

I pull my leather jacket around my torso a little tighter as I catch up with Harley on the sidewalk.

"Ready to party, lil' sis?"

She glances over at me, concern still evident in her eyes, but she forces it down and plasters a smile on her face. She's sixteen now, most would probably say too young for the kind of debauchery happening under the roof of the house in front of us. But we're Creek kids. We grew up surrounded by this. She's already seen worse than what might be happening here tonight. Hell, I was up to all sorts of shit I don't want to even consider Harley getting involved with when I was sixteen.

Shaking my regrets from my head, I take her hand in mine and together we make our way through the crowds to find Skylar and my old group of friends.

Music booms from the speakers someone has set up in the living room, making the floor rattle as we make our way through the kitchen.

"Here," I say, handing Harley a Solo cup with a weak vodka orange inside. Mine, however, isn't so weak. The prospect of bumping into the enemy forces me to splash a little extra alcohol in mine to help take the edge off my nerves.

I drink half down in one go, reveling in the burn as the vodka slips down my throat and begins to warm my belly.

My muscles ache to join the crowd that I know will be in front of the speakers and let go.

College is great. New York is fantastic but still, you can't beat a Creek party.

"Come on, I know where they'll be." I take Harley's hand once more and we push our way through the mass of people toward the living room.

Most pay us little attention as we pass, but a few recognize us and nod or smile in greeting.

There would have been a time when everyone would have spoken to us, but we gave up that right when we packed all our shit and moved.

We're outsiders now, and I feel it more and more every time I come back here.

I see a flash of blonde on the other side of the living area that's been turned into a makeshift dance floor for the night, and I head that way.

"Letty," Skylar squeals the second she sees me, she steps away from the guy she's dancing with and throws her arms around my shoulders. "It's so good to see you." The slur in her voice indicates just how much she's had to drink already, and when she pulls back, I notice her eyes are blown too.

"You too, Sky. It's been too long. Happy Birthday."

"Come on, let me introduce you to the guys." She threads her fingers through mine and drags me toward her group of friends. Most I know from school but there are a couple of new additions, including the guy who quickly drags her away from me and wraps her in his arms.

Jealousy burns through me at the way he stares down at her. So much love and adoration it makes my chest hurt.

"This is Matt," she says, happiness laced through her voice.

I know all about him. When we've spoken recently, he's all she talks about.

Hearing how happy she is back here is about the only thing that makes me homesick. Not for Harrow Creek, but for those I love.

"Sky says you're at Columbia. Impressive."

"T-thanks," I stutter. "It's pretty awesome."

Going to college—especially a college like Columbia —makes me an anomaly around those I grew up with. Only a few from the Creek get a shot at college, most don't even graduate. And if they do, it's more likely they'll

7

end up at Harrow Community College, where Sky and Matt are. A few lucky ones get out, I know of a handful who are at Maddison Kings—the closest college to the Creek—but that's got more to do with connections than it has to do with ability.

"Being back here must suck after New York," Sky mutters.

"Nah, it's home."

Truth? This place is hell. If it weren't for Dad or the few friends I still have from here, then I'd never return.

The whole place is depressing.

"How's college?"

"Yeah, it's good. It's Harrow College, doesn't get better than that," she jokes.

Sky always had big dreams to get out of the Creek just like I did. Only her life and her plans didn't quite go the way mine did.

I have my mom to thank for everything. If we were still here, still living in Dad's damp old trailer, then I doubt that I'd have ever had a shot at a college like Columbia. No doubt I'd be at community college and enjoying it about as much as Sky's face shows she really is.

"I'll go and get you ladies more drinks." Matt nods at Harley who's been standing beside me awkwardly listening to this conversation as if she's a part of it.

"Baby Hunter, how's it going?" Sky asks. "Bry is around here somewhere." She looks around for her little brother but with the number of bodies filling her house, it's no surprise she doesn't spot him.

"I'm sure I'll catch up with him. Happy Birthday."

"Thanks, sweetie."

Matt quickly reappears with some very strong drinks

for us and after a few minutes, Flo Rida pumps through the speakers and we forget our shouted conversation in favor of moving to the beat.

Matt pulls Sky's ass into his crotch and they move together in perfect sync while I dance with Harley.

"You need to slow down," I warn. We've only had a couple of drinks but already her eyes are looking a little wild.

"I'm good. Just enjoy yourself."

"I know you're on edge about this, but it will be fine." Discreetly, I look over her shoulder, not feeling as confident with my statement as I should.

Sky assured me that he wasn't going to be here. But looking at this house right now, almost every teenager in the Creek has turned up. Why wouldn't he show his face?

Swallowing down my unease with a large mouthful of vodka. I turn my attention to dancing and enjoying myself.

I'm not scared of him. And I have every right to be here for my friend's birthday.

One song blurs into the next until the back of my neck is hot with sweat and I've got a nice buzz going on thanks to Matt's attentiveness in supplying us and the birthday girl with drinks.

"I need to pee," Harley shouts in my ear. "I'm gonna—"

"I'll come," I say, slipping my hand into hers.

"I don't need a babysitter," she snaps.

"I'm aware." She might be my little sister, but we're all Creek kids. No matter our age, we know how to look after ourselves, and these kinds of wild parties aren't new to us. "I need to go too."

We drop our empty cups in the kitchen before

making our way toward the upstairs bathroom in the hope there's less of a line.

There's not.

"Ugh," Harley complains when she sees the length of it. "One good thing about the houses in Rosewood... the extra bathrooms."

She's not wrong. Everything about our lives in Rosewood—the next, more wealthy town over—is a world away from this place.

"Sky seems happy," Harley says, changing the subject. Most people are looking at us as if we don't belong, we really don't need to be standing here obviously discussing the difference between this shithole town and our new one.

Thankfully, the line goes pretty quick, and not too long later we're back with Sky with fresh drinks and Bry in tow when Harley literally bumped into him on the way to the kitchen.

He smiles at her like she's the most incredible thing he's ever seen. It's no secret that Sky's little brother has always had a crush on my little sister. Sadly though, the feelings are not mutual and Harley friend-zoned him a long time ago.

But thanks to the vodka pumping through her veins, she allows him to pull her into his body and they dance together effortlessly.

I push aside the fact no one has made a beeline to dance with me and immediately push the thoughts of one person from my head. He's not going to be here tonight, in-person or in my imagination.

I down my drink and focus on the music.

I'll be out of here tomorrow afternoon and heading back to New York. I can put this place, all my memories and mistakes behind me and continue with my new life as if this little visit never happened.

We're still dancing when a couple of guys descend on Matt, one immediately locks his eyes on me. I've never seen him before, which is unusual for a place like the Creek. Maybe he's been unlucky enough to move here.

"Hey, beautiful," he says, taking my hand and lifting my knuckles to his lips.

Yeah, he's so not from here.

"Hey."

My body heats as he obviously checks me out, his eyes lingering on my chest for a little longer than should be allowed for two strangers.

"Dance with me, beautiful."

He doesn't wait for my agreement and steps into my body anyway. The second he does, the scent of alcohol on his lips hits my nose and I understand his forwardness.

The front of his body burns against mine and I throw caution to the wind and slide my free hand up his chest and wrap it around the back of his neck as our hips move together.

"Whoa, someone's got some moves," he says into my ear as his hands land on my waist. His voice is so low and rough, it sends shivers skating down my spine, causing warmth to bloom in my belly.

With his spicy scent and heat surrounding me, I lose myself in him. So much so that I don't notice anything has changed until Harley slaps my shoulder, dragging me from my own drunk head.

"What?" I snap at her, annoyed that she's bringing me back to reality.

She tips her chin to the other side of the room. "The Harris twins just walked in."

My stomach drops into my toes.

"He told me himself. He's not coming. Got other plans." Sky's words from our conversation when she invited me to this party come back to me.

My mouth goes dry as I watch them step farther into the room and look around as if they own the place. I fight the urge to swallow and to appear unfazed by their appearance.

So what if they're here. It doesn't mean he is.

"Are you okay?" the guy whispers in my ear.

"Umm..." Unlike when we first started dancing, my body doesn't react to his closeness or his breath racing over my neck.

I'm numb.

Numb and scared. Not that I'd ever admit that.

CHAPTER TWO

Kane

"I thought you said we weren't going tonight?" Ezra asks from the passenger seat of my Skyline.

"We weren't," I spit, not wanting to explain myself to him.

"And yet we're here," he muses, staring at Skylar Marshall's house.

I glance over at him and whatever he can read on my face shuts him up instantly. He holds his hands up in defeat and sinks down in his chair as he watches a few girls in the driveway. One is bent over throwing up while her friends help, simultaneously flashing anyone who's looking their way in their short skirts.

Ezra widens his legs and pulls at his jeans.

"You're a fucking dog," I mutter.

"What? You're saying you wouldn't. That one—" He points out the window. "Isn't even wearing panties. I could slide right—Ow," he complains as his twin leans forward from the back seat and slaps him in the back of the head.

My cell buzzes in my pocket and I forget about the two of them or the pussy on show and open the message.

Devin: Confirmed.

"Let's go," I demand, killing the engine and shouldering open the door.

The second my foot hits the sidewalk, Kyle, my little brother, emerges from behind me. His eyes find mine but they don't focus, thanks to the beer I plied him with earlier.

It was either that or find a way to get rid of him for the night, and I knew that wasn't happening after he discovered who was attending this party.

"You gonna be good tonight, little bro?" I ask, grabbing him in a headlock and messing up his hair.

"Hey," he complains, trying to fight me off.

Car doors slam as the twins climb from my car and the rest of our guys emerge from the others parked down the street.

I nod at Reid and Gray and the two of them head toward the house, the other guys hot on their tail.

They didn't take much convincing to come here tonight, any excuse for them to shift some gear and make some cash, and they're there.

Ezra looks at me from over the hood of the car, concern in his eyes, much like were in Kyle's earlier but I ignore it.

I know what they're thinking. Hell, they're probably right to be concerned, but this is the first chance I've had in months and I'm not going to pass it up because they're worried.

They might know parts of the story but they don't know everything, they don't know how deep the betrayal runs. They have no idea how much my need for revenge eats at me with every day that passes.

I let them all go first, more than happy to hang back in the shadows until the right time.

"Are you really sure—" Kyle starts.

"Get in that fucking house and find your girl, bro. Her brother isn't here. You've got a free pass tonight. Make the fucking most of it," I encourage, fed up with him pining after a girl he can't have.

I push him forward and he walks into the house just behind the twins, his head twisting from side to side to find the girls we're both looking for.

I know the second he sees them, his entire body jolts. I follow his eyeline into the living room at the mass of bodies dancing to the heavy bass being pumped through the house.

Bingo.

Her dark hair fills my eyes as she stares at the twins in horror.

A satisfied smile tugs at the corner of my lips.

Good to see the message that we weren't coming got through loud and clear.

I stand in the shadows out of sight as she looks around.

My heart pounds and my fists curl. It doesn't matter that her eyes are wide in fear. My need to get to her consumes me.

And she should be scared. She's eluded me long enough.

It's time for her to pay for her mistakes. It's long overdue.

"Let's go get a drink," Devin says, stepping up beside me and all but dragging me to the kitchen.

He uncaps a couple of bottles of beer for us and I down mine the second he passes it over.

"I told you this was a bad idea," he warns.

"And I told you to butt the fuck out of my business," I seethe.

He rolls his eyes at me and it does nothing to calm the beast that's raging inside me.

We've been friends since we were in diapers, he should know by now that I do what I want, regardless of what he, my little brother, or anyone else thinks.

"Fine, but I want it on record that you're probably going to make a huge mistake tonight."

"Whatever," I mutter, taking a pull from the bottle but I'm disappointed when the beer hits my throat. It's not strong enough and I feel like I'm going to need more to get through tonight.

Tension radiates from me as we stand there in silence. The music continues to pound and other partygoers come and go. All of them glance at us, the usual wary expression on their faces and they soon disappear again.

Now we're inside, there's no way the news of our arrival isn't going to hit her ears.

I just need to make sure that doesn't make her run.

"What are you going to do?" Devin inquires.

I blow out a long breath, throwing my bottle into the trash at the other side of the room with a perfect shot.

I shrug. "I just want to talk to her," I lie.

"Bullshit. You really expect me to believe that after everything?"

"I don't give a shit what you believe, Dev."

He eyes me suspiciously. He has a right to. He knows

how much I hate Scarlett Hunter and despite that, how much she gets under my skin.

It was never meant to be this way for us. But she made it happen.

It's all her fault things got fucked up.

There was a time I wanted to protect her. Now all I want to do is hurt her for all the pain she has caused me.

Leaving town was probably the best thing that ever happened to her, and not just because of the opportunities it allowed her, but the fact she's managed to escape me for the best part of three years.

"Those Hunters look hot as hell, man," Ezra says, joining us in the kitchen.

My teeth grind with the knowledge that he's had a better look at her than I have.

"You're supposed to be watching her," I grit out.

"Ellis has it covered, man. Just getting drinks."

He steps up to me, and I have his shirt in my fists in seconds. His eyes go wide in surprise for a beat but then I'm sure an inkling of amusement flickers through them.

I lean into his face, our noses only a breath apart.

"Don't go anywhere fucking near her," I warn, my voice low and menacing.

Of all my boys, he's the only one who'd accidentally go there. He's a fucking dog and has zero shame or morals when it comes to getting pussy.

"Bro, man. I got it. Hunters are off-limits. We got that message about a decade ago." He rolls his eyes as if this is all one big joke. And despite the fact I want to break his fucking nose for running his mouth, I release him and push him away from me.

He stumbles over his own feet and unfortunately for me, Ellis appears in the doorway right before he plummets to the ground and catches his twin at the last second.

"What the hell?"

"She good?" I ask Ellis, ignoring the scowl on his face.

"Uh..." He looks between his brother and me. "Yeah, just dancing with her friends."

"She know we're here?"

He raises a brow as if to say, 'we walked in, every motherfucker knows we're here.' "Kyle's with Harley."

"Course he is," I chuckle. That boy's got the bluest balls for baby Hunter. Too bad he's too much of a pussy and scared of her big brother or he'd have made a move years ago.

"You gonna let that happen?" Devin asks from behind his bottle.

"Of course. My issue isn't with Harley. Kyle can do whatever he likes."

Turning my back on them, I grab another beer and storm out of the room.

They're supposed to be keeping an eye on her so she doesn't escape, but they all seem to be talking to me in an entirely different room.

They don't get it, I know that. But they need to fucking listen.

The warnings they've given me fall on deaf ears.

While they might give her a free pass for what went down. I won't.

She's screwed me over one too many times and it's time for her to pay.

I slip into the living room. I want to say I go unnoticed, but I'm Kane fucking Legend, barely anything I do in Harrow Creek goes unnoticed. Eyes follow my every move.

I nod at a few guys while their girls blatantly check me out as I pass. But no matter how beautiful they might be, I have no interest in them.

I've got my sights solely set on one woman tonight.

I finally get to a spot where I can remain hidden while watching her—exactly what my brothers should be doing—and look up. I find Harley and Kyle instantly where they're laughing and dancing together. I roll my eyes at the goofy smile I find on Kyle's face and rip my eyes away, more interested in the older Hunter sister.

But she's gone.

"Fuck," I breathe, scanning the room, looking for a glimpse of her dark hair.

Knowing she wouldn't have left Harley behind for the wolves, I set off through the house, more than ready to make my move.

It's been a long fucking time coming.

CHAPTER THREE

Letty

My heart is racing as I bolt through the house to find somewhere to catch my breath.

My hands tremble as I take in the long line for the upstairs bathroom once more.

"Fuck this," I mutter, walking to the end of the hallway and blasting through Sky's parents' bedroom door. It's off-limits tonight and everyone knows it—although most will ignore it.

The room is still as it should be as I make my way through and directly to the en suite on the other side.

I close the door and lock it behind me, dragging in a lungful of air as I turn my back to the wood.

"This is not happening," I mutter to myself. Although, I don't know why I'm really surprised, or why I believed Sky when she said he wouldn't be here.

I don't think she lied to me. Our friendship might not

be what it once was, but she wouldn't knowingly hurt me, or willingly hand me over to him.

The bass of the music from downstairs vibrates through the floor.

My cell burns a hole in my purse. It would be so easy to message Harley and get the hell out of here, preferably before I have to see him.

But why should I run? I didn't actually do anything wrong.

I blow out a slow breath, trying to ground myself, to push through the haze from the vodka and make a sensible decision.

I go about my business, pull my lipstick out of my purse and reapply the deep red coating my lips, hoping it's all the armor I'm going to need tonight.

I might be blowing it totally out of proportion. He might not even want to see me. He might not know I'm here.

Keep lying to yourself, Letty. It won't make this any better.

"Fucking hell."

I stare at my reflection in the mirror as I smooth my hair down.

My skin is flushed from dancing. I think back to the guy I left behind when my need to run got the better of me.

He seems like a good guy, he certainly knows how to move his body.

I should go back downstairs, shove Kane Legend inside the lockbox that lives in my head for all the things I don't want to deal with, and focus on him—whatever his name is. Maybe that's where I need to start.

With newfound confidence, I drag the door open and

make my way out of the bedroom I never should have been in.

The second I step out, a shiver races down my spine and I'm reminded of all the reasons I ran to the safety of that room to begin with.

I keep my head down, not waiting to acknowledge that his stare alone affects me but as I get to the stairs, I'm forced to stand aside as a drunken couple stumbles toward me, locked in their heated kiss and I stupidly look over the bannister.

I gasp the second my eyes land on his blue ones and my stomach flips.

Everything around me, the people, the music, the commotion, it all fades to nothing as tension crackles between us.

My hands tremble and my mouth goes dry as he ensnares me in his gaze.

My heart thuds against my ribs and my need to grab Harley and run almost gets the better of me when his eyes narrow in warning.

This has been a long time coming, thanks to me avoiding him at every cost until now.

I always knew my time was running out. This meeting between us was inevitable.

As much as I hoped he might let it go. I knew he wouldn't.

That's not the kind of person Kane Legend is.

He doesn't let anything go.

And he thinks I owe him for the mistake I made.

Some movement behind me finally rips me from my trance and I come back to myself.

Swallowing down my anxiety and the giant lump of

emotion in my throat, I force a blank expression on my face and find my fighting spirit.

I'm Scarlett fucking Hunter. I don't bow down to the likes of him. No matter what he's pegged me as being guilty of.

With my head held high, I make my way down the stairs and to the kitchen. I need another drink after that exchange.

To my amazement, he doesn't appear and I make it back to Harley and Sky without having to deal with him.

I have no doubt that's all in his plan though.

He wants to freak me out. Let me know he's watching so he can strike at the right moment.

I might be a Hunter, but right now I'm fully aware that I'm his prey. I also know that I have no chance of escaping his clutches.

Do you really want to?

I shake that thought from my head and plaster a smile on my face as I approach the others.

"Everything okay?" Harley asks me the second she notices I've rejoined them. I run my eyes down the front of her body, noticing Kyle's hands possessively on her hips and I smile.

Unlike his older brother, Kyle is a nice guy, and it's no secret that he's been hot for Harley for, well... forever. But he used to be our brother's best friend, and Zayn made it quite clear what would happen if any of his friends touched his little sister. Although it looks like all bets are off tonight. I wonder if that would be the case if Zayn were here instead of back in Rosewood with his football team.

I plaster a fake smile on my face and nod at her. "Of course. You look like you're enjoying yourself."

Her face flushes with embarrassment but she makes no move to pull away from Kyle.

Turning away to give them some privacy, I turn back to the guy I was dancing with.

"I thought you'd left me," he faux whines.

"Why would I do that?" I look up at him through my lashes, a seductive smile playing on my lips as I press my body against his.

I know it's wrong to use him like this, but with my skin tingling with the awareness that only comes with being watched by a certain cold pair of eyes, I can't help myself.

He wants to punish me, he's made that clear in the past, what he doesn't realize is that I'm not opposed to playing this game.

He scares me, yes. I know what he's capable of.

But that's not what this is.

I don't think.

I roll my hips into the guy and he eagerly follows my lead.

I don't take any notice of the song that's playing. My only focus is his attention.

I spin around, thrusting my ass into the guy's crotch and search him out through the masses of heads surrounding us.

I find the twins once more. Ezra has some poor girl backed up against the wall. No surprise there.

I might have left Harrow Creek at sixteen, but he was already well on his way through both the senior and junior girls.

Ellis stands a few feet away, his focus zeroed in on his cell as if there's not a party booming around him. I even spot Devin talking to a crowd of adoring fans.

But I don't find him.

He can see me though, and it sends a thrill racing down my spine.

I drop down low, dragging my ass up the guy's body as he growls in delight at my move.

His hard length presses into my ass as I brush against him.

"You're killing me, baby," he groans in my ear, licking his tongue around the edge as his giant hand splays across my tummy.

I feel bad for the guy. He has no idea I'm using him right now.

I should walk away, let him down gently so he can go and find another girl to spend his evening with. But I can't.

If I push him away, it'll be an invitation to our hidden spectator.

Closing my eyes, I rest my head back on his shoulder and allow the thoughts to drift from my head.

Just for a moment, I feel free.

I can imagine the tingles and desire coursing through my body are for him.

I can allow myself to be swept away thinking that tonight could have a good outcome. That I could have the fun I was hoping for when I agreed to come.

But I know it's not going to happen.

Drinks arrive courtesy of Matt once more, and I eagerly drink down every one he hands over.

My head spins a little more with every sip and reality soon begins to melt away.

Although, *he* never does.

He remains wherever he is, just watching like a creepy fucking psycho.

Whatever.

I turn back to the guy—Leo, I think I heard Matt call him—and stare up into his eyes.

"I'm so fucking glad I came tonight," he slurs, his eyes bouncing between mine.

"Yeah?"

Verdict's still very much out on whether I'm regretting my appearance or not. The night is still young.

"Yeah, but I need to tell you something."

My heart drops a little. If I find out he's one of Kane's crew and that he's been playing me, I'm going to bitch slap him.

I wonder briefly if there's something wrong with me because I'm more concerned about that than I am of him possibly about to confess he's got a girl.

He leans into me and my breath catches in my throat as his races against my ear and sends a shiver skating down my spine.

"I need to pee."

I throw my head back and laugh, the tension that momentarily locked up my muscles immediately gone.

"Go," I say, pressing my hand to his chest.

"Don't go anywhere," he warns, his eyes dropping down my body.

"As if." I roll my eyes and he laughs as he backs away from me.

I try to fight it. But the second he turns and gets swallowed up by the crowd, I feel vulnerable.

I keep moving in time with everyone else around me, but they're all coupled up and I feel like an idiot. I'm just about to push my way through the crowd to go and get a drink when the lights go out and everything falls silent.

What the—

The second a body presses against my back, I know my time is up.

My lips part, ready to scream but I don't get a chance to make a sound because a giant hand covers half my face as my feet are lifted from the ground.

I thrash in his hold, kicking my legs and flailing my arms, hoping that I'll make contact with him, hurt him, anything, for him to put me the fuck down.

He navigates out of the house as if the entire place isn't in darkness. I can barely see the people in front of us, let alone the exit, but it doesn't seem to bother him.

In only a few short seconds, the cool outside air hits my skin.

Sky's house is on the edge of the Harrow Creek woods and the thought of him taking me into the darkness and killing me has a renewed surge of energy flowing through my limbs and I fight harder.

"Fight as much as you like, Princess. I'm not letting you go."

I scream behind his hand, my feet flying backward in the hope of connecting with his shin, but somehow he dodges every attempt I make.

He continues forward into the darkness, twigs snapping underfoot and leaves rustling as we get deeper into the undergrowth.

The sound of rumbling thunder in the distance only adds to my misery.

Thoughts of our surroundings and possible drenching are soon cut off when he slams me up against a tree.

My breath rushes from my lungs in shock as the music from the house starts up in the distance.

His fingers thread into my hair and he drags my head to the side so he can see me but I can't quite see him.

"Are you going to do this the easy way or the hard way?"

"Fuck you, Kane," I spit the second he removes his hand from my mouth.

There's no point screaming or crying for help.

If there's anyone else out here in the woods with us then they're probably a murderer. Or worse, Kane's crew who'll do whatever he commands.

I'm not sure if being alone with him or part of a group right now is better or worse.

"Shut the fuck up," he growls, pulling harder on my hair until it begins to sting. "You're playing a dangerous game, Princess."

"I'm not playing anything," I argue innocently, although it's a lie. I knew exactly what I was doing with Leo. I knew it would infuriate Kane.

"Nice try. I know you better than that, Scarlett." The way he growls my name sends an electric bolt down my body in a way that Leo couldn't. Where his touch felt... nice, Kane's is pure fire.

It's always been this way with us. It's why things have spiraled so far out of control between us.

"Whatever. You've made your point, can I go back now?"

The laugh that rumbles up his throat is pure evil and reminds me of the reason most people are scared of him.

Me though? I remember the boy before the anger, the hate.

Seeing that blond-haired, blue-eyed boy softens him to me somewhat.

"You're fucking delusional."

"You want to hurt me. Punish me. Make me pay. I get it, Kane. But it's not going to change anything."

"Maybe not," he says, taking a step toward me, the length of his body burning the skin of my back. "But it'll make me feel a little bit fucking better."

"Do your worst," I say with a resigned sigh.

CHAPTER FOUR

Kane

"*Do your worst.*" Her defeated tone rings in my ears.

Oh hell no.

A loud crack of thunder echoes into the night as the sound of approaching rain gets louder.

Ripping her from the tree, I spin her and press her back against it. She glances back to the house, and for the briefest moment, I wonder if she's about to try to run.

Part of me wants her to try.

I run my eyes down the length of her. Her black dress wraps around her curves, showing them off perfectly, and thanks to me carrying her out here, the hem sits dangerously high on her thighs.

My mouth waters for her, my cock strains against the zipper of my pants.

I work my way up over her slim waist, full breasts, and

slender neck, but it's not until I get to her eyes that I see the fire I was expecting.

"You're lying to me, Princess."

"Oh?" Her head tilts to the side slightly as if she's innocent.

She's not fucking innocent. A long way from it.

I take a step forward, the scorching heat from her body damn near burning mine.

"You can't play me, Princess. I'm in charge here."

My knuckles brush up the side of her body and I don't miss the gasp of surprise that rips up her throat as I skim the side of her breast.

A satisfied smile threatens to pull at my lips knowing that she's as aware of our connection as I am.

I've always fucking felt it.

My need to linger, to make her do it again, is almost too much to bear. But I fight it, instead, lifting my hand higher until my fingers wrap around the smooth skin of her throat.

She swallows nervously under my touch but she shows no other signs of fear knowing that I could end her life in a few seconds flat like this.

This is part of why I can't stay the fuck away from her.

Even after all the shit I've thrown at her over the years. She's never fucking reacted to me.

I need it. I fucking crave it.

She's been inside my head since the first day I laid eyes on her, yet I'm nothing to her. Fucking nothing.

My fingers tighten with irritation as our past flashes through my mind like a fucking movie.

I thought I hated her when we were fourteen.

But apparently, it was a momentary lapse in

judgment because I wasn't the one she was letting her walls down for.

My teeth grind as our eyes hold. Hers silently challenging mine in a way that holds me captive, just like they have for damn near fifteen years.

"You're not welcome here," I breathe. "No one fucking wants you here."

"You're wrong. *You* are the only one who doesn't want me here. Sky, *Leo*—" She smirks, knowing that mentioning his name is going to hurt and she wants a reaction out of me. She's going to be damn out of luck though because all she's getting is my fucking wrath. "They want me here. In fact, they're probably looking for me."

"Sky is currently getting fucked six ways from Sunday and won't have even noticed you gone. And Leo —" I spit his name in disgust. I know him. I know everyone in this town and he's a fucking pussy. Nowhere near good enough for the likes of Scarlett Hunter. "I'm doing you a favor."

"I highly doubt that," she seethes. "Anything that involves spending time with you, is never a good thing."

A growl rumbles up my throat at her words and a smile curls at her lips.

"Am I supposed to be impressed by that little stunt to get me out here?" she sasses. "It's nice to know you're aware of how much I hate you and that I'd never have come willingly."

"Shut up," I spit, my fingers tightening as the first droplets of rain find their way through the trees above us and hit me on the head. The cool water landing on my overheating skin.

"You want a girl to comply while you attempt

to *punish* her, then I can assure you that you picked the wrong one to play with."

My head spins as I stare at her full, dark red lips as she speaks.

"You need me to—"

My body moves without instruction from my brain and I cut off her words with my lips, plunging my tongue into her mouth.

She doesn't move as I step into her body, pressing her back into the tree.

It's the first time I've kissed her, and fuck, if it's nothing like all the times I imagined it over the years.

"Ow, you fucking—" I pull back, lifting my hand to my lip, finding a drop of blood on my finger when I finally rip my eyes away from her murderous ones. "You fucking bit me," I say in disbelief.

"Then stay the fuck away from me."

"Oh, Princess, I think we both know that's not going to happen."

The clap of skin sounds out a beat before the pain hits me. My cheek burns with the strength of her hit. I have no doubt I've got her handprint glowing on my skin.

Our eyes hold. Hate, anger, and desire crackle between us as the party continues without us in the distance.

The rain gets heavier, beginning to come down in sheets, but our eyes don't part, both of us daring the other to move, to take the next step.

Her chest heaves as my breaths race past my lips.

"You're going to fucking regret that," I bark, lunging for her.

She gasps in surprise when I wrap my fingers around her throat once more, applying more pressure than before, and I pull her head back with the other so she has no choice but to look up at me.

"You sorry?"

"Fuck yo—"

I make the most of her parted lips and push my tongue past them once more. "You fucking will be," I mutter into her mouth, my fingers tightening in warning, although not enough to cut off her air supply.

"Fuck you, Kane. Fuck. You."

"Yeah, Princess. That's what I'm thinking too."

She squeals when I release my hold on her and lift her off the ground.

Her legs wrap around my waist, although I have no doubt it wasn't by choice.

"Kiss me," I demand, my voice rough with my desire.

"No."

"I don't remember you always being this stubborn."

"Then maybe you should have looked closer."

"Trust me, Princess. I've done nothing but fucking look."

"Kane, what the fuck?" she squeals when I pull her from the tree and lower us both to the ground, dropping her in a quickly forming puddle.

The rain soaks my shirt and jeans, the fabric sticks to every inch of my skin, but I barely feel it while she's beneath me.

I press my palm to her chest when she tries to get up, shoving her back down into the mud.

"No," I growl, pushing her legs farther apart and leaning over her. "You're not in fucking charge here."

"Kane." I'm pretty sure it's supposed to be a warning, but all I hear is a plea.

"Yeah, Princess?"

"I hate you."

"Not as much as I hate you."

Reaching out, my fingers wrap around the top of her dress and I drag it down, ripping the thin straps in the process.

"What are you—fuck—" she moans the second I wrap my lips around her nipple and suck hard before sinking my teeth in.

Her hips grind against me and I stifle the moan that threatens to erupt from my throat at the feeling of her against my cock.

"You holding out on me, dirty girl?"

"Kane." Her warning might hold a little more conviction if it wasn't said around a needy panting breath.

"Don't worry, Princess. Your punishment doesn't end there."

Sitting up, my hands land on her wet knees. She watches completely enthralled as my fingers slide down her thighs, pushing the rain droplets lower as I go until her dress is bunched up around her waist, exposing her tiny black lace thong.

The sound of the party in the distance has been swallowed by the rain blasting through the trees and soaking into the earth around us.

The only thing here is us and the elements. Exactly as it should be.

Coldness seeps into my knees and I can only imagine how it feels to be lying in it like Letty is.

"Pretty. But not enough to save," I mutter. The lace practically disintegrates in my hands and I discard the scrap of fabric in the mud.

Letty's eyes blaze with heat and anger when I make my way back up her body.

Her hair is sodden, tendrils sticking to the sides of her face, the length swamped by the muddy puddle she's in.

Her dress is rucked around her middle, her full tits and pert nipples on full display. Her legs parted and her pussy slick and ready for me

Fuck. She's never looked better. And Letty is always fucking beautiful, so that's really saying something.

"Kane, we can't—"

My hand finds her throat once more and I squeeze tight enough to cut off her words as I run the fingers of my other hand through her folds. She shudders, her teeth sinking into her bottom lip to stop her from moaning in pleasure.

But fuck, I need that sound.

"So fucking wet for me, Princess. Anyone would think you want me."

"Never," she breathes as I tease her entrance.

"I think you're lying to me again. You like the pain. You like the punishment. You like the games. It's why it's taken us this long to get here."

"No," she cries, her head thrashing from side to side in denial, but we both know the truth here.

This moment has been a long time coming.

It should have been us all this time. But it wasn't.

She ruined that.

She ruined everything.

CHAPTER FIVE

Letty

"No," I cry weakly as he spears his fingers inside me.

Oh my fucking God.

My chest heaves as he finger fucks me like a pro. Finding that spot inside me almost instantly that would send me crashing over the edge in only minutes.

This shouldn't be happening.

I bit him. I slapped him for fuck's sake.

He should be clawing my eyes out not... not...

"Oh my God," I pant, my back arching in the mud beneath me.

I squeeze my eyes shut as the rain lashes down on me so I can focus on the sensations and attempt to forget who I'm with.

"Eyes. On. Me," he demands as his fingers slow down

allowing the release I was racing toward to almost vanish into oblivion.

My eyes flicker open, the raindrops that had caught in my lashes dropping into my eyes and making my sight of him blurry.

He's still too fucking pretty for his own good.

His dirty blond hair falls over his brow and into his eyes, water dripping off the strands and running down his sharp jawline. A jawline that is way too good for an asshole like him.

Why are all the bad boys gifted with the looks?

His lips are full, still a little swollen from our brief kiss and a little blood is still in the corner from where I sunk my teeth into it.

Fuck, did that feel good after all these years of him tormenting me.

I'm not a violent person. Anything but. But damn if I don't want to do that again. The way his eyes darkened with shock and desire. How his hand trembled against me.

A rush of heat floods my core as I think about his reaction.

"Tell me what you're thinking about," he demands.

"Hurting you," I admit.

His eyes flash once more and his nostrils flare.

He thrusts deeper and my fingers curl in my need to grip something but like fuck am I reaching for him. Instead, I end up with fistfuls of squelchy mud.

"Oh God," I whimper as he rubs just the right spot.

"Don't come," he growls, his voice so low and deep it pushes me closer to where he doesn't want me to be.

But fuck him. He's not the boss here.

"Scarlett," he growls again, obviously feeling my core tightening.

"Oh God. Oh God."

His eyes narrow in warning, but even if I had the power to stop myself right now, I wouldn't.

"Fucking asshole," I scream when he rips his fingers from me right at the last minute.

"Do you ever do what the fuck you're told?" he spits, but his anger has been replaced by lust as he tears at the fabric around his waist and pushing it low enough to pull his cock out.

Fuck.

My eyes lock on where he holds himself. My mouth going dry.

Fuck.

"You. Ruin. Everything," he spits again as he lines himself up with my entrance and surges into me in one swift move.

"Holy—" I gasp, my words vanishing when he pulls out and immediately slams back in without giving me even a second to adjust.

But that's just the way Kane is. He always has been.

He takes what he wants and fuck the consequences.

Another reason why I'm amazed we haven't ended up in this position before. Hell knows we've come close.

"Fuck, Princess. Who knew the devil felt so good."

His fingers dig into my hips as he crashes our bodies together as if he's trying to get even deeper.

His grip hurts and I already know I'm going to be sporting the evidence of this mistake for days to come.

Just what I need. A reminder when I'm sober and of sound mind.

My back slides through the mud, making the mess worse.

"So fucking tight," he breathes, but I think he's talking to himself more than anything else.

His eyes continue to hold mine as we move together in sync. It's as if he's trying to brand himself on my soul as well as on my body.

I bite on the inside of my cheeks to refrain from assuring him that it's not necessary. He's been in my head for years. Forever.

Along with my family, he's been the other constant thing in my life. I could always rely on him showing up at exactly the wrong time and making my life hell, reminding me why I hate him so much.

If he wasn't taunting me in class for being a nerd, he was starting rumors about me being frigid, and when that didn't work, he started on the 'Scarlett is a slut' angle.

None of it worked. Well, not that I allowed anyone to see.

Being alone in my bedroom at night reliving it was another matter entirely. But I was young, naïve, and easily played.

I'm older now. Wiser.

Strong enough to take on Kane fucking Legend and win.

"Oh fuck," I cry, my thoughts falling away as he leans over me, changing the angle.

His forearm lands in the mud beside my head, dirty water splashing over my face as his lips lower to mine.

"You have any idea how long I've imagined what this might be like?"

I keep my lips shut. Mainly because I know my

answer would be, "as long as I have," and I can't allow him to think he's taken up any of my thoughts over the years.

He's the bad boy. The one mothers warn their daughters to stay away from.

But I'm like a moth to a fucking flame and fuck it if I get burned.

His lips claim mine in a savage, bruising kiss.

I want to fight the feelings every possessive sweep of his tongue ignites within me, but with every second that passes, I feel myself falling farther and farther under his spell.

He sucks on my tongue as his fingers flex around my throat, his thumb softly caressing my pulse point and I briefly wonder if he's even aware of the soft move when every other one of his touches have been so rough.

I can't help the moan of pleasure that erupts from my throat when he mimics my action from earlier and bites down on my bottom lip.

The bite of pain shoots straight to my core, sending me dangerously close to falling over the edge before the taste of copper fills my mouth.

"I can give back much worse than I receive, Princess. You're not going to win."

Lifting my arms, I touch him for the first time, slipping my hands under his shirt, I dig my nails into the taut skin of his back and scratch down.

His eyes roll back in pleasure.

"Fuuuuck."

His thrusts become more and more erratic, his kiss becomes dirtier and his touches even more explosive.

The cold rainwater pounds down on my bare skin stopping me from combusting as his fingers release my throat and slip down between us and pinch my clit, ensuring I cry out in a mix of pain and desire.

I gasp for breath, now able to breathe unrestricted without his punishing grip.

I bite down on my tongue as my orgasm begins to crest, not wanting to give him the satisfaction of calling out his name, but at the same time desperate to, just to cement in my mind that it's him I'm with, that he's the one making me feel this good.

Everything about it is wrong. Everything.

And the fact I'm currently sliding around in a mud puddle, soaked to my bones, is only one indicator.

But right now, I don't care.

I don't care about any of it, apart from what he can give me.

I'll worry about the weight of my mistake and drown in regrets tomorrow once the vodka has faded from my system and all I'm left with is my memories and the bruises on my body.

"You. Are. Going. To. Remember. This," he barks on each thrust. Both his movement and words making me fly even higher.

"Come, Scarlett. Give me everything."

He sits up and pinches my clit hard one more time and I lose all control, falling over the edge without a care for where I end up landing, although already knowing that it's going to be painful.

I'm desperate to keep my eyes on him, but as the most intense wave hits me, I have no choice but to slam them closed and focus on the pleasure.

My back arches, my muscles quiver as I ride out every inch of the one good thing he can give me.

"Scarlett, Princess, fuuuuuck," he groans and I rip my

eyes open just in time to see him throw his head back and roar out a string of curses as his body locks up and his cock jerks violently inside me.

The moment he looks back down at me, my breath catches in my throat at the expression on his face.

His mask is well and truly back in place and the coldness of his eyes, the pure hatred in their depths, sends a shiver racing down my spine.

The chill from the rain and ground seeps into me, despite the fact we're still connected, and I fight the need to scramble up and run away from him as fast as my legs will carry me.

Our eyes hold as a smirk pulls at the corner of his lips. But there's no joy, no happiness after what we just did.

There's only warning.

Threats of more to come.

Of how this is about to get worse for me.

He drops down over me and I force myself to swallow over the giant lump in my throat.

"This is the least of what you deserve, whore." His words threaten to slice me wide open, but I don't allow him that much power as I force myself not to react to his barbed words.

"Wha—I—" I stutter, not able to scramble any words together with his hate stare burning through me. I'm desperate to cover up, to hide from him, but I can't move.

"I've been waiting for you for a long time, Princess. If only I knew revenge would taste this fucking sweet, I might have come for you earlier."

"Kane, please—"

"No, the time for begging is long gone. You killed my best friend. It's time to pay."

THE REVENGE YOU SEEK

1

LETTY

I sit on my bed, staring down at the fabric in my hands.

This wasn't how it was supposed to happen.

This wasn't part of my plan.

I let out a sigh, squeezing my eyes tight, willing the tears away.

I've cried enough. I thought I'd have run out by now.

A commotion on the other side of the door has me looking up in a panic, but just like yesterday, no one comes knocking.

I think I proved that I don't want to hang with my new roommates the first time someone knocked and asked if I wanted to go for breakfast with them.

I don't.

I don't even want to be here.

I just want to hide.

And that thought makes it all a million times worse.

I'm not a hider. I'm a fighter. I'm a fucking Hunter.

But this is what I've been reduced to.

This pathetic, weak mess.

And all because of *him*.

He shouldn't have this power over me. But even now, he does.

The dorm falls silent once again, and I pray that they've all headed off for their first class of the semester so I can slip out unnoticed.

I know it's ridiculous. I know I should just go out there with my head held high and dig up the confidence I know I do possess.

But I can't.

I figure that I'll just get through today—my first day—and everything will be alright.

I can somewhat pick up where I left off, almost as if the last eighteen months never happened.

Wishful thinking.

I glance down at the hoodie in my hands once more.

Mom bought them for Zayn, my younger brother, and me.

The navy fabric is soft between my fingers, but the text staring back at me doesn't feel right.

Maddison Kings University.

A knot twists my stomach and I swear my whole body sags with my new reality.

I was at my dream school. I beat the odds and I got into Columbia. And everything was good. No, everything was fucking fantastic.

Until it wasn't.

Now here I am. Sitting in a dorm at what was always my backup plan school having to start over.

Throwing the hoodie onto my bed, I angrily push to my feet.

I'm fed up with myself.

I should be better than this, stronger than this.

48

But I'm just... I'm broken.

And as much as I want to see the positives in this situation. I'm struggling.

Shoving my feet into my Vans, I swing my purse over my shoulder and scoop up the couple of books on my desk for the two classes I have today.

My heart drops when I step out into the communal kitchen and find a slim blonde-haired girl hunched over a mug and a textbook.

The scent of coffee fills my nose and my mouth waters.

My shoes squeak against the floor and she immediately looks up.

"Sorry, I didn't mean to disrupt you."

"Are you kidding?" she says excitedly, her southern accent making a smile twitch at my lips.

Her smile lights up her pretty face and for some reason, something settles inside me.

I knew hiding was wrong. It's just been my coping method for... quite a while.

"We wondered when our new roommate was going to show her face. The guys have been having bets on you being an alien or something."

A laugh falls from my lips. "No, no alien. Just..." I sigh, not really knowing what to say.

"You transferred in, right? From Columbia?"

"Ugh... yeah. How'd you know—"

"Girl, I know everything." She winks at me, but it doesn't make me feel any better. "West and Brax are on the team, they spent the summer with your brother."

A rush of air passes my lips in relief. Although I'm not overly thrilled that my brother has been gossiping about me.

"So, what classes do you have today?" she asks when I stand there gaping at her.

"Umm... American lit and psychology."

"I've got psych later too. Professor Collins?"

"Uh..." I drag my schedule from my purse and stare down at it. "Y-yes."

"Awesome. We can sit together."

"S-sure," I stutter, sounding unsure, but the smile I give her is totally genuine. "I'm Letty, by the way." Although I'm pretty sure she already knows that.

"Ella."

"Okay, I'll... uh... see you later."

"Sure. Have a great morning."

She smiles at me and I wonder why I was so scared to come out and meet my new roommates.

I'd wanted Mom to organize an apartment for me so that I could be alone, but—probably wisely—she refused. She knew that I'd use it to hide in and the point of me restarting college is to try to put everything behind me and start fresh.

After swiping an apple from the bowl in the middle of the table, I hug my books tighter to my chest and head out, ready to embark on my new life.

The morning sun burns my eyes and the scent of freshly cut grass fills my nose as I step out of our building. The summer heat hits my skin, and it makes everything feel that little bit better.

So what if I'm starting over. I managed to transfer the credits I earned from Columbia, and MKU is a good school. I'll still get a good degree and be able to make something of my life.

Things could be worse.

It could be this time last year...

I shake the thought from my head and force my feet to keep moving.

I pass students meeting up with their friends for the start of the new semester as they excitedly tell them all about their summers and the incredible things they did, or they compare schedules.

My lungs grow tight as I drag in the air I need. I think of the friends I left behind in Columbia. We didn't have all that much time together, but we'd bonded before my life imploded on me.

Glancing around, I find myself searching for familiar faces. I know there are plenty of people here who know me. A couple of my closest friends came here after high school.

Mom tried to convince me to reach out over the summer, but my anxiety kept me from doing so. I don't want anyone to look at me like I'm a failure. That I got into one of the best schools in the country, fucked it up and ended up crawling back to Rosewood. I'm not sure what's worse, them assuming I couldn't cope or the truth.

Focusing on where I'm going, I put my head down and ignore the excited chatter around me as I head for the coffee shop, desperately in need of my daily fix before I even consider walking into a lecture.

I find the Westerfield Building where my first class of the day is and thank the girl who holds the heavy door open for me before following her toward the elevator.

"Holy fucking shit," a voice booms as I turn the corner, following the signs to the room on my schedule.

Before I know what's happening, my coffee is falling from my hand and my feet are leaving the floor.

"What the—" The second I get a look at the guy

standing behind the one who has me in his arms, I know exactly who I've just walked into.

Forgetting about the coffee that's now a puddle on the floor, I release my books and wrap my arms around my old friend.

His familiar woodsy scent flows through me, and suddenly, I feel like me again. Like the past two years haven't existed.

"What the hell are you doing here?" Luca asks, a huge smile on his face when he pulls back and studies me.

His brows draw together when he runs his eyes down my body, and I know why. I've been working on it over the summer, but I know I'm still way skinnier than I ever have been in my life.

"I transferred," I admit, forcing the words out past the lump in my throat.

His smile widens more before he pulls me into his body again.

"It's so good to see you."

I relax into his hold, squeezing him tight, absorbing his strength. And that's one thing that Luca Dunn has in spades. He's a rock, always has been and I didn't realize how much I needed that right now.

Mom was right. I should have reached out.

"You too," I whisper honestly, trying to keep the tears at bay that are threatening just from seeing him—them.

"Hey, it's good to see you," Leon says, slightly more subdued than his twin brother as he hands me my discarded books.

"Thank you."

I look between the two of them, noticing all the things that have changed since I last saw them in person. I keep up with them on Instagram and TikTok, sure, but nothing is quite like standing before the two of them.

Both of them are bigger than I ever remember, showing just how hard their coach is working them now they're both first string for the Panthers. And if it's possible, they're both hotter than they were in high school, which is really saying something because they'd turn even the most confident of girls into quivering wrecks with one look back then. I can only imagine the kind of rep they have around here.

The sound of a door opening behind us and the shuffling of feet cuts off our little reunion.

"You in Professor Whitman's American lit class?" Luca asks, his eyes dropping from mine to the book in my hands.

"Yeah. Are you?"

"We are. Walk you to class?" A smirk appears on his lips that I remember all too well. A flutter of the butterflies he used to give me threaten to take flight as he watches me intently.

Luca was one of my best friends in high school, and I spent almost all our time together with the biggest crush on him. It seems that maybe the teenage girl inside me still thinks that he could be it for me.

"I'd love you to."

"Come on then, Princess," Leon says and my entire body jolts at hearing that pet name for me. He's never called me that before and I really hope he's not about to start now.

Clearly not noticing my reaction, he once again takes my books from me and threads his arm through mine as the pair of them lead me into the lecture hall.

I glance at both of them, a smile pulling at my lips and hope building inside me.

Maybe this was where I was meant to be this whole time.

Maybe Columbia and I were never meant to be.

More than a few heads turn our way as we climb the stairs to find some free seats. Mostly it's the females in the huge space and I can't help but inwardly laugh at their reaction.

I get it.

The Dunn twins are two of the Kings around here and I'm currently sandwiched between them. It's a place that nearly every female in this college, hell, this state, would kill to be in.

"Dude, shift the fuck over," Luca barks at another guy when he pulls to a stop a few rows from the back.

The guy who's got dark hair and even darker eyes immediately picks up his bag, books, and pen and moves over a space.

"This is Colt," Luca explains, nodding to the guy who's studying me with interest.

"Hey," I squeak, feeling a little intimidated.

"Hey." His low, deep voice licks over me. "Ow, what the fuck, man?" he barks, rubbing at the back of his head where Luca just slapped him.

"Letty's off-limits. Get your fucking eyes off her."

"Dude, I was just saying hi."

"Yeah, and we all know what that usually leads to," Leon growls behind me.

The three of us take our seats and just about manage to pull our books out before our professor begins explaining the syllabus for the semester.

"Sorry about the coffee," Luca whispers after a few

minutes. "Here." He places a bottle of water on my desk. "I know it's not exactly a replacement, but it's the best I can do."

The reminder of the mess I left out in the hallway hits me.

"I should go and—"

"Chill," he says, placing his hand on my thigh. His touch instantly relaxes me as much as it sends a shock through my body. "I'll get you a replacement after class. Might even treat you to a cupcake."

I smile up at him, swooning at the fact he remembers my favorite treat.

Why did I ever think coming here was a bad idea?

2

LETTY

My hand aches by the time Professor Whitman finishes talking. It feels like a lifetime ago that I spent this long taking notes.

"You okay?" Luca asks me with a laugh as I stretch out my fingers.

"Yeah, it's been a while."

"I'm sure these boys can assist you with that, beautiful," bursts from Colt's lips, earning him another slap to the head.

"Ignore him. He's been hit in the head with a ball one too many times," Leon says from beside me but I'm too enthralled with the way Luca is looking at me right now to reply.

Our friendship wasn't a conventional one back in high school. He was the star quarterback, and I wasn't a cheerleader or ever really that sporty. But we were paired up as lab partners during my first week at Rosewood High and we kinda never separated.

I watched as he took the team to new heights, as he

met with college scouts, I even went to a few places with him so he didn't have to go alone.

He was the one who allowed me to cry on his shoulder as I struggled to come to terms with the loss of another who left a huge hole in my heart and he never, not once, overstepped the mark while I clung to him and soaked up his support.

I was also there while he hooked up with every member of the cheer squad along with any other girl who looked at him just so. Each one stung a little more than the last as my poor teenage heart was getting battered left, right, and center.

With each day, week, month that passed, I craved him more but he never, not once, looked at me that way.

I was even his prom date, yet he ended up spending the night with someone else.

It hurt, of course it did. But it wasn't his fault and I refuse to hold it against him.

Maybe I should have told him. Been honest with him about my feelings and what I wanted. But I was so terrified I'd lose my best friend that I never confessed, and I took that secret all the way to Columbia with me.

As I stare at him now, those familiar butterflies still set flight in my belly, but they're not as strong as I remember. I'm not sure if that's because my feelings for him have lessened over time, or if I'm just so numb and broken right now that I don't feel anything but pain.

It really could go either way.

I smile at him, so grateful to have run into him this morning.

He always knew when I needed him and even without knowing of my presence here, there he was like some guardian fucking angel.

If guardian angels had sexy dark bed hair, mesmerizing green eyes and a body built for sin then yeah, that's what he is.

I laugh to myself, yeah, maybe that irritating crush has gone nowhere.

"What have you got next?" Leon asks, dragging my attention away from his twin.

Leon has always been the quieter, broodier one of the duo. He's as devastatingly handsome and as popular with the female population but he doesn't wear his heart on his sleeve like Luca. Leon takes a little time to warm to people, to let them in. It was hard work getting there, but I soon realized that once he dropped his walls a little for me, it was hella worth it.

He's more serious, more contemplative, he's deeper. I always suspected that there was a reason they were so different. I know twins don't have to be the same and like the same things, but there was always something niggling at me that there was a very good reason that Leon closed himself down. From listening to their mom talk over the years, they were so identical in their mannerisms, likes, and dislikes when they were growing up, that it seems hard to believe they became so different.

"Psychology but not for an hour. I'm—"

"I'm taking her for coffee," Luca butts in. A flicker of anger passes through Leon's eyes but it's gone so fast that I begin to wonder if I imagined it.

"I could use another coffee before econ," Leon chips in.

"Great. Let's go," Luca forces out through clenched teeth.

He wanted me alone. Interesting.

The reason I never told him about my mega crush is

the fact he friend-zoned me in our first few weeks of friendship by telling me how refreshing it was to have a girl wanting to be his friend and not using it as a ploy to get more.

We were only sophomores at the time but even then, Luca was up to all sorts and the girls around us were all more than willing to bend to his needs.

From that moment on, I couldn't tell him how I really felt. It was bad enough I even felt it when he thought our friendship was just that.

I smile at both of them, hoping to shatter the sudden tension between the twins.

"Be careful with these two," Colt announces from behind us as we make our way out of the lecture hall with all the others. "The stories I've heard."

"Colt," Luca warns, turning to face him and walking backward for a few steps.

"Don't worry," I shoot over my shoulder. "I know how to handle the Dunn twins." I wink at him as he howls with laughter.

"You two are in so much trouble," he muses as he turns left out of the room and we go right.

Leon takes my books from me once more and Luca threads his fingers through mine. I still for a beat. While the move isn't unusual, Luca has always been very affectionate. It only takes a second for his warmth to race up my arm and to settle the last bit of unease that's still knotting my stomach.

"Two Americanos and a skinny vanilla latte with an extra shot. Three cupcakes with the sprinkles on top."

I swoon at the fact Luca remembers my order. "How'd you—"

He turns to me, his wide smile and the sparkle in his

eyes making my words trail off. The familiarity of his face, the feeling of comfort and safety he brings me causes a lump to form in my throat.

"I didn't forget anything about my best girl." He throws his arm around my shoulder and pulls me close.

Burying my nose in his hard chest, I breathe him in. His woodsy scent mixes with his laundry detergent and it settles me in a way I didn't know I needed.

Leon's stare burns into my back as I snuggle with his brother and I force myself to pull away so he doesn't feel like the third wheel.

"Dunn," the server calls, and Leon rushes ahead to grab our order while Luca leads me to a booth at the back of the coffee shop.

As we walk past each table, I become more and more aware of the attention on the twins. I know their reps, they've had their football god status since before I moved to Rosewood and met them in high school, but I had forgotten just how hero-worshiped they were, and this right now is off the charts.

Girls openly stare, their eyes shamelessly dropping down the guys' bodies as they mentally strip them naked. Guys jealousy shines through their expressions, especially those who are here with their girlfriends who are now paying them zero attention. Then there are the girls whose attention is firmly on me. I can almost read their thoughts —hell, I heard enough of them back in high school.

What do they see in her?

She's not even that pretty.

They're too good for her.

The only difference here from high school is that no one knows I'm just trailer park trash seeing as I moved from the hellhole that is Harrow Creek before meeting the boys.

Tipping my chin up, I straighten my spine and plaster on as much confidence as I can find.

They can all think what they like about me, they can come up with whatever bitchy comments they want. It's no skin off my back.

"Good to see you've lost your appeal," I mutter, dropping into the bench opposite both of them and wrapping my hands around my warm mug when Leon passes it over.

"We walk around practically unnoticed," Luca deadpans.

"You thought high school was bad," Leon mutters, he was always the one who hated the attention whereas Luca used it to his advantage to get whatever he wanted. "It was nothing."

"So I see. So, how's things? Catch me up on everything," I say, needing to dive into their celebrity status lifestyles rather than thinking about my train wreck of a life.

"Really?" Luca asks, raising a brow and causing my stomach to drop into my feet. "I think the bigger question is how come you're here and why we had no idea about it?"

Releasing my mug, I wrap my arms around myself and drop my eyes to the table.

"T-things just didn't work out at Columbia," I mutter, really not wanting to talk about it.

"The last time we talked, you said it was everything you expected it to be and more. What happened?"

Kane fucking Legend happened.

I shake that thought from my head like I do every time he pops up.

He's had his time ruining my life. It's over.

"I just..." I sigh. "I lost my way a bit, ended up dropping out and finally had to fess up and come clean to Mom."

Leon laughs sadly. "I bet that went down well."

The Dunn twins are well aware of what it's like to live with a pushy parent. One of the things that bonded the three of us over the years.

"Like a lead balloon. Even worse because I dropped out months before I finally showed my face."

"Why hide?" Leon's brows draw together as Luca stares at me with concern darkening his eyes.

"I had some health issues. It's nothing."

"Shit, are you okay?"

Fucking hell, Letty. Stop making this worse for yourself.

"Yeah, yeah. Everything is good. Honestly. I'm here and I'm ready to start over and make the best of it."

They both smile at me, and I reach for my coffee once more, bringing the mug to my lips and taking a sip.

"Enough about me, tell me all about the lives of two of the hottest Kings of Maddison."

"Okay... how'd you do that?" Ella whispers after both Luca and Leon walk me to my psych class after our coffee break.

"Do what?" I ask, following her into the room and finding ourselves seats about halfway back.

"It's your first day and the Dunn twins just walked

you to class. You got a diamond-encrusted vag or something?"

I snort a laugh as a few others pause on their way to their seats at her words.

"Shush," I chastise.

"Girl, if it's true, you know all these guys need to know about it."

I pull out my books and a couple of pens as Professor Collins sets up at the front before turning to her.

"No, I don't have diamonds anywhere but my necklace. I've been friends with them for years."

"Girl, I knew there was a reason we should be friends." She winks at me. "I've been trying to get West and Brax to hook me up but they're useless."

"You want to be friends so I can set you up with one of the Dunns?"

"Or both." She shrugs, her face deadly serious before she leans in. "I've heard that they tag team sometimes. Can you imagine? Both of their undivided attention." She fans herself as she obviously pictures herself in the middle of a Dunn sandwich. "Oh and, I think you're pretty cool too."

"Of course you do." I laugh.

It's weird, I might have only met her very briefly this morning but that was enough.

"We're all going out for dinner tonight to welcome you to the dorm. The others are dying to meet you." She smiles at me, proving that there's no bitterness behind her words.

"I'm sorry for ignoring you all."

"Girl, don't sweat it. We got ya back, don't worry."

"Thank you," I mouth as the professor demands everyone's attention to begin the class.

The time flies as I scribble my notes down as fast as I can, my hand aching all over again and before I know it, he's finished explaining our first assignment and bringing his class to a close.

"Jesus, this semester is going to be hard," Ella muses as we both pack up.

"At least we've got each other."

"I like the way you think. You done for the day?"

"Yep, I'm gonna head to the store, grab some supplies then get started on this assignment, I think."

"I've got a couple of hours. You want company?"

After dumping our stuff in our rooms, Ella takes me to her favorite store, and I stock up on everything I'm going to need before we head back so she can go to class.

I make myself some lunch before being brave and setting up my laptop at the kitchen table to get started on my assignments. My time for hiding is over, it's time to get back to life and once again become a fully immersed college student.

"Holy shit, she is alive. I thought Zayn was lying about his beautiful older sister," a deep rumbling voice says, dragging me from my research a few hours later.

I spin and look at the two guys who have joined me.

"Zayn would never have called me beautiful," I say as a greeting.

"That's true. I think his actual words were: messy, pain in the ass, and my personal favorite, I'm glad I don't have to live with her again," he says, mimicking my brother's voice.

"Now that is more like it. Hey, I'm Letty. Sorry about—"

"You're all good. We're just glad you emerged. I'm West, this ugly motherfucker is Braxton—"

"Brax, please," he begs. "Only my mother calls me by my full name and you are way too hot to be her."

My cheeks heat as he runs his eyes over my curves.

"T-thanks, I think."

"Ignore him. He hasn't gotten laid for weeeeks."

"Okay, do we really need to go there right now?"

"Always, bro. Our girl here needs to know you get pissy when you don't get the pussy."

I laugh at their easy banter, closing down my laptop and resting forward on my elbows as they move toward the fridge.

"Ella says we're going out," Brax says, pulling out two bottles of water and throwing one to West.

"Apparently so."

"She'll be here in a bit. Violet and Micah too. They were all in the same class."

"So," West says, sliding into the chair next to me. "What do we need to know that your brother hasn't already told us about you?"

My heart races at all the things that not even my brother would share about my life before I drag my thoughts away from my past.

"Uhhh..."

"How about the Dunns love her," Ella announces as she appears in the doorway flanked by two others. Violet and Micah, I assume.

"Um... how didn't we know this?" Brax asks.

"Because you're not cool enough to spend any time with them, asshole," Violet barks, walking around Ella. "Ignore these assholes, they think they're something special because they're on the team but what they don't tell you is that they have no chance of making first string or talking to the likes of the Dunns."

"Vi, girl. That stings," West says, holding his hand over his heart.

"Yeah, get over it. Truth hurts." She smiles up at him as he pulls her into his chest and kisses the top of her head.

"Whatever, Titch."

"Right, well. Are we ready to go? I need tacos like... yesterday."

"Yes. Let's go."

"You've never had tacos like these, Letty. You are in for a world of pleasure," Brax says excitedly.

"More than she would be if she were in your bed, that's for sure," West deadpans.

"Lies and we all know it."

"Whatever." Violet pushes him toward the door.

"Hey, I'm Micah," the third guy says when I catch up to him.

"Hey, Letty."

"You need a sensible conversation, I'm your boy."

"Good to know."

Micah and I trail behind the others and with each step I take, my smile gets wider.

Things really are going to be okay.

3

KANE

"**W**hoa, look who decided to show their face. Classes started this morning, you know," Devin barks as I join him and the twins in their kitchen.

"Fuck off," I grunt. "I was busy."

"Our old man taking liberties again?"

"Something like that," I mutter. "One for me?" I ask, nodding at the beer in Devin's hand.

"Sure thing, man."

He pulls one from the refrigerator and throws it over. I catch it easily and knock the top off.

"Behind before you've even started. Not the best start to your college career, Legend."

"Whatever, nerd." I rub my hand on Ellis's head and jump up on the counter. "So, what have I missed?"

"They wouldn't know. Both were so fucking hungover they missed classes."

"And you're giving me shit?" I balk at Devin and Ezra.

"Was worth it though, right?" Ezra says, looking at Devin with a smirk.

"Hell yeah, she was a filthy bitch."

"Christ, I'm gonna unpack."

I leave them behind to relive their previous night's antics and I'm not surprised to hear another set of footsteps behind me as I jog up the stairs to the bedroom I know is mine.

"You ready for this?" Ellis asks me and when I look over my shoulder, I find him leaning back against the doorframe with his arms folded over his chest.

"Of course, man." His brow rises suspiciously. "I earned this just as much as you did."

"I know, I know," he says, holding his hands up in defeat. "I'm not saying you're an idiot or anything."

"Right, so what are you saying?"

"That you're about to piss a lot of people off."

I can't help but laugh. "Yeah, that's half the fun. The Panthers have no clue what's about to hit them."

"Coach is gonna be pissed you missed today."

"Probably. He'll get over it."

Turning away from him, I open my bag and start pulling my clothes out, ready to find homes for them.

"How was your first day seeing as you were the only one who made it?"

"It was good. Different."

"Most places are, compared to Harrow Creek High," I mutter, thinking of the jungle we've all thankfully left behind.

Ellis and Ezra have only just graduated, whereas I've been out of that shithole for over a year now after retaking my senior year.

I should have been here a year ago, but life got in the way in the form of my brother getting a one-way ticket to juvie for a year and I had other things aside than my own future to think about.

But a year later, and I'm ready to take Maddison Kings by storm, or more importantly, their championship winning football team.

A smile curls at my lips as I think about the reactions I'm going to get tomorrow when I walk into the locker rooms to join the team.

As far as I know, Coach Butler hasn't announced my impending arrival.

I can almost picture the look on the Dunns faces in my mind and it sends a thrill shooting down my spine.

Those fuckers walked all over the Harriers every single game we played in high school. Not to mention they took a certain golden-skinned beauty under their wing after she left Harrow Creek.

Anger burns through me as I think about her and how we left things at that party last year. It was never my intention to let her go like I did. But the second the sirens started and the sound of everyone fleeing from the house filtered down to us, I had no choice but to run with them.

If I knew what was going to unfold, I might have done things a little differently.

I sigh, dropping to the end of my bed as I think about leaving Kyle behind in our home in Rosewood to follow my dream of college football.

He's eighteen now, more than capable of looking after himself but without any other family, it's my job to worry about him.

Thanks to his stint in juvie, he's retaking his senior year as well. He's already secured his place playing for the Rosewood Bears and has even scored vice-captain.

I can only hope I can get my new ball career off to such a flying start. I think it might be wishful thinking.

"You okay?" Ellis asks, startling me. I'd totally forgotten he was watching me.

"Yeah, just worried about Kyle."

"He'll be fine. Plus, he's got his girl with him, right?"

"Yeah," I say with a laugh, thinking of Baby Hunter.

Trust my fucking brother to fall in love with the sister of the girl who's ruined my life. I know I've done plenty of bad things in my twenty years, but fuck karma, she really is a bitch.

"He's a good kid, he'll be fine," Ellis says as if they're not the same age.

"He is," I agree. Juvie wasn't his fault.

Okay, so yeah, his pockets were full of blow and he was found with a drugged girl in his arms. But neither were his fault.

My fists curl as I think of the one responsible for everything that night.

"You want my notes from our business class earlier?"

"You mind?" I ask, glad to have something else to think about than everything we've left behind.

"Get yourself sorted then come find me. I can't help with the others though, you'll need some other sucker for that."

I think about the other class that I missed today. When it became apparent that I wasn't going to make it this morning, I sent an apology email to my professors spouting some bullshit about food poisoning and my sincere apologies. I have no idea if they bought it, and I don't really give a shit, to be honest. One has replied with his presentation and information on the first assignment but I have yet to hear from the others. Probably not a good sign.

I make quick work of putting my clothes away before dropping my books to my desk and plugging my charger in by the side of the queen-sized bed.

The room isn't much. It's the smallest of all the ones in this house but I can't complain seeing as I don't actually have to pay for it, well not with actual money anyway.

I glance around the small room. The walls are dark gray, the dresser, bedframe, nightstand, and small desk are all black and there's a cracked mirror in the corner, I'm hoping that the bad luck that came with that left with the room's previous resident because hell knows I've had enough bad luck to last a lifetime.

With a notebook and a pen in hand, I leave my room behind and go in search of Ellis. He's probably the only Harris brother that deserves his place here at MKU but thanks to who their father is, both Devin and Ezra have found themselves here, along with me, although their intentions for this experience vary hugely from mine.

I want a future. A chance.

They're having their puppet strings pulled by their father.

"Hit me with it," I say, dropping down onto Ellis's bed, ready to embark on this whole college thing.

———

I sit bolt upright in bed the next morning the second my alarm starts blaring from my cell on the nightstand.

It's still dark and my brain fights to come to life and remember why the hell I need to be awake so early.

Hell, right now I don't even know where I am.

It's not an unusual feeling after the past couple of years, and one I'm hoping to see the back of soon.

Glancing around in the darkness, realization sets in and a smile begins to twitch at my lips.

Today's the first day of the rest of my life. The first day of putting Victor Harris and his demanding, controlling ways behind me and embarking on the life I've always dreamed of.

With my body suddenly on board with the situation, I throw the covers off, drag on a pair of shorts followed by the MKU Panthers jersey I ordered when all of this was set into place. I needed a reminder that everything could turn out as it should after all the shit.

Shoving my feet into my sneakers, I throw my duffel over my shoulder and make my way down to the kitchen.

I make myself a quick protein shake and throw a couple of bottles of water into my bag before heading out.

The house is still in silence behind me as I pull the front door closed.

Turning the key in my old Nissan Skyline, I turn the volume up and back out of the driveway, my thumb tapping the wheel along with the beat.

There's a lightness to my body that I haven't felt in... forever.

I know what's to come isn't going to be straightforward. I'm aware that the chances of being welcomed to the team with open arms and wide smiles is unlikely but knowing there's fuck-all Luca Dunn or any of the others can do about it makes it that much sweeter.

The drive to the training facility is short and by the time I'm pulling to a stop beside the other cars already in the lot, excitement is buzzing through my veins.

I jog to the door and wrench it open, stepping through

and breathing in the scent of the slightly overpowering air freshener they use, I assume to cover up the smell of the sweaty guys who are constantly filling the space.

The entrance is empty but as I get closer to the locker room door, the sound of muffled voices filters down to me.

I clench my fists as my excitement almost becomes too much to bear.

I slow to almost a complete stop outside the door, suck in a few deep breaths and run my fingers through my hair, pushing it back from my brow for a few seconds.

I want to remember this moment. The moment I show those assholes on the other side of the door that I'm not the nobody they think I am. That I'm not the loser captain of the Harriers who bombed out of the division every single year. That I'm not forever going to be held back by the shithole place I was unlucky enough to be born into.

I'm Kane fucking Legend and the Panthers have no clue what's about to hit them.

I nod to myself and widen my shoulders and slam my palm down on the purple door.

The chatter gets louder for a few seconds as I step into the room. The scent of the air freshener dies out and is replaced by the familiar scent of sweat, mud and deodorant as slowly, almost every set of eyes in the room turn on me and the silence and tension becomes almost overbearing.

I look from each face to the next. Most are oblivious as to who I am and the importance of this moment but then I find a familiar set of eyes. They're narrowed and filled with an anger I'm all too used to.

We've hated each other on and off the field for years. Despite the fact we've never actually spent any time together outside of a stadium, we both know that the mutual hatred and rivalry that festers inside of us will always stop us from being friends.

"What the fuck?" Luca barks, his lips curling in disgust as his fists curl at his sides.

"Don't tell me Coach didn't tell his beloved starting quarterback that he's expecting a new wide receiver any day now." The smugness in my tone rings out loud and clear through the locker room.

There are a couple of gasps from the few guys who know who I am, one in particular over Luca's shoulders looks about ready to murder me right here on the spot— rightly so after the shit I've put his sister through, I guess.

"You're lying," Luca grits out as his sidekick and twin brother steps up beside him.

I smile at Leon although it's totally insincere. I have no intention of making friends with any of these assholes.

I'm here for one reason and one reason only.

To play fucking football.

I was scouted during my first attempt at senior year. Our team might have been beyond abysmal, but I never was. I was the best thing the Harrow Creek Harriers had seen in a very long time, but even as good as I might be, my skill can hardly carry an entire team.

I did my best, and it was helped when Kyle, my little brother, stepped up to play with me but still, we were never going to turn the rest of the pilled-up, hungover, trailer trash that surrounded us every practice into a real team of winners, it just was never going to happen.

But without enough credits to graduate, I couldn't accept my place as a Panther. So I retook the year, fucking bossed it, and was ready to make the move to Maddison until my little fucking brother got himself locked up.

But I guess, like they say, everything happens for a reason, because here I am about to claim my rightful place right alongside the Dunn twins as first string wide receiver. A position I'm sure many guys who are staring at me right now would give their left testicle for.

"Am I?" I ask, throwing my duffel down on the bench before me and unzipping my hoodie to reveal my Panthers jersey beneath.

"Y-you have to be. You can't just turn up like this. That's not how shit works."

"Not in your world, maybe. But in mine, I'm right where I should be."

Turning back to him, I find Luca's lips pressed into a thin line, the muscles down his neck and across his shoulders straining to the point I wonder if they could snap, and his fist clenched, ready to throw a punch that I know he's been desperate to land for a few years now.

My smile widens as my eyes hold his.

I take a step closer and I swear everyone around us sucks in a deep breath, preparing for us to go up against each other.

"Do you happen to know which locker is mine?" I ask innocently.

"This is not fucking happen—" His words are cut off as the door at the other end of the long room swings open and crashes back against the wall.

While some of the others around us go back to what they were doing before I entered and interrupted things, Luca and Leon don't move, and neither do I. It'll be a cold day in hell before I cower down to the fucking Dunn twins. So what, their daddy is ex-NFL. So what, they've got more money than I'd know what to do with.

"Ah good, I see you're getting to know our new receiver."

Luca's eyes narrow to slits before he turns to Coach.

"Yeah, about that—" Luca starts marching toward the man in charge. "Do you know who he is?"

Silence once again descends on the locker room, most of them probably wanting to know the answer to that question.

"Yeah, the best damn receiver in the state. No offense, Dunn," he says, his eyes briefly flicking to Leon.

"I don't give a shit how good he is, he shouldn't be here," Luca barks, trailing after Coach when he turns toward his office.

"Get in there, Dunn," he chastises. "Get your asses in the gym, ladies. Your muscles ain't gonna strengthen themselves." At his word, everyone jumps into action. "Legend," he says, tilting his chin up in greeting. "Good to see you're feeling better. Welcome to the team, son."

I smile at him, it's the most genuine one I've given anyone in a pretty long time.

I might not be wanted here by many, but fuck, I feel more at home here already than I have in years, even with the hate stares still being thrown my way from a few, mainly Zayn Hunter.

4

LETTY

Everything feels different when I wake the next morning. I feel lighter, the tightness in my chest that I've become all too used to has lessened.

The guys took me to a bar and grill off campus and we spent the evening laughing and eating. It was the most normal night I've had in a very long time.

Every time one of them made me laugh, I felt the stress and loss of my past begin to melt away. It was such a freeing feeling after drowning under the weight for such a long time.

Flicking my bedside light on, I look around my room. It's not unlike my dorm room at Columbia and that's kinda comforting. The walls are an off-white with dirty marks where the previous occupant must have had posters up. As well as the twin bed I'm curled up in, there's a single closet, a chest of drawers and a desk. Plus, and I've no idea how Mom managed to secure it at the last minute, a private bathroom.

I curl back up and think of how incredible yesterday was. From bumping into Luca and Leon, my classes, my roommates and the possibility of actually being happy here.

I can't wipe the smile off my face as I finally throw my sheets off and plod through to my bathroom. The tiled floor is like ice against my bare feet and I hop around as I brush my teeth and wait for the shower to warm up.

The second I'm ready, I don't hesitate in pulling open my door and joining whoever is already crashing around in the kitchen for breakfast. The scent of frying bacon is too much to resist.

"Good morning," Violet sings from her spot by the stove.

"Morning."

"I hope you're hungry." My stomach rumbles right on cue.

"You have no idea."

Panic flickers inside me as I look down at myself but I quickly talk myself down because there's no way anyone here would know that I'm two dress sizes down on what I've always been, thanks to the stress of the past year.

"Grab yourself a coffee and it'll be ready in a few."

"I can help," I offer, heading for the coffee machine.

"We have a food rota. You're tomorrow and Friday. The guys luck out during the season, but we'll ensure they make up for it once it's over."

"You're assuming I can cook."

"You don't have to cook. Buy a box of cereal if you like, order something. You're just in charge of those days."

I smile at her, loving how the six of them work like a well-oiled machine. If I'd have known about this before I moved in, I might have been intimidated about joining them, but they've welcomed me as if I've always been here and I couldn't be more grateful.

They're the family I didn't know I needed and it's only day two.

I'm sipping on my coffee when Ella and Micah join us and Violet begins plating up.

"Still here then?" Micah jokes.

"Yeah, you didn't all put me off too badly last night."

"And here I thought West and Brax's jokes might have been the end of you."

I laugh, recalling some of their worst pickup lines last night. "They're harmless."

"There are a few broken hearts walking around campus who probably wouldn't agree with you."

I roll my eyes. "Football players. I know all about them." I think of Luca and his ways with women over the few years I've known him.

"Oh, so..." Ella pipes up. "You never actually explained how you know them," she digs.

"You need to get over yourself. They don't want you," Violet groans as she sits down with us to eat. "She's been chasing them around like a lost puppy for two years. It's becoming pathetic."

"I haven't chased anyone. And..." she points out, poking her knife in Violet's direction. "As you well know, I was with Sawyer for most of freshman year."

"Ugh," Micah complains. "We know. No need to remind us."

I watch as the three of them bicker like siblings and I realize why the vibe in this dorm works so well, they really are a little family.

"So, the twins," Ella prompts once again, ignoring the others and their attempt at a topic change.

"I moved to Rosewood when I was sixteen. Luca was

my lab partner in my first week and we just hit it off. The rest is history."

"You slept with them?" she asks, leaning forward on her elbows and soaking up my every word.

"Err..."

"Oh my God, you have. Tell me they tag teamed you, please." The excitement in her eyes is amusing as hell and I realize that I'm going to have to introduce her to them for the comedy value alone. She'll lose her shit.

"No, I haven't been in a Dunn sandwich, so I can't feed your fantasy, sorry."

"Ugh, what kind of use are you?" she sulks.

"I'll introduce you next time we see them."

"Yesss," she hisses. "Oh, maybe I shouldn't eat this. If this happens today I don't want to be all bloated and gross."

We all stare at her. "For real?" Violet asks, her brows raised.

She's got a point, Ella's got a banging body and the most insane curves. Any guy would be lucky to get their hands on her.

"Just eat the damn bacon, El. No guy wants a skinny bitch anyway."

None of them look my way, and I know that the comment isn't in any way directed at me, but still, I feel myself retreat a little. I hate how I look right now. I hate that when I look in the mirror, my ribs and hip bones are so visible. I miss my curves, my breasts, my ass.

Silently, I cut into my breakfast and pop each bite into my mouth but I don't taste any of it. Thoughts of my body take me back there and I'll do anything to keep my head in the present.

"So what do you say, Letty? You in?"

"Uh..."

All three of them are staring at me but I have zero clue as to what they're talking about.

"Party Friday night. You in?"

Dread sits heavy in my stomach at the mention of a party. I should say no. I should make an excuse about the amount of work I have to do and hide in my room.

But as I look between them and the hope in their eyes, I realize that I can't be that scared little girl anymore. I'm here and it seems like I might have already landed some incredible friends. I need to embrace it.

"It's a football party at the Dunn's place," Ella adds. "They'll probably invite you anyway."

"Oh, um..." The thought of Luca and Leon being there makes me feel better and I quickly find myself agreeing.

"Sweet. We'll get ready here, head over fashionably late, hopefully, catch some eyes." Ella wiggles her brows.

"Girl, the twins don't want you," Micah spits, sounding totally exasperated by her.

"I wasn't talking about them. I'll take any athlete. I'm not choosy."

"We know. We have to listen to you, remember."

"Aw, Micey." She pouts while his face hardens at the awful nickname. "You're just jealous because you haven't gotten laid in..." She starts counting on her fingers as if she has actually worked it out.

"Fuck off, El." He pushes his thick-rimmed glasses up his nose and stands with his empty plate in hand. He turns his dark eyes on me. "Sorry, Let. I hope you have a good day."

He damn near throws his plate in the sink, drills a hate stare at Ella and storms from the room.

Interesting.

"Girl, do you have to push his buttons?" Violet snaps at Ella who just shrugs innocently.

"Not my problem that he can't get over his ex."

"He's over her and you know it. Cheating bitch doesn't deserve any more of his thoughts."

"Amen to that. Chloe was a bitch with a capital b."

"You finished?" Violet asks me, glancing at my empty plate.

"Yes. Thank you, it was delicious. Feeling the pressure for tomorrow."

"It's not a test, Let. Just make sure there's something to eat and we're all good. Ah, here come the boys. Get that pan on the go, Vi."

The booming sounds of West and Brax's voice filter down to us a few seconds before they come bounding through the door.

They're both freshly showered by looking at their hair. They throw their duffels in the direction of their bedrooms and simultaneously pull out a chair each and sit down.

"Where's the food, Vi? Two starving athletes here."

"You're back early," Ella mutters. "You might even get to class on time today."

"Session was cut short. New guy turned up and caused havoc." West waves it off as nothing as the sizzling of bacon fills the room once more.

"I'm just gonna get sorted," I say, pointing to my room and then quickly head that way to gather my books ready for class.

I'm not really interested in the football drama. I did my best to stay away from it all in high school—which was easier said than done when my best friend was the freaking captain and best quarterback in the state.

I roll my eyes at his undying love for the game and pack everything up. If there's one thing I intend to do during my time here, it's to stay as far away from football, hell any athletes, aside from those who are already my friends—or quickly turning into my friends. Nothing good comes from football players.

"You heading in?" Ella asks me when I meet her out in the living area also with her bag over her shoulder ready to get to class.

"Yep. Sociology, you?"

"Marketing. I'm in the next building to you so I'll walk you."

"Let's do it."

She links her arm through mine and together we leave the others behind.

"Just so you know, I'm not some sex-starved whore," she says a little too seriously as we make our way across the quad.

"I didn't think that," I say lightly. "I know they were just ribbing you."

"I'll admit, I've had my fair share of less than memorable relationships and one-night stands. They seem to forget that they're the same. Well, apart from Micah, he's quieter than the rest of us."

"He's got the nerd look down."

"Yeah, girls at MKU generally pine after the athletes."

"You say that like it's different at any other college. Columbia was exactly the same."

"I blame books."

I snort a laugh. "How so?"

"You know, all those hot romances make the guys out

to be players and whatever but then there's that one who takes one look at you and forgets everyone else and you get to run off with him while he earns a shit ton in the NFL or NBA or whatever." She sighs dreamily.

"That what you want?"

"No, not really." She laughs. "I want a career. But we can all dream, right?"

"Sure can." I think back to my own obsession with Luca over the years and I totally understand the fascination.

Ella opens the door for me when we get to the building I apparently need and I step through.

"I think your cell is buzzing," she says, quickly catching up with me.

"Oh."

Swinging my purse around, I dig through it as we head up to the second floor.

"Is that Mary Poppins' purse or something?" she mutters when she looks over to find me still searching.

"Ah-ha," I exclaim as I pull it out.

"Jesus, someone wants you," she mutters, staring down at the screen as I do.

Seventeen missed calls from Zayn.

My heart drops into my feet as I think about what that many missed calls could mean.

Mom, Dad, Harley... fuck.

My hand is trembling as I attempt to call him back. I can barely breathe through my panic as I wait for the call to connect.

If something has happened to them, I'm not sure I'm going to cope. Not after...

The call rings twice before he answers.

"What's wrong? Is everyone okay?" I rush out, my voice cracking with emotion.

Ella's concerned stare burns into the side of my head but I keep my eyes trained on a spot on the wall down the hall in the hope the nothingness might somehow calm me.

"What? Yeah, everyone's okay," he says, sounding a little regretful about sending me into a meltdown.

"Thank fuck. Don't ever do that to me again, okay?"

"Shit, I'm sorry. I didn't mean... it doesn't matter. Um... you might want to sit down for this."

The panic that had started to subside returns full force.

"Zayn?"

"Okay, um... I'm not sure how to... fuck..."

"Just spit it out."

"Okay, so a new player showed up at our session this morning and—"

His voice fades into oblivion as a person walking up the hallway I'm staring down catches my attention.

My heart slams against my ribs and my head begins to spin.

No. No, it can't be.

No.

Our eyes connect and it's like someone's just hit me with a fucking truck.

This cannot be happening to me.

No.

No.

"No," I cry, although my voice doesn't sound like my own.

My cell slips from my hand. I can vaguely hear Zayn shouting down the line as I wrap my arms around my middle and stumble back, needing to put as much distance between us as possible.

"Letty?" A soft voice hits my ears and I remember that Ella is with me but all I can see is him.

Kane Legend.

Walking down the hallway as if he's about to attend my sociology class.

No. No. No.

When my eyes focus again, I find him standing stock-still outside the door and staring at me as if I can't possibly be real.

God, please let this be a dream—or a fucking nightmare.

Hate crackles between us as we just stare at each other as if we're not really there.

I guess at least I know he didn't plan this.

He's as shocked as I am.

His lips part and for a second, I think he's actually going to say something but at the last minute, he closes them again and swiftly disappears into the auditorium.

I release the breath I had no idea I was holding and my legs give out.

I slide down the wall until my ass hits the floor and I wrap my arms around my knees.

"What the hell was that?" Ella asks, dropping down to her haunches beside me and placing her warm hand on my shoulder.

"T-that... that was my worst nightmare."

"Uh... o-okay." She looks to the door where Kane vanished and then back to me. "Do you want to go back to the dorms?"

I'm about to say yes and I'm almost climbing from the

floor in my need to escape but at the last minute, I stop myself.

"No. I need to go to class."

"But—"

I push up from the floor and brush myself off.

I refuse to be the girl I've been for the last year. If I'm her, then he'll crush me without even trying.

I need to find the girl who stood up against him the night of that party. The night that tilted my world on its axis.

I blow out a breath and reach down for my cell, looking it over, grateful that I didn't crack the screen, and then grab my purse.

I take a step toward my class but Ella's hand on my arm stops me.

"A-are you sure this is a good idea?"

No, it's probably not. "Yes, it'll be fine." I refuse to stop my life for a moment longer because of him. He's already taken enough from me. That has to stop now.

After tapping out a quick message to Zayn, I square my shoulders and hold my head high as the professor slips into the room.

Perfect timing.

"I can come?"

"No, you have a marketing class. I'll be fine."

She hesitates, not wanting to leave me.

I understand. If I'd just witnessed her react like that to merely seeing someone, I'd be concerned too.

"Unlock this," she says, lifting my cell up.

I do as she says and she takes it from me, quickly tapping out her number.

"If you need me... anything. Call me. I'll be right here."

"Thank you," I whisper. "I-I should go. I don't want to miss anything."

"Okay."

She doesn't leave, instead just watches me walk into my class.

The seats are almost full as I scan my eyes around the room, hoping like hell my eyes don't find him.

Spotting an empty seat about halfway back, I hitch my purse up higher and make my way there as the professor begins introducing himself and what today's class will entail.

I can't have taken more than ten steps before a tingle of awareness races down my spine.

He's watching me.

As discreetly as I can, I look around the room trying to find him, but I'm unsuccessful. All I find are eager students listening to whatever is being said at the front of the class.

My blood is still whooshing in my ears long after I sit down and get my books out. I try my best to focus and get my head around what this semester has in store for me in this class but all I can see are his blue eyes as he stared at me in the hallway.

He looked exactly as he did that night. Like he left and wasn't affected by what happened between us.

Why should he? It's not like we saw each other or even spoke after that night.

The second he heard the sirens in the distance, he bolted, leaving me there in the dark forest, damn near glued into that muddy puddle he'd fucked me in.

I was a mess. If only I knew that it was a sign of what was to come, it might not have felt so bad.

Hindsight is a great thing because if I had known

what was going down in Skye's house then I might have swallowed down my pride and walked back inside to find my sister.

But I didn't. I fixed my dress the best I could, got in my car, and made my way home, confident that Harley would be safe with Kyle and the others. She doesn't need babying, we're all Harrow Creek kids and we know how to look after ourselves.

But if I had known...

I try to swallow down the messy ball of emotion that clogs my throat.

I have so many regrets from that night. There are so many things that shouldn't have happened and what went down between Kane and me was only one of them.

Harley ended up in the hospital being questioned by police and Kyle ended up in juvie.

No doubt he blames all of that on me along with the already very long line of crimes he thinks I'm guilty of.

I let out a shaky sigh as images from my past play out in my head like a freaking movie.

It's two hours later when our professor brings the class to a close after explaining our first assignment but I haven't heard a word of it. I breathe a small sigh of relief when he tells us that notes will be online shortly because I have no clue as to what's happened this morning.

Everyone around me begins packing up their things and making their way toward the exit but I find myself frozen to the spot.

Still, my skin prickles with awareness telling me that he's still here.

Why can't he just leave with everyone else, forget I exist and continue on with his life.

Out of nowhere West and Brax's comment from this morning hits me.

"New guy turned up and caused havoc."

Holy shit, Luca.

He hates Kane almost as much as I do. Something I never discouraged during my time in Rosewood, although I never confessed to the feeling being mutual. I made a point of being busy every time the Bears and the Harriers had a game and I never once mentioned my connection to him aside from us being at school together. Neither of them ever asked either, not that I'd have told them the truth if they had. I'd run away from my high school bully and that was the end of it. I was just glad that the Bears ruined the Harriers every time they played. It made everything feel a little better in my head.

But now... now he's here and if he's on the team.

Fuck.

This is not good.

No.

This is really, really fucking bad.

5

KANE

I find myself a seat at the very back of the auditorium and sink into the shadows as more students pour in behind me, filling the seats around me.

The room around me spins and blurs into nothing as I try to get my head around what just happened out in the hall.

She's here.

Scarlett Hunter is at MKU and looking like she's about to attend class.

But she goes to Columbia. Or at least, she did.

I haven't seen or heard from her since that night. But my brother is dating her little sister. How didn't I know this?

Probably the same reason why they don't know you're attending, asshole, a little voice pipes up in my head.

I never meant to hide college from Kyle, from anyone really. But the thought of saying it out loud and then it all falling through at the last minute terrified me. Everything I've done these past few years has all been to get here, to provide my brother and me with a better life but to get here, I've relied on others coming through on promises they could quite easily break. The risk was too high and I didn't want to get Kyle's hopes up. He already thinks he had a hand in ruining my life when he went down that night.

If I'd told him then I might have gotten the heads up I needed about her being here. Or word would have got back to her that I would be and she'd have changed her mind.

I let out a sigh as I think about the woman who's consumed so many of my thoughts over the years. There were so many differences between that woman outside this room and the one at that party eighteen months ago.

When I first clocked her at the other end of the hall, I didn't even think it was her, just my mind playing games with me.

But the closer I got, I knew, my body knew.

Her face was thinner, her cheeks hollow and her complexion pale. Her body was so much thinner than it was the night I had my hands on her and my immediate reaction was concern. Something has clearly happened to her, but then I remembered everything she's done to me, all the ways she hurt me, and the anger decimated the concern and raced to the surface.

I clench my fists over and over, trying to expel some of the pent-up anger but it does little to help. I need to get up, to move to go and punch something—or someone. Luca fucking Dunn is top of that list after the drama he caused with Coach this morning, accusing him of breaking the NCAA rules by letting me in as he has. That really ticked Coach off because everyone knows that Coach Butler never does anything against the regulations. It just shows how much trust he has in Coach. I expected him to question me, but I didn't think he'd be quite that angry about my arrival.

It was hard not to smile as we all heard Luca shouting his frustrations at his leader and threatening to go to the athletic director about the decision.

His reaction was everything—and more—than I expected. And now, running into Letty. Well, today couldn't actually get much better.

I shift in my chair, still fighting to keep a lid on things as our professor begins his lecture. I've got my pen poised and ready to start at least one class the way I'd like when the side door opens and a familiar figure steps into the auditorium.

Most are too focused on Professor Nelson to notice the late arrival, although he gives her a hard stare as she makes her way into the room.

Unlike out in the hall, she's got her head held high and her shoulders squared.

I barely manage to contain my laughter at her attempt to look in control.

Clearly, she's forgotten that around me, she has zero control.

I watch her every move, wishing like hell I could easily get up and make my way to sit near her, anything just to torment her a little.

I smile to myself. It's like high school all over again. Only, back then, I just wanted to teach her a lesson for betraying me. Now I want to ruin her for how everything turned out.

I've lost so much because of her, yet she got everything she wanted.

Although her being here right now instead of her

beloved Columbia makes me question things, but I don't care enough about her problems to let it affect me.

I slump down in my chair, half-listening to Nelson but mostly focusing on her, picking out all the differences I see in her from last year.

I never should have touched her that night. I knew that before I even laid a finger on her but the temptation after all the years we'd danced around each other way too strong. Then when I had her body pressed up against mine, writhing and begging for more, I knew I'd made a colossal mistake.

My cock swells, tenting my pants, as I vividly recall taking her in the muddy puddle as the party raged behind us.

But as good as my memories are about finally claiming what should have been mine all along, I can't forget what was happening inside that house.

I drop my head, thinking of my brother and everything he went through because I was distracted. Because of her.

The class passes faster than I thought possible but I barely hear any of it. Today might be turning out to be better than I expected, but I kinda hoped I'd make a better start with my classes. I missed two yesterday and I've just fucked this one up.

It really is just like high school all over again. Too distracted by a dark-haired beauty to focus on what I should be listening to.

I'm slow packing up, mostly on purpose because I want to watch her run from the room like her ass is on fire.

She might want to appear that she's not affected by my appearance, but it's all lies.

She's terrified.

Exactly as she should be.

In the end, I'm one of the last out of the auditorium. There are a few guys I vaguely recognize from our session this morning but none of them so much as attempt to talk to me. I get it. Their loyalty is to their captain.

Pulling the folded up piece of paper from my back pocket, I stare down at the campus map and try to figure out where I can find some food before my statistics class in an hour.

I grab myself a sandwich when I finally locate the campus coffee shop and by the time I've eaten it and then found the right building for my next class, I'm almost late.

The auditorium is abuzz with student chatter as I step through the door, almost all the seats taken.

I scan the room, looking for a place to sit when my eyes land on a familiar bowed head.

Bingo.

The seats on either side of her are taken, but that's not going to stop me.

I march up the stairs toward where she is and come to a stop by the guy who's getting his iPad set up ready for the lecture beside her.

"You're in my seat," I say, making him stop what he's doing to turn to look up at me. Something about him is familiar and I'm not the only one who sees it because his eyes flash with recognition.

Next to him, Letty tenses at the sound of my voice but she refuses to look up despite the fact her body has locked up tight at the prospect of having to sit beside me.

"Sorry, but I'm pretty sure seats haven't been allocated in this class. Go find another."

"Huh." I tilt my head to the side as if I didn't

understand his words. "Clearly, you didn't hear me properly. I said... you're in my seat, asshole."

The students surrounding us begin to pay attention but still, Letty doesn't so much as breathe while I stand here.

"Everything alright?" another guy says, coming to stand beside me but keeping his eyes on the guy who's sitting.

"It's okay," a quiet voice says from beside the guy. "Go and sit with Brax somewhere."

An accomplished smile twitches at my lips.

"But—" the guy argues, ripping his narrowed eyes from mine to look at Letty.

"It's okay." She smiles at him. Anyone else would think she meant it, but I see more than most, and she's anything but happy about this.

"Is everyone ready to start?" the professor says from behind me as the guy begins collecting up his things.

"We'll just be down there." He points to a couple of empty chairs a few rows down.

She nods at him and smiles again and he hesitantly gets up but he doesn't leave right away, instead, he levels me with a look that might have lesser guys running scared. Clearly, he has no idea who I am or what I'm capable of.

"Shoo," I say with a flick of my hand before dropping down into the now vacant seat and unpacking everything I need.

She's like a stone beside me, not moving and I swear not even breathing as she waits for what I'm going to do next.

Professor Richman begins going over his expectations for this class, but his words fade off into the background.

Yet another ruined first class then, I muse to myself as I watch Letty out of the corner of my eye.

After what seems like forever with her sitting beside me and her floral scent filling my nose and driving me insane, I lean toward her slightly.

Her spine straightens as she prepares for my next move.

"Get lost on your way to Columbia, Princess?"

Her lips flatten as she fights the need to say something back to me.

That's the fun with her. She can't help herself.

Her chin drops and I suck in a breath waiting for her response.

"I'm trying to listen."

She leans forward on her desk, effectively putting me behind her. It's a move that pisses me off beyond belief, that she can discard me, forget about me that easily.

I chuckle and after a few seconds, she glances back at me, her eyes are narrowed in anger as she attempts to pin me with a look that she hopes will shut me up. I'd like to think she knows better than that by now.

The gold flecks in her eyes shine under the harsh fluorescent lighting above it. It's only this obvious when she's angry or turned on. I like to think with me this close that it's a little of both, but I know I'm only lying to myself. The reality is that I need to be sleeping with one eye open because she's likely to stab me in the middle of the night. Her and the line of others which will probably be headed up by Luca Dunn himself.

"What?" she snaps. Her eyes briefly flicking around my face as if she's looking for differences in me like I have with her.

She's going to be disappointed if she was hoping to

find a weakness because in the eighteen months since we last saw each other, I'm only angrier, tougher, stronger, and more hardened to the realities that lie outside of this campus.

There's only one of us who has any kind of weakness here, and only one of us is going to end up broken because of all the mistakes they've made.

The other is getting revenge.

I just wish I knew she was going to be here so I wasn't so blindsided by her.

I continue smiling at her, trying to hide how I really feel.

"It's just like high school again. You're the nerd taking all the notes and I'm—"

"The arrogant, asshole jock intent on failing everything?"

"Ouch, Princess," I say, lifting my hand to cover my heart. "You wound me."

"Fuck off, Kane. I need this class."

"Yeah about that, what happened to—"

"If you're not going to listen, you can walk out of my lecture right now and never return," Professor Richman booms across the auditorium, a ripple of tension following his words.

I hold Letty's eyes for two more seconds before turning toward the front, nodding at the professor who's throwing his hate stare in my direction and pick up my pen, ready to get to work.

"I will not tolerate any more interruptions."

"Hard ass," I mutter to myself, and I soon realize that I was wrong. No one snickers around me, and when I glance up every single person is focused on the front of class. Nope, this is nothing like high school.

I look at Letty once more. Allow myself a few seconds to really take her in and register all the differences in her.

She knows I'm looking, her breathing hitches under my inspection but she doesn't stop what she's doing or turn to look at me again.

I tell myself that I don't care what's happened to her, but I know deep down that I do.

Because if she's hurting, then I want to be the one who's delivered that pain.

This class, I swear, is the longest of my life.

I force myself to listen and take notes because hell knows I'm already behind in my other three and I need to be on top of my classes before the season starts. These few weeks before our first game are going to fly and then once we start, I can only imagine how full on it's going to be. Especially as I have no doubt that Luca will be continuing to ride my ass. My foot bounces against the floor in excitement. *Bring it on, asshole. I'm ready for you.*

As our professor brings the class to a close with a detailed description of yet another assignment I need to embark on, I don't move. Unlike the rest of the auditorium who jump into action and begin moving toward the door at lightning speed.

I sit back and watch Letty as she packs her things away.

"Excuse me," she says abruptly as she stands.

Her eyes hold mine before I release her stare in favor of getting a close up look at her body.

She's wearing a pair of leggings under a floral dress and a leather jacket. I can't deny that she looks hot, she's Letty Hunter, she always looks fucking hot. But it's unmistakable that she's damn near half the woman she used to be.

My fists clench as I consider the possibility of someone hurting her at Columbia and that being the reason she's here.

Did some motherfucker ruin her dream of graduating from the college she spent her whole life dreaming about?

"Kane," she barks, getting exasperated, but still, I don't move. "Fine, whatever."

She spins and is about to make her way down the row of now empty seats at her back when I reach for her arm.

I stand as she fights to slip her wrist from my grip but I hold tighter.

"Ow, that hurts," she complains.

I pull her back and she stumbles, falling into my body.

Every single one of my muscles tenses at her touch and the blood racing through my veins turns to lava.

"You think I care, Princess?"

"Let go of me," she demands, her voice low and husky as she once again attempts to pull herself free.

"Why are you here?"

Her eyes lift from my chest until her dark ones collide with my blue angry ones.

"Why are *you* here? Last I heard you failed to graduate."

A laugh falls from my lips as I lower my head down a little to her. To anyone around us, it might look intimate, like I want to kiss her. The reality is very different.

"Princess," I growl and her lips twist in anger. She hates that nickname, always has. It's the exact reason I still insist on using it. "There is a lot you don't know about me."

"Letty, is this asshole bothering you?" a familiar voice asks from behind me.

"No, he's not," I answer for her, knowing that the two

goons from earlier are burning holes in the back of my head.

"We weren't talking to you, asshole."

"I'm fine. Thank you," Letty says, her eyes not once leaving mine. "I know how to handle this *asshole*."

My chest grows tight as my anger burns hotter within me.

I lower my face down, regretfully ripping my eyes from her until my lips are right next to her ear.

A shudder rips through her as my breath cascades over her exposed skin, I feel it all the way down her arm.

"That is where you are very, very wrong, Princess."

"Threaten me all you like. You can't break what's already broken."

With that, she pulls her arm free. My shock from her words allowing her to do it easily and she takes off through the small gap in the chairs.

"You need to watch who you make enemies of around here," one of the guys warns. "Stay away from Letty. Hell, stay away from all of us."

I spin around to respond but the pair of them are already at the bottom of the stairs and making their escape.

6

LETTY

The second my wrist slips from his grasp, my legs can't carry me away fast enough.

I don't look back as I flee from the lecture hall and I don't come to a stop again until I run into a very solid chest.

A familiar scent surrounds me as strong hands clamp down on my upper arms to steady me.

"Whoa, Letty are you okay?"

A sob bubbles up my throat as his concerned deep voice hits my ears and I only just about manage to contain it.

"Y-yeah, I'm fine. Can we just get out of here please?"

"Uh... sure. Let me take th—" His words trail off as he reaches for the books in my arms, but I don't need to look behind me to find out what's captured his attention. I feel it. I feel him.

"Legend," Luca spits as if his name tastes bitter on his tongue.

He looks down at me and then back to Kane once

more. His jaw is set while anger and confusion battles in his eyes.

He has no reason to know there's anything between Kane and me. I never told him for a very good reason.

They already hate each other enough.

I didn't need Luca going after Kane and risking the career he was building for me. Because I knew he would in a heartbeat if he knew the truth.

"Luca, let's just go, please?"

"Y-yeah, sure. Come on."

He turns, putting his back to Kane and wraps his arms around my waist, pulling me tight into his body, a move that I'm sure pisses Kane the fuck off.

I've never been Kane's but for some fucked-up reasons he can't stand anyone else having me. Well, one person aside.

I blow out a relieved breath as Luca quickly navigates us out of the building and away from Kane's hateful stare full of wicked promises and the pain he's planning to inflict.

What he doesn't realize is that I've already suffered the worst kind of pain because of him and anything else will be like child's play compared to the past year of my life.

"What the hell was that?" Luca asks, coming to a stop once we're safely away from him, the building, and anyone else who might be interested in listening.

"Not here. Don't you have practice?"

"I've got an hour," he says softly, lifting his hand so his fingers tuck under my chin to stop me from hiding from him, which he knows I'm desperate to do. "Wanna show me your dorm?" he asks, giving me a cheeky wink.

"You're a nut. Come on." I thread my arm through his

and turn toward where I think my building is, but just before I spin, I find *him* watching us.

Our eyes hold for a beat, the tension cracks so violently between us it feels like a physical blow to my body.

Luca notices my hesitation and follows my eyeline but he's too late, Kane's slipped into the shadows.

"You're in a dorm with West and Brax?" Luca asks as we approach the main door.

"Yeah. Please don't tell me they're bad guys," I beg as we walk into an almost empty communal area.

Micah is the only one sitting at the dining table with his laptop open.

"Afternoon," he says to me before doing a double-take at Luca.

"Christ, don't let Ella know he's here or she'll be clawing at your door like a cat in heat," he says in a disgruntled tone as I lead Luca to my room.

Luca snorts as if it's a totally normal thing to say to him.

"You didn't see us, okay?"

"Sure thing, Princess."

My steps falter at his use of that nickname for me.

"W-what did you call me?"

"P-princess? Sorry, I didn't mean to offend you. It's just, he's the king and... it was meant to be a joke. Forget I even said anything."

"I'm sorry," I say quickly feeling bad for assuming anything ill of him. Micah is good people. All the guys here are. I need to not let Kane get inside my head and force me to start questioning everyone. He's the only twisted motherfucker around here.

He looks a little sheepish behind his laptop.

"I'm just not a fan of the nickname. Queen suits me better."

Luca snorts a laugh behind me and thankfully, Micah smiles before I unlock my door and gesture for Luca to step inside.

He whistles as he takes in the small room.

"Momma Hunter did good scoring this place at the last minute."

"Right? I have no idea how she did it. I'm not complaining though. I'm loving not having to share a bathroom."

"It's pretty sweet. You know where is better though?"

"No," I say suspiciously, narrowing my eyes at him, as I drop down onto my bed while Luca takes the chair at my desk.

"We've got a spare room at our place. If you'd have—"

"No," I say cutting him off. "I need to do this myself. I can't live under your shadow for the next few years. Plus, I refuse to live with sweaty, smelly football players."

He pretends to be offended by my words but he knows just how smelly they can be.

"It's not just football players. A couple of girlfriends live with us too."

"Which I am not."

He stares at me for a beat too long. The teenage girl inside me starts jumping to conclusions but I quickly shove her back down. So much time has passed and so much has happened since she had her all-consuming crush on her best friend. It's too late for all that now.

"Maybe not but—"

"No, Luc. I appreciate the offer, I really do. But after —" I cut myself off, not wanting to start down a path I have no intention on continuing with. "I just need my space. I need to start over myself."

"You've had space, Let. You've been gone for two years. I..." He drags his eyes away from mine and stares down at his feet for a beat. "I missed you."

I gasp when his green eyes find mine once more.

My heart aches for the vulnerable boy I see hiding behind the king of football persona that everyone else sees.

"You were my best friend, Let, and... and..."

"And I left," I finish for him.

He laughs to himself. "Shit, that sounds like I blame you for chasing your dream. That's not what I meant at all."

"I know, Luc. I get what you mean. We lost touch. I'm sorry."

"Me too," he says sadly, standing from the chair and coming to sit beside me on the bed.

He reaches for my hand and threads our fingers together, staring down at them.

"What happened earlier, Let? What aren't you telling me?"

He looks up at me, his green eyes darkening around the edges in concern as he begs me to open up to him.

"N-nothing." It's not a lie, nothing did happen other than I freaked out and then he spent the entire class trying to get a rise out of me. He was right, it was just like high school all over again.

I let out a sigh. I thought all that shit was over the day we drove out of Harrow Creek in favor of Rosewood all those years ago. It seems fate had other ideas.

"Don't lie to me, Letty," Luca snaps, a hard edge to his voice. "You ran out of there terrified. What did that motherfucker do to you? Is he trying to get to me through you?"

I pull my hand from his and push from the bed so I can pace back and forth as I try to decide how much I'm willing to share right now. I already know I can't go the whole way because I fear it might send me straight back into the black hole that I've only recently managed to claw my way out of.

"I never... um..." *Fuck.*

I lift my hands to my hair and push it back from my face as I continue with my inner battle.

If Luca knows the kind of shit Kane has pulled over the years then he'll go after him, and I don't want to make the war that's already brewing between them any worse.

"Letty, just tell me."

I glance at my best friend as he rests his elbows on his knees, his dark hair falling down into his eyes, his teeth already deep into his bottom lip as he chews it while waiting for me.

Fuck it.

"I never told you everything about my time at Harrow Creek."

"Go on," he encourages, still watching my every move.

"Kane, he..." Out of the corner of my eye, I see Luca's entire body tense just at the mention of his name. "He hates me."

Luca's lips part to say something but only air rushes out.

He's silent for a few seconds as my words sink in.

"As in he avoided you at all costs, hates you, or he made your life hell, hates you."

I come to a stop in front of him.

"What do you think?"

"Fucking hell, Letty. Why didn't you ever tell me this? I'd have flattened the motherfucker for ever hurting you."

"That," I say, pointing at him. "That is the exact reason why I never told you."

"So I wouldn't hurt him?" His brows draw together in confusion. "That's fucked up, Let."

"No, you idiot. I don't give a shit about protecting him. I was protecting you."

"What?" He jumps up and reaches for me, stopping me from wearing the floor out and forces me to stop in front of him.

He's a whole foot taller than me at six-four and he stoops down so he can look into my eyes.

"How badly do I need to hurt him?"

"No, Luc. No." I throw my hands up in exasperation. "I don't want you in the middle of this. That's the whole point. You need to focus on the game, on your future."

"Fuck that, Let. I'm not letting him get away with hurting you. That's bullshit."

"He hasn't hurt me." *Not for eighteen months anyway.*

Luca's brows rise in suspicion.

"Please, Luc. Just stay out of it. It's not your fight."

Lifting his hands, he cups my cheeks and I can't help but lean into his heat. He always makes me feel so safe and secure.

"If he hurts you, then he hurts me, Let. I wish you'd told me this years ago."

I shrug. "It doesn't matter," I say, trying to play it down.

"It really fucking matters."

Leaning in, he presses his lips to my forehead and wraps his arms around me.

His scent and warmth surround me and I soon lose myself in the feeling of his hard body against mine.

"You're my girl, Letty. I'll do anything for you."

"I know," I mumble against his chest, tears filling my eyes faster than I want them to.

I can't cry. I'm scared that if I allow myself to do that again then I might not stop.

I swallow down the giant lump in my throat and pull back from him.

"Thank you," I whisper, staring up into his soft eyes, needing him to know how much I appreciate his support. "I'm sorry I allowed us to lose each other."

"Me too."

He pulls me into him once more and drops his lips to the top of my head.

"He just let him walk onto the team," Luca says when I return with a drink for each of us a while later. I know our time is running out, he needs to get to practice but now I've got him alone, I don't want to let him go.

"Can he do that? Isn't there protocols to follow or something?" I ask because really, I have no clue about any of it. I've tried to remember all the things Luca and Leon have attempted to explain to me about football over the years but mostly it goes in one ear and out the other.

"Yeah, you'd think. Coach is adamant that it's all above board. He's planning on making him first string. He's going to be playing alongside Leon and me. Fucking joke."

"He is good," I say, after taking a sip of my water. "What?" I ask when he stares at me as if he wants me to go up in flames. "You know it's true. You've said it yourself before now."

"Ugh." He drops his head into his hands and pushing his fingers through his hair, dragging it back painfully from his face. "I know, I know. I just wish I wasn't blindsided by this."

"You need him, don't you?" It's no secret that the Panther's best wide receiver opted to enter the draft early in the spring and got snapped up to play for... someone. I have no clue where he went other than he went.

"Do I have to answer that?"

"No, it's written all over your face."

Silence falls between us but it's not uncomfortable. Things are never that way between the two of us, it's one of the things I love about him so much.

"Zayn told me to come to meet you after class. He's worried about you. Should we be?"

Yes. "No, of course not. I can handle Kane. You need to focus on the upcoming season."

He nods but I know it's not going to be that easy. There's already more tension than there should be between teammates, I really don't need to add to it.

"I wish I could stay and hang out more."

"I've got a ton of work to do, don't worry about it."

He leans over and drops a lingering kiss on my cheek.

"If you need anything, if he so much as looks at you the wrong way, you know where I am."

"I know, but it won't be necessary."

He climbs from the bed and walks to my door.

"Oh, party Friday night. You in?" Excitement sparkles in his eyes at the prospect of letting it all go for a night.

"You got it."

"Sweet. See you tomorrow?"

I smile at him as he slips through the door and disappears.

I'm making myself dinner later that evening when Brax and West come stumbling into the dorm, both fresh from the shower.

"Evening, beautiful," Brax sings. "That smells insane. Enough for three?"

"Funny you should say that," I mutter as he wraps his arms around me from behind and peers over my shoulder.

"Giiiirl, I think I love you."

I laugh at his antics as he smacks a wet kiss on my cheek.

"Just gonna dump this and you can fill us up good."

As they both disappear to their rooms, I pull down three plates and start dishing up.

I didn't need to make this much, but something told me others would be grateful.

After Luca left, I figured I'd be safe because Kane would be at practice with him, so I headed to the on-campus store for ingredients for dinner and everyone's breakfast in the morning.

Cooking always used to be something that helped me to relax but I've barely done it recently, but with all the nervous energy zipping through me after the events of the day, I knew I couldn't just sit in my room and attempt to work on my assignments.

"How was practice?" I ask when they both return and take their seats.

"Brutal. And Luca was fucking pissed."

"I've never seen him like that before," West adds.

My stomach knots knowing that I didn't help with that situation.

"What the fuck was that with you and the new guy earlier?" Brax asks, his eyes drilling into the top of my head as I stare at my dinner.

I knew the question was coming. They were unlikely to forget jumping to my defense in statistics earlier.

"It was nothing?"

"Nothing?"

"Luca wants to kill him and he treated you like a piece of shit."

"He barely spoke to me," I argue.

"Maybe not, but the way he looked at you. It was like he wanted you to go up in flames right in that spot."

KANE

"**D**id you know?" I ask, throwing my bag at the wall in the living room as I stare at the three assholes sitting around the dining table stuffing their faces with dinner.

The bag hits with a thud leaving a dark mark on the wall before crashing to the floor. But it doesn't make me feel any better.

Right now, nothing aside from getting my hands on her will go anywhere near making me feel any better.

Okay, maybe landing a punch on Luca's smug fucking face like I've been holding myself back from for the past fucking three hours might do something.

The three of them stare at me as if I've sprouted another head.

"Know what?" Devin finally asks.

"Did you know she was here?"

"She?" Ezra asks, his brows drawing together. "Wh—"

"Holy shit," Devin interrupts, clearly having a light bulb moment. "No fucking way. She's not?" His eyes are so wide, I wonder if they're about to pop out.

I stumble back on aching legs until my calves hit the couch and I drop down, lowering my head into my hands as three confused sets of eyes drill into me.

"She's here like... she goes here now?" Ezra asks, obviously up to speed on the situation.

"She was in my class, so I'm assuming so," I mutter into my palms.

Silence echoes around the room as they wait to see my reaction to this and also try to figure out what to say.

Scarlett Hunter has been a touchy subject for me for... a long time and they all try to avoid talking about her at all costs because they never know how I'm going to react—and nor do I.

"So..." Devin says inquisitively, testing the water. "What happens now? You're... you're staying, right?"

I drag my head from my hands and meet his concerned stare. Out of everyone, he knows just how hard I've worked to make this happen, which means only he really understands just how much I would be throwing away if I were to turn my back on it—on her.

"Of course I'm fucking staying," I bark. "I haven't gone through everything I have for her to ruin everything."

"O-okay good," he stutters while the twins look at me bemused.

"It's nothing," I say with a wave of my hand but we all know it's a lie.

To get here, I had to have the help of their father and we all know that Victor Harris' help comes with a serious cost.

"You want some food, man?" Ellis finally asks. "There's plenty of leftovers."

"Yeah, that would be awesome. Thank you."

Him and Ezra collect up their plates and disappear into the kitchen while I make my way over to the table.

Devin pushes a bottle of beer toward me but I decline. I need to start taking shit seriously so that I can prove my worth to the team and show them that Luca is wrong, that they need me to help take them all the way this year.

They had an incredible season last year but it's all up in the air with a new team hitting the field this season. Just one person can change the dynamics of a team, and I fear that if we fuck it up this year, then the blame is going to be entirely placed on me.

"Did you talk to her?" he asks, pushing the remaining food around on his plate.

"Yeah... kind of. She's... she's different, man. I don't know." I slump down in my chair as I picture her in my mind. "She was so skinny, tired."

"You think something happened?"

I shrug. "She wouldn't have given up Columbia without a fight."

I might not have known Letty well for a lot of years, but she was dreaming of that place before most of us even knew what a college was. It was her ultimate dream.

So the fact she's here right now raises huge questions.

"Something bad must have happened," he muses, mirroring my thoughts. "You hear of girls getting attacked and shit all the time, dropping out and—"

"Really?" I ask him, turning to stare at the side of his face.

"Sorry, I was just saying."

"Well don't." I've already got enough images racing

through my mind as to the reason she could be here. Him adding more—or encouraging the ones I already have—isn't helpful.

"Here. Enjoy," Ellis says with a smile, sliding a plate over. The scent of the tomatoey Bolognese assaults my senses and my mouth starts watering.

"You perfected anything else yet?" I ask him, knowing this is the only dish he ever cooks.

"Nope, I'm a one-dish kinda man."

I shake my head at him as Ezra calls something about not being a one-woman man from the kitchen.

"You need to talk to her. Put all this shit behind you and move on."

My fork pauses halfway to my lips.

"Wait... you're fucking serious?"

"Bro, I know, I get it. But don't you think it's time to let it all go? You're both here, starting over. Just..." He trails off, not really needing to say the words out loud.

But while he does understand. He has been beside me through it all, he suffered some of the same loss I did, it doesn't run as deep for him as it does for me. And no matter how hard I might want to walk away, to do what he just suggested, I know I'm not going to be able to.

I'm not going to be able to watch her walk around, embarking on her new life and stay on the sidelines. I already know that it's not going to happen while we're here together.

"Yeah, I know." I shovel Ellis's Bolognese into my mouth and savor the flavors for a second, it's the perfect distraction, although it doesn't last very long.

"You're not even listening right now, are you?"

"Of course I am."

"Sure. That little issue aside, how's it feel to finally be a college student?"

"I'm sure it'll be great if I ever manage to drag my head out of the past," I mutter.

"You didn't hear a word of your classes, did you?"

"One or two. It's all online. I'll figure it all out. Things can only get better, right? I mean, the girl I hate is in my classes, the captain of the team hates me and wants me gone. It's a pretty solid start to my college career."

"Dude, you're so fucked." He laughs, slapping me on the back.

I'm glad my life amuses someone.

Once I've finished eating, I begrudgingly agree to clean up the kitchen before shutting myself in my room to attempt to fix the tiny issue that is me fucking up all four of my classes only two days into the semester.

Dropping onto my bed, I flip my laptop open and log into the college website so I can locate the class notes from today.

My head spins as I read through everything, but my mind keeps dipping in and out and taking me back to that auditorium where she was sitting beside me.

I start to wonder what she's doing right now?

Is she in the dorms, or does she have a house with friends?

I sit bolt upright. Does she live with him?

My heart begins to race as I think about the familiarity between them when she rushed into his arms at the first opportunity earlier. He was waiting for her to finish class, that much was obvious.

I knew they were friends in high school, but I never saw any evidence they were any more than that. If I had, then our games might have been even more brutal if I had any suspicion he'd touched her.

Did she move here for him?

It's that thought and the image of her in his arms that has me dumping my laptop on the end of the bed and jumping up. I might have had our session this morning followed by a hardcore practice but the only way I'm going to expel the energy that's twitching at my muscles is to get up and move.

Pulling on a black hoodie, I shove my feet back into my sneakers and head out of the house, popping my AirPods in, I pull the front door closed behind me and take off.

It's dark out now and I have no clue where I'm going but I don't really give a shit. I'll find my way back eventually. All I know is that I need to at least try to outrun some of my demons and attempt to get my head together before it all starts again in the morning.

I smile as my muscles start burning.

This right here is something I have control over. The rest of my life, not so much, it seems. But this, my body, this is all me.

I push harder, sweat beginning to stick my hoodie to my skin as I move.

My feet pound against the sidewalk as I eat up the miles.

I don't realize where I've ended up until the bright lights of the campus coffee sign come into view.

I look around, seeing all the unfamiliar buildings but knowing exactly where I am.

Is she here somewhere?

I spin around looking at all the lights in the surrounding dorm room buildings.

My fist clench as I imagine her looking down at me right now.

My eyes flick around in an attempt to search her out.

"Where are you, Princess?" I whisper to myself like a complete psycho. "You can only hide for so long."

8

LETTY

I sit at my desk working on my assignment with my eyes burning and my body begging me to give up for the night and head to bed.

Spinning around, I stare out of the window and up at the dark night sky.

With all the light pollution from campus, it's impossible to see if there are any stars out tonight.

Pushing from the chair, I walk toward the window and rest my forearms on the sill, staring up and squinting in the hope of seeing a twinkle.

When I returned to Rosewood with my tail between my legs to confess to Mom that I was now a college dropout, I spent a lot of time out in the backyard or sitting on the beach watching the sun go down and getting lost as the darkness engulfed both me and my surroundings.

Staring up at those twinkling stars made me forget about everything that had led to the moment I broke down in Mom's arms and told her everything I'd been

It felt good to finally get it all out. I openly bled out my pain and to have someone cry with me.

The look on Mom's face as she held my face in her hands and sobbed with me is one I'll never forget.

I was terrified to go home and to tell her what a mess I'd made of my life. I knew she'd be disappointed in me. Her main focus since the day we were all born was ensuring we had everything we needed to make a success of our lives and there I was crumbling and losing control of the life I thought I was making for myself.

I should have had more faith in her because although, yes, she was disappointed that I'd turned my back on Columbia, she supported me wholeheartedly and chastised me for suffering alone for so long.

Maybe if I had come clean sooner, I might have been able to continue with my life with her support. But it's too late to wonder now.

All of that is done and here I am.

Starting over and trying to put all of that behind me.

But I can't, because he's here.

Taunting me.

Reminding me.

Threatening to drag me right back into the darkness.

With a sigh, I turn away from the window, shrug my hoodie from my shoulders, I throw it over my chair and crawl into bed.

I lie there staring at the ceiling knowing that really I should flick the light off and attempt to get some sleep but something stops me from doing it.

The rest of the dorm has been in silence for over an hour, everyone disappearing to their own rooms to do their thing, so when a sharp knock sounds out on my door it makes me squeal in fright.

My heart jumps into my throat and my hands begin to tremble.

My initial thought is that it's him. That he's found me already.

I didn't tell anyone not to let him know where I live but I'm sure there are a million and one ways to find out if he wanted to.

He's always been pretty resourceful. I mean, he got himself here after all.

Hesitantly, I pull the covers back and lower my feet to the cold floor.

Every single muscle in my body screams for me to stay where I am and hide.

But I know that if it is him, that he won't stop until he gets to me, even if that means kicking the door in.

I'd rather just accept my fate than wake the entire dorm and have them witness my shitshow of a life.

My breaths race out so fast that I'm almost hyperventilating by the time my hand wraps around the door handle.

If this is him then... then anything could be about to happen.

My entire body jolts when whoever it is knocks again.

It's okay. It's okay. Just open the door. It might not even be him.

I suck in a long breath before pressing the handle down, the loud click of the lock disengaging echoes through my silent room.

I pull the door open quickly. It's too late to turn back now.

"Holy fuck," I breathe, relief racing through me so fast that I sway a little on my feet. "It's just you."

A lopsided smile appears on Leon's face as he steps toward me, his eyes darkening with concern. They're so similar to his brother's but they're darker with a little hazel mottled within when you look close.

"Who were you expecting? Wait... don't answer that. Can I come in?" he asks and I jump back, realizing that I'm still standing with the door half open and totally blocking his way.

"Oh, yeah. Of course."

I pull the door wide and walk into the room, leaving him to close it behind him.

The second he turns his eyes on me, a tingle runs down my spine and I'm suddenly very aware of what I'm wearing—or not, as the case may be.

"Sorry, I was in bed," I mutter, embarrassed about showing too much of my body right now.

"Hey," he says, turning me toward him.

He steps into me a little and tucks his fingers under my chin so I have no choice but to look at him.

"You're beautiful, Letty."

I fight to look away but he doesn't let me.

"It's me, Let. You never have to hide from me."

Tears burn my eyes at the emotion in his voice.

"I know. It's just... it's hard."

He nods in understanding. That's the thing about Leon, he just always seems to know how I feel, the right thing to say or do to just make me feel better about whatever the situation is.

"Why don't you get back into bed? I just came by to check in on you. Luca mentioned what happened earlier."

"Of course he did," I mutter, although not expecting anything different from them. They're nothing if not protective.

"He's worried about you."

"He doesn't need to be. Everything's fine."

His brow lifts in argument but he doesn't say anything. Well, not about my blatant lie anyway.

"Go on," he says, placing his giant hands on my slender shoulders and pushing me toward my bed. "Get in before you get cold."

I crawl under the covers and look up at him.

"Keep me warm?" I offer, lifting the corner to show him the space beside me.

"Thought you'd never ask."

My chest swells at the smile that lights up his face and it just proves how much I needed this—someone—right now.

I watch his movements as he toes off his sneakers, drags his hoodie over his head, revealing his sculpted chest and abs.

My mouth waters as I trace the lines down to his waistband.

"Don't you go getting any ideas, Hunter." He winks at me, and I giggle like the schoolgirl I'm sure he remembers me as. "I'm here purely in a friendship capacity."

"I know. And I really appreciate it. You... um..." My cheeks heat as he drops his jeans and dives toward me. "You look really good."

"Aw, you getting all shy on me, Cupcake?"

Curling into his side, I bury my face into his chest in an attempt to hide the fact my face is burning up.

He wraps his arm around my back, holding me tight against him and I pull my face away and snuggle in. He's surprisingly comfortable seeing as he's a solid body of muscle.

"Coach Butler works us really fucking hard," he admits. "My fucking brother is a bit of a slave driver too."

"Is it what you thought it would be?" I ask, staring across the room as the steady beat of his heart beneath my ear grounds me.

The fear that consumed me when the first knock on my door is long gone with him here now.

Anything could happen and I know without a doubt that Leon would protect me.

Luca was always the one who was utterly obsessed with the game. Sure, it was Leon's dream too, but he wasn't quite as dedicated to the cause as Luca was.

Luca has always lived and breathed the game whereas Leon sees other things. He's deeper, doesn't wear his heart on his sleeve and he keeps his walls up for almost everyone. I've only seen him let a couple of people in over the years and I'm so grateful that I'm one of them. Because the person he hides behind those walls is genuinely beautiful.

"Yeah, I guess."

"Wow, spell it all out for me why don't you," I joke, walking my fingers across his ribs and to his other side.

"I don't know. It's really hard work but the payoff is pretty sweet."

"The throng of adoring girls?"

He chuckles. "Sure can't complain about them but they weren't exactly what I was talking about."

He never was one to put it out like Luca. He was a little more choosy about his women. I can only assume that's the same now.

"Enough about me. What's put the sadness in your eyes, Cupcake?"

His old nickname warms me from the inside out but I

don't think anything will ever be enough to make me willingly share. Not yet at least. The pain is still all too raw.

"I... I can't, Lee."

Wrapping his other arm around me, he holds me tighter.

"Sleep, Cupcake. You look exhausted."

I don't need telling twice because not two minutes after he says that does my body succumb to the rest it needs.

Being in the safety of his arms means I sleep the whole night.

Part of me expected him to slip out once I had drifted off but when an unusual ring starts up at God knows what time the next morning, I find I'm proved wrong because I'm still plastered against his hot body.

And by hot, I mean quite literally because I am freaking melting with him in this small bed.

"What time is it?" My voice comes out raspy and deep as I attempt to detach myself from him.

"Five a.m."

"Five a.m.," I echo. "Why the fuck do you have an alarm set for five freaking a.m.?"

"Training."

"Hardcore."

"You have no idea, Cupcake."

A smile curls at my lips as he drops a kiss to my forehead and climbs from the bed.

The temptation to get another close up look at his body is too much to deny and I crack my eyes open.

It's still dark, but the light coming from the partly open window curtains is enough to show me the sharp lines and hard planes of his body. And there is one hard part that most definitely stands out as I run my eyes down his front.

"I know you're staring, Letty."

"No... uh... I was—"

He laughs at me as he shoves his legs into his jeans and tugs them up.

Sitting up in bed, I pull the covers up to my chin and continue watching him. It would be rude now that he knows I am.

"You're the beautiful one, you know that, right?"

"On the outside maybe."

"Lee," I chastise. "You are one of the kindest, sweetest people I know."

"I only let you see what I want you to see, Cupcake."

"Bullshit, Leon. I see you."

I know he's hiding something, and I fear it might be something dark that he refuses to deal with but whatever that is doesn't change who he is. I wish he could accept that.

"I see you too, Let. And you need to talk. Whatever it is, is eating you alive."

"Pot calling the kettle black?"

"It's different," he insists, pulling his hoodie on.

"No, it's not. Let's make a deal." He stills and looks over at me, a flicker of fear on his face about what I might be about to say. "When you're ready to talk, come and find me and we can have it out. Lay all our truths on the table."

His lips part but no words come out for a few seconds.

"Wow, pulling out the big guns, huh?"

"Tit for tat, big boy."

"Hmm... I take the tit, Cupcake."

"You're an idiot." I laugh as he closes the space between us.

"Aw, don't pretend like it wasn't fun."

His words send me back a few years to something we swore we wouldn't talk about ever again.

"Are you breaking the rules, Mr. Dunn?"

"They were made to be broken, Cupcake." He drops his lips and plants a kiss on my lips.

My heart skips a beat at the move. I'm used to the pair of them being very affectionate with me, it's how it's always been but I can't help feeling there's more to that simple kiss.

But like almost everything else in my life, I shove the thought deep inside the box within that hides the hard to deal with stuff.

"Thanks for the sugar."

I chuckle, trying to cover up how I really feel as he walks toward the door.

"Do you have class this morning?"

"Um..." I wrack my brain for what day it is let alone what classes I might have. "Yeah, I think I have psych."

"Want me to walk you?"

"It's okay. I've got Ella," I say but instantly regret it because I'd quite like to see her reaction if one of the twins came to collect me just to walk me to class.

"I'll see you later. Call if you need me."

"Thank you. I really appreciate you coming to check on me."

"Always, Cupcake." He smiles at me before slipping out of the door.

Sliding out of bed, I rush over and flip the lock. I know I'm being paranoid but I can't help it.

Kane let me walk away with Luca yesterday and I know for a fact that it would have pissed him off beyond belief.

He might be trying to be patient, maybe even do the right thing in his own fucked up way. But that patience will wear out and I need to be ready for when it does.

———

I'm looking over my shoulder the whole way to our psych class as if Kane's about to jump out of a bush and attack me at any moment.

I know I'm being paranoid but one of Kane's specialties is pouncing when I'm least expecting it. Just like that night eighteen months ago.

I let out a sigh and force myself to focus on where we're going.

"Have you started the assignment yet?"

"Uh-huh," I agree although really, I barely heard her question.

"Letty." Ella places her hand on my arm, halting our progress toward the Anderson Building. "Is everything okay?" Her huge honey-colored eyes staring back at me in concern.

"Y-yeah, it's fine."

"Is it the guy Brax and West mentioned?"

"Fucking hell," I mutter, realizing that my drama has gone around our dorm like wildfire.

"They were worried and asked me if I knew anything. We're just looking out for you, Let. I promise. You're one of us now, we look after our own."

Relief floods me and emotion burns the back of my eyes. She has no idea how much what she just said means to me.

"Thank you," I whisper.

"It's nothing really." *I hope.* "Just old high school drama."

"They said—"

"I'm okay. It's okay," I assure her when she looks like she wants to dig more. "I'm putting it behind me and looking forward. Tell me about the Dunns party on Friday, is it gonna be huge?" We take off walking again as she squeals in excitement.

"Girl, it's gonna smash all your Columbia parties out of the fucking water. They are banging."

"You mean, you wanna be banging..."

"Well, duh. That place is going to be wall to wall hot athlete."

"Have they been warned?"

"I'm pretty sure someone put the word out because none of them seem interested in what I have to offer." She sulks as we approach the building.

"The ex you mentioned... not an athlete?"

"Oh yeah, he's on the team."

"So he's warned them all off you."

"He'd fucking better not, the cheating fuck," she spits.

"O-okay," I say with a wince, clearly having hit a soft spot. "Things ended well then."

"Oh yeah, we're the best of friends."

I can't help but laugh at her blatant lie.

We find our seats in class and chat away about Friday night and she delights in telling me some of the debaucheries that have gone down at previous Dunn parties. I can't wipe the smile off my face as she talks about what they get up to with their friends. I can picture them acting like clowns, drinking and letting go. They deserve it, hell knows they work hard enough.

Class passes quickly and after grabbing a coffee and lunch together, Ella heads to her afternoon class while I go in search of the library to get some work done.

There's a big part of me that screams to go back to the dorms and eradicate the chances of bumping into Kane. But the rational side of me knows that the chances of seeing him on a campus this size with this many students is slim to none. So I pull up my big girl panties and force myself not to cower to a non-existent threat.

With my books in my arms, I walk around the library, checking out each floor to familiarize myself with where everything is. I finally find a group of almost empty tables on the third floor and make myself at home.

I tap away at my keyboard, totally lost in what I'm doing when a shiver runs down my spine.

I tried to push aside my concern when I sat here and ignored the fact that there are a lot of hiding places should someone want to torment me. I'm surrounded by rows and rows of books and dark corners.

Forcing myself to ignore it, I continue working, telling myself that I'm just being paranoid once again.

After another two minutes, the shiver becomes more violent and the feeling of being watched becomes impossible to ignore, I turn around and scan the area.

There are a few others sitting at tables working but none of them are looking in this direction and there's no one standing around.

Blowing out a shaky breath, I turn back to my screen to continue but the feeling never abates.

"Hey, fancy seeing you here," Micah says, marching up to my table with an armful of books. "You alone?"

"Sure am."

"You mind?"

"Of course not."

As he pulls out the seat opposite me, I take the opportunity to look around once again.

Still nothing.

"Oh, are you meeting someone?" he asks when he notices what I'm doing.

"No. I just thought I heard something," I lie. "So, what have you got there, it looks..." I run my eyes down the spines of the IT programming books he's piled between us.

"Boring?"

"Uh..." I hesitate, not wanting to diss anything he clearly loves.

"It's fine. I know it's boring as fuck to most people."

"As long as you enjoy it, that's all that matters." I smile at him and he quickly returns it. "Who gives you shit? Let me guess, the football players of the group."

He chuckles. "Yeah, but they mean well. They're just jealous because they'll be washed up ex-NFL players by thirty-five and I'll be just getting better and better."

I bark out a laugh as he rubs his hands together in delight.

"I think I landed in the right place with you all."

"Our bark is worse than our bite. Well, actually, I'm not so sure about Violet." He winks at me and I laugh, forgetting all about the uneasy feeling I couldn't shift.

We fall into a comfortable silence and get some work done before his cell starts dancing across the desk.

"It's the guys," he says, looking up from the screen.

I smile at him.

"Has no one added you to the group chat yet?"

"Umm... no."

"Assholes. You'll probably regret it because it's mostly Brax posting totally inappropriate memes every five minutes, but at least you'll know where to find us should you ever..."

I roll my eyes. West and Brax got to him as well then.

"We're just—"

"Looking out for me, I know. I appreciate it."

"Give me your number then."

I rattle it off and only a few seconds later, my cell starts blowing up in my pocket.

By the time I pull it out, there are twenty messages welcoming me to the chat. Mostly from Brax, and as promised more than one meme that makes me snort out a laugh.

"I'm not sure whether to thank you or..."

"Don't say I didn't warn you."

I silence my cell knowing that I'll never get any work done if they continue at this rate and shove it deep into my purse.

9

KANE

I didn't mean to fall into creepy stalker territory. I was legitimately in the library when she walked in all wide-eyed and excited as she took in all the books.

I stepped into the shadows so she wouldn't notice me as she passed and began walking up and down each of the aisles of books.

The temptation to follow her was strong but I told myself as I stood in the middle of the quad last night that I wasn't going to search her out, instead just make the most of our classes together for now.

I've got plenty of time to up the ante over the coming weeks and months. I want her looking over her shoulder, waiting for me to strike then when she realizes that maybe I'm not, that's exactly when I'm going to make my move. When she least expects it and has lowered her guard.

Then... then she's mine.

My intention was to leave but I walked in here for a reason, so I stepped out of the shadows and discovered

That's how I find myself hiding behind a row of books on the third floor watching her work.

I know I shouldn't but there's something fascinating about the way her fingers fly over the keyboard of her laptop.

She's got her long hair piled up on top of her head with not one, but two pens shoved through it, and the level of concentration on her face is mesmerizing.

I stand there for way too long just watching her work.

Images of the things I want to do to her flicker through my mind like a movie as my need for revenge surges around me.

I want her alone where we'll have no witnesses.

I want her all to myself.

My fists curl as I picture walking up to her and demanding she leaves with me. She would, I know she would because she hates causing a scene.

She'd rather deal with me in private than have everyone else privy to what goes down between us.

Silly girl.

I'd have thought that she'd have learned before now that being alone with me is the most dangerous place to be.

I've almost convinced myself to walk away when someone else approaches her.

It's clear she knows who he is. The way her face lights up as she notices him makes my chest constrict and my fists tighten.

Again, I try to make myself leave and damn, am I glad I don't. I'm close enough that I can hear every single word they say to each other and the second they start talking about a group chat, I move closer still.

I fumble to get my cell from my pocket when he asks

her for her number and I just get mine unlocked quick enough to type it in.

I smile to myself as I stare down at it.

She has no idea what she's just done.

Beginning to creep myself out with the level of stalking I've lowered myself to this afternoon, I slip from the aisle of books and set about finding what I came for before leaving the library and heading to the cafeteria for some lunch before my next class and then our practice session.

———

Letty is like a deer caught in headlights during class on Thursday morning. Knowing she was going to be there, I made sure that I was early and I sunk into the shadows at the back of the auditorium long before she arrived so I could watch her.

When she finally arrives, she has protection in the form of my two idiot teammates flanking her sides—the same assholes who tried to stand up for her on Tuesday.

It's weird because, at practice, they barely pay me any attention, preferring to do their own things and keep their heads down. But put them anywhere near Letty and it seems their inner cavemen come out and they do all they can to protect their girl from the big bad wolf.

I have no idea how she knows them. My unwanted feud with seemingly the entire team at Luca's request means that I don't have anyone to subtly ask all these questions to.

I want to know who they are, why they feel the need to look after her, and most importantly if they're going to be a problem for me.

One of them wraps his arm around her shoulder as he leads her to some empty seats about halfway back.

If she's trying to be discreet as she looks around for me, then she's failing miserably because I can almost feel her nerves from here as her eyes flit around trying to find me.

I sink down in my chair as she continues to search, and I know the very second her eyes lock on me. The crack of electricity between us is almost enough to alight the room. I feel it right down to my soul.

A smile curls at my lips. I try to make it a soft one but my need to hurt her means it turns into a snarl all too quickly.

Her bodyguards soon notice who is holding her attention as she fights to rip her eyes from mine, and they manage to move her so they can get ready for class to start.

Satisfaction fills me once again as she sits ramrod straight in her chair throughout the entire lecture as if she can physically feel my stare burning into the back of her head.

She never once turns around. I bet it's fucking killing her.

"Hey, aren't you Kane Legend?" a sickly sweet voice says from behind me as I'm leaving the auditorium not long after Professor Richman has left our class.

I didn't hang around and wait for her and her goons to leave. I didn't want her to think that what she did had any impact on me. I never planned on getting accosted as I left but it's kind of perfect.

News of my arrival hasn't spread all that far yet, seeing as Luca fucking Dunn is doing his damnedest to get rid of me. He's somehow managed to put a halt to most of the gossip, which, I must be honest, is kind of impressive.

Maybe he does have more power around here than I gave him credit for.

"Yeah, who's asking?" I spin on my heels and lock eyes with a pretty blonde girl with the bluest eyes I think I've ever seen.

"Hey." Her smile widens to show off perfectly straight white teeth. "I'm Clara." She takes a step forward, right as movement over her shoulder catches my eye. "Would you like to go and grab a coffee sometime?"

Ripping my eyes away from where Letty and her goons are, I look down at Clara.

My skin prickles with awareness as she gets closer. I don't need to look up again to know she's shooting me a death stare.

"Careful, girl. That one bites." The desire to throw my head back and laugh at Letty's little warning almost gets the better of me.

The fact she cares enough to even try to warn this girl tells me everything I need to know.

"It's okay, hon. I can handle rough. Right, Brax?" She lifts her chin in the direction of one of Letty's followers and his chest expands.

"Hell yeah she can," he brags, much to the other guy's irritation if his dramatic eye roll is anything to go by.

"Let's go," he barks. "I need food." Gently pushing Letty forward, although it seems that she doesn't need too much encouragement before she races down the corridor calling, "Don't say I didn't warn you," over her shoulder.

I smirk. It amuses me that she cares enough to get involved.

"So, coffee?"

"Now?"

"Sure." Her eyes light up as she tugs her purse up higher on her shoulder.

I, on the other hand, don't feel even a flicker of excitement. That is until we get to the end of the hallway to find Letty and the guys disappearing behind the closing elevator door.

Racing forward, I shove my foot into the gap and watch in delight as horror floods Letty's face.

"Stalker territory, Legend," one of the guys mutters as I step inside the small space with them.

In an ideal world, I'd stand right beside Letty, even behind her, so she couldn't see what I'm doing. But with her personal protection both taking a step closer to her, I know I've got no choice. I'll have to settle for my presence pissing her off.

The second Clara steps in beside me, I reach an arm out and wrap it around her waist, pulling her into me.

"Anyone ever told you that you've got the most mesmerizing eyes?"

"Yes, but I prefer hearing it from you."

Someone makes a gagging sound behind me but I ignore them, sliding my hand from the small of her back to her ass.

"I think we're going to enjoy spending time together, *Princess*."

Letty's gasp of shock sounds out loud and clear around the enclosed space.

I know how much she hates the nickname I gave her when we were just kids, but it seems as much as she might dislike it, she doesn't want anyone else to have it either.

"I sure hope so," Clara breathes, running her palm up my chest.

Her touch is... nice. But it doesn't stir a fire within me like I know someone else does.

We might have only been together once, but fuck it if didn't make all the other girls of my past pale in comparison.

The second the elevator pings to say we've hit the ground floor she storms out of the enclosed space, her shoulder slamming into me as she passes sending a bolt of electricity straight to my dick.

If she felt it then she doesn't show it because she doesn't so much as look back as she exits the building as if she's being chased.

"What's her problem?" Clara purrs, wrapping her hand around the back of my neck and staring into my eyes.

"Probably jealous that she's not as pretty as you."

"You're an asshole," one of Letty's protectors barks as they follow her out.

"I know. It's fun."

He flips me off over his shoulder as Clara threads her fingers through mine and pulls me from the elevator.

The second we step outside and I realize that Letty is nowhere to be seen, I pull my cell from my pocket and stare at it as if I'm reading something.

"I'm sorry, baby, I'm going to have to call a rain check. One of my boys needs me."

"I can come with," she offers, stepping forward and pressing her breasts against my chest as if it's enough to change my mind.

No fucking chance, love.

"Sorry, maybe another time."

She sticks her filler-filled lip out in a pout but all I do

is spin away from her and walk away, not giving two fucks about dropping her like a stone.

She's a jersey chaser. I'm sure there's plenty of other team members she can run off and dig her claws into.

I get myself some lunch and manage to get some work done on an assignment I've been working on before making my way to my afternoon class early, just like this morning.

I have no idea if I'll have the pleasure of making her squirm uncomfortably in this class as well seeing as I missed our first lecture on Monday but I can only hope.

"He really is an asshole," Brax mutters as he and West catch up with me after I all but sprinted from the elevator.

The second I heard him call her by my name, all I could think about was getting away from him.

I never want to hear him say that again, but I didn't realize just how hearing him say it to another girl would affect me.

The jealousy that surged through me was almost too much to contain and I was about two seconds away from wrapping my non-manicured nails into her hair extensions and dragging her away from him.

Thankfully, the doors opened just in time and allowed me an escape.

The second the outside air hit me, I sucked in a huge breath that wasn't laced with his masculine, woodsy scent and forced myself to relax.

I hated that I showed that he affects me by storming out the way I did, but I couldn't help it.

I was losing control and I had to get away.

"He is."

"What's his issue with you anyway?"

"It's..." I think of all the things he hates me for. The majority, things that were totally out of my control and not my fault, but that doesn't seem to matter to him. "Just stuff from the past that he can't let go of."

"Well, he needs to. It's bad enough he hates Luca, we don't need him causing you shit too."

I shrug. "I'm used to Kane. I know how to handle him."

They both turn their eyes on me but I ignore the fact that they've both witnessed me fail to deal with him twice now.

"Come on, I'll buy you both lunch."

"I know just the place."

The three of us pile into Brax's car and he floors the accelerator taking us away from campus. I'm more than happy to get away and reduce the risk of bumping into him again.

"Didn't think you were ever going to get here," Violet says when we walk up to where she's waiting outside the diner.

"Stop whining," West mutters, pushing the door open and stepping inside.

There are college kids everywhere but thankfully, he's not one of them.

Our time off of campus passes all too quickly and before I know it and with belly's full of pizza, we head back so I can get to my American lit class on time.

I take off toward the Westerfield Building after insisting that I didn't need escorts and the others head back to the dorms seeing as they've got the afternoon free.

I'm almost at the entrance when two very welcome faces come into view.

"Letty, looking gorgeous as ever," Luca says, pulling me into his arms and swinging me around dramatically while everyone within a fifty-foot radius stares at his over-the-top greeting.

"Put me down," I squeal when he continues to twirl us.

When he finally places my feet back on the ground, my head spins and I can't stop laughing.

"You're a goof." I pull him into my arms and give him a hug, quickly repeating the action with Leon.

"You okay, Cupcake?" he whispers in my ear, holding me for a beat longer than acceptable for friends.

I feel the jealous stares of all the girls around us burning into my back but I'm used to it. I've been friends with these two long enough to deal with the haters.

"Yeah, you?"

"Always." He winks at me when I pull back.

"Ready to hit class?"

"Hell yeah," I state. How could I not be with a Dunn twin on each arm.

I'm ready to face the fucking world.

Unfortunately, my confidence dwindles a little when the three of us step into the lecture hall and my eyes immediately lock with an angry set of blue ones.

My steps falter and both Luca and Leon notice.

"What's—oh. Is that motherfucker stalking you or something?"

"I'm pretty sure he's probably just in this class." I shrug. "Just ignore him."

"Hard to do when he seems to be everywhere I

fucking turn. If I make it to the first game of the season without breaking his nose it'll be a fucking miracle."

"Don't let him get to you, and don't give him the satisfaction of ruining your season. If your coach says it's all above board then you need to let that shit go and focus on the games."

He stares at me in amusement for a few seconds. "Who are you and what have you done with my football hating best friend."

"I don't hate football, I just—"

I can almost see the light bulb go off in his head. "You wanted to stay away from him. You never came to our Harrow Creek games. Ever."

"Guilty as charged."

Anger washes through him and his expression pulls tight as we make our way to our seats.

"I wish you'd have just told me, Let," he grits out after a few minutes of silence.

"If I knew it would turn out like this, then I would have. I don't want him ruining your chances at the NFL."

"That fucker isn't going to ruin anything." He reaches out and grabs my hand under the table. "I won't fucking let him."

I smile at him and rest my head on his shoulder. "You're a good person, Luc."

"So are you and I won't let you get poisoned by the likes of him."

"We've got your back, Letty. No matter what," Leon adds right before our professor starts the lecture.

I feel his stare throughout the entire class but I never once look back. And when we get up to leave first, I continue looking where I'm going.

Kane is a part of my past. A part I'd rather forget. It's time to focus on my future.

I breathe a sigh of relief as I walk out of sociology late Friday morning. It's my last class of the week and I've got my first MKU football party to get ready for.

Ella has already warned me that her and Violet have the face packs and fireballs ready.

I can almost feel the alcohol burning down my throat as I think about it.

I haven't had a drink in... I can't even remember how long. So I know I'm going to need to take it easy tonight.

The last thing I want is to end up passed out or sick and embarrass Luca and Leon at their own party.

I practically skip back to the dorms with excitement stirring in my belly. It's a feeling I've missed.

Hanging with the girls and getting ready to spend the night dancing and forgetting about the stresses of college is one of the reasons I was so excited to embark on this chapter of my life.

No parents, no one watching your every move.

I push through the door to our dorm and already there's music booming through the small space and Ella and Violet are dancing around the kitchen.

"We're making tacos and margaritas. You want?"

"Serious question?"

I dump my bag and books into my room before joining them and helping where I can.

The guys never appear and I wonder if that's because they got class or if they've been banished from the dorm so we can all hang out.

It's not until hours later when I'm sitting on Ella's bed with some purple junk on my face while she paints my nails fire engine red to go with the dress she insisted I wear tonight that we hear them return to the dorm.

"It's Friday," one of them bellows before their doors all close, I assume so they can get ready for tonight.

I was happy with a pair of skinny jeans and a top but she point-blank refused and pulled out a dress that was hanging in my closet with the tag still attached.

I have no idea why I kept it. I'd bought it with every intention of wearing it on a night out at Columbia, but everything turned to shit and it never saw the light of day again.

I almost gave it to goodwill when I packed up but something about it made me keep it. Maybe it was the hope that one day I could pull it on and somehow find the confidence I used to have and realize that life can return back to normal. That I can go out and enjoy myself once again without drowning in the past.

"You still hating on me for that," Ella says, following my eyeline to see me staring at the dress that's now hanging on the back of her door.

"N-no," I stutter.

"It's gonna look killer. Those Dunn boys won't know what's hit them."

"It's not like that with us," I argue.

"Girl, have you seen the way both of them look at you. It's literally like you personally hung the moon or some shit."

"Nah, we're all just friends. If you want my permission to make a play then you're more than welcome. Either of them would be lucky to have you."

A smile splits her face at my words. "I'm not sure

they'd even notice I existed. I could walk in naked and I'm pretty sure they'd both still have their eyes firmly focused on you."

I squirm uncomfortably.

"That's not—"

Ella holds her hand up.

"It's not how it is, I got that memo. But I think you might need to look a little harder because I think you might be missing something."

I stare at her.

"What?"

"Nothing. Pass me my drink?"

Ella quickly fills my glass from the pitcher we made earlier.

I've been keeping it slow all afternoon, unlike her and Violet who polished off the first pitcher between them in no time.

"Where's Violet? I thought she was just going for a shower. That was like, over an hour ago."

"Come on," Ella encourages, pushing from the chair she's sitting on and pulling her door open.

"The guys are now sitting in the kitchen with bottles of beer but they pay us little attention as we sneak across the hall with our hair in curlers and goo on our faces. I'm sure it's something they've seen a million times living with these two.

"Shhh." Ella holds her finger up in front of her lips and quietly pushes Violet's door open.

I stifle a laugh when she comes into view curled up in a ball fast asleep on her bed.

Ella's hand lands on my forearm stopping me from backing out to let her rest.

"Get ready," she mouths, before holding her hand up and counting down from three.

On one, she screams before running at Violet, who sits up like the world is exploding around her. The alcohol that's trickling through my veins ensures I burst into fits of laughter as the two of them begin wrestling on Violet's bed as footsteps race our way.

"Oh hell yeah. Micah, go get the chocolate sauce," West announces, his eyes locked on the girls.

Ella's robe falls open flashing us all her black lace bra while they continue to fight.

"Fuck the party," Brax adds. "We can just have an orgy right here."

He dives onto the bed with them, wrapping his arms around both of their waists and pulling them into his body.

"I'm more than happy to take on both if you two pussies don't want to get involved. Let?" he adds, his eyes locking on mine. "There's more than enough of me to go around."

"You're a fucking idiot," Ella squeals as he slaps her ass and she scrambles away from him.

"That's a good look, girl. You look hot." He blows her a kiss as she walks to me.

Her curlers are everywhere and the junk on her face mostly rubbed off on Violet's bedsheets.

"I guess I should have that shower now then, eh?" Violet asks, unattaching herself from Brax and walking toward her bathroom. He quickly follows. "Alone. Thank you."

"It's like none of you want to sleep with me," he mutters, pulling a sad puppy dog look.

"That would be because we don't," Ella announces.

"But you're all about the players, baby." He runs his eyes down her robe-clad body.

"Hmm... not this player. I've seen what you're hiding down there, and I've got to be honest, I wasn't all that impressed."

Everyone in the room falls about laughing before we all turn to leave Violet alone to shower.

"I can't help that I'm a grower," Brax barks, causing us all to laugh again.

"I swear to God, we have the best dorm on campus," Ella says, walking to her own bathroom to wash her face.

When she returns her skin is clear and her blonde hair is hanging around her shoulders in soft waves. She's really beautiful.

She walks to her closet in just her underwear, not batting an eye about me being here. Her confidence reminds me of how I used to be. But since losing as much weight as I have, I do everything I can to hide my body.

Reaching for my drink once more, I down the contents, hoping the alcohol will help me find the old me who would have owned that dress like a fucking queen.

"This or this?" she asks, spinning to me with two equally revealing dresses in both hands.

"Because you're making me wear that." I point to my scrap of fabric. "I say that one." I wiggle my finger in front of the one that looks the smallest.

"Done. It should at least get me some attention." She drags it on and flicks her hair over her shoulder.

"Y-yeah, it should do that." She looks like a freaking model. My shoulder slump knowing that I'm never going to match up to her.

"Don't," she barks. "Get those stupid thoughts out of your head right now."

My lips part to argue but she pins me with a look that tells me she understands exactly how I feel.

Turning around, she pulls a scrapbook from her top drawer, flips it open and passes it over.

I look down at a photo of a teenage girl sitting on a porch. It's immediately obvious that it's Ella because her honey eyes shine just like they do now but her face doesn't show the happiness I'm becoming used to.

"I haven't always looked like this. I was the school's chubby girl who got bullied every day of her life. I know you're not happy about how you look right now. But it's not forever. Only you can make it so you love yourself."

"I used to, that's what's so hard. I used to be like you now."

She drops down beside me and takes my hand.

"What happened?"

"I lost myself."

She's silent for a beat as if she's expecting me to say more, but she'll be disappointed because that's all the sharing I intend to do. I want to enjoy tonight, not fall back into the past.

"Okay, so let's work on making you love you again. I go to yoga twice a week, you should come with."

"That sounds... good, actually. Thank you."

"I know hearing it from me means nothing because up here." She taps the side of my head. "Is full of your own opinions, but you're beautiful, Letty. And I know you don't want to hear it, but Luca, Leon, those idiots out there, they all see it too."

I smile at her. "Thank you."

"Anytime, sweetie. Now, shall we party?" she asks, refilling both our drinks and passing mine over.

"Hell, yeah. I am ready to dance the night away."

"Amen to that. And maybe an athlete who knows what to do with his... stick." She chugs down her drink. "Makeup, then we leave."

She walks over to the door. "Vi, you got your shit together yet?"

"Yeah, I'll be right there, boss."

"Okay. Sit," she demands, pointing to her desk chair and lifting her massive makeup box from the bathroom.

"Do your worst."

"Oh, girl. I fully intend to." She winks and sets to work.

I t's almost two hours later when we finally walk up to Luca and Leon's house.

"Holy crap, this place is insane," I mutter, swaying a little on my feet as we pass groups of students loitering around the front yard.

The huge colonial-style house looms over us. It's got more windows than I can count after the number of margaritas I've consumed already tonight.

It's seriously impressive.

"Rumor has it that Daddy Dunn pays for it," one of the boys says from behind me.

"Of course he does." Just hearing Mr. Dunn's name being mentioned leaves a bitter taste in my mouth. He might be my best friend's dad, but man, I hate him.

He's a pretentious, opinionated, belittling asshole. I've no idea why Maddie stayed with him as long as she did. I think people assumed it was his money and fame, but I don't think it was. She wasn't that kind of fame-hungry wife. She's really sweet. A great mom. I guess she had to be to make up for their forceful, pushy and demanding father.

Although I was gutted for the twins that their family had broken up, but I can't lie, I was relieved for Maddie's sake when I heard that he'd left and was living in New York.

I should have reached out to Luca and Leon when it happened, but I couldn't. I could barely look after myself at that time, having compassion and concern for them as well really would have pushed me over the edge.

"Well, whoever owns it, I'm grateful we have somewhere to party," Violet announces, marching forward and entering the house as if she owns it.

"Looks like we're going in," Ella laughs beside me as we follow Vi inside.

The house is packed as we make our way through to the kitchen to find drinks.

West and Brax end up getting dragged off by other members of the team and although I've been assured time and time again that he's not going to be here, I find myself looking around for Kane.

I've been told once before that he wouldn't be at a party and look how that ended, with me getting royally fucked in a muddy puddle.

A shudder rushes down my spine as I allow my brain to remember just for five seconds how fucking good that puddle was. Then, I lock it down tight.

Ella makes me a mixer drink before passing the Solo cup over. Her eyes lock on someone over my shoulder and for a second, my heart drops thinking that it's him, but then a wide smile spreads across her face and excitement twinkles in her eyes and I know exactly who is approaching. Well, technically there are two options but I'm happy with either.

"Scarlett Hunter, you are fucking banging," Luca announces loudly to the whole room as Ella's smile gets wider.

"Told you so," she mouths to me, a large pair of hands land on my hips before his arms wrap around my middle as his front presses against my back.

"Hey," I say, looking back at him. "How much have you had to drink?" I ask when his eyes struggle to focus on mine.

"We had a bet, I lost. Shots." He winces.

"What was the bet?"

"Can't, babe." He lifts his hand to his lips and zips them closed before twisting and throwing away the key.

"Bro code, got it." I laugh.

"Man, you're so perfect, Let. You always just get it." He plants a sloppy kiss on my cheek and squeezes me tighter.

"Okay, you really are drunk."

"Come meet the guys."

"Uh... sure."

He releases me and takes my hand instead, dragging me away from a smug-looking Ella and through the throngs of people partying in his house.

"This place is incredible," I say when we emerge onto the back deck where there are huge couches—all full with football players presumably—surrounding a large firepit.

"Boys, this is my girl right here," he announces loudly, making me cringe and for my face to burn hot. "Letty, meet my boys."

The majority just nod at me in greeting. A few of their eyes take a leisurely trip around my body. I want to curl into Luca's side to hide but the heat in their eyes means I hold my head high and let them get their fill, knowing that they'll probably end up with a black eye when Luca notices.

"Evan, eyes on her fucking face, man." The guy in question immediately locks eyes with me and I instantly recognize him from sociology this morning. He wasn't hard to spot with his little crowd of jersey chasers vying for his attention while the rest of us were just trying to get through the door. "Do I need to say it again? Letty. Is. Off. Limits."

"Even to me?" Leon says, coming to a stop on my other side and pulling me out of Luca's hold.

"Girl, you're going to need to watch your back around campus with these two claiming you as theirs. The girls are going to have their claws out," Colt, the guy I was introduced to in my first American lit class with these two pipes up.

"I know how to handle myself around your admirers."

Luca snorts a laugh, probably remembering the couple of fights I might have ended up in with the cheersluts of Rosewood High.

"Don't underestimate her." Luca drops down onto one of the empty couches. "Sit, babe."

Tugging at the short hem of my dress so I don't flash every guy here a shot of my panties, I step from Leon's hold but before he lets me go, he drops his lip to my ear.

"You look stunning, Let. Save a dance for me later, eh?"

"Always." I smile at him before dropping down beside Luca who immediately places his large, burning hot hand on my thigh.

Leon's eyes stare at his possessive hold for a beat before he sits on the other side of me.

"So, golden boy here tells us you were at Columbia." I wince waiting for the standard questions but I'm relieved when they never come. I've no idea if that's because these guys don't care about my reason for leaving New York, or they've been warned not to pry, whatever it is, I'm grateful. "Their team is shit, no wonder you came back to be part of a winning one."

"Hell yeah," one of the guys bark, holding his bottle in the air for a few of them to tap.

I fall into easy conversation with the twin's friends, and I smile to myself as I realize that it's just like high school all over again. Me with all the boys. Every girl who walks past and gets shunned by the guys sends a scathing look my way, but I just smile sweetly. Not my issue that they want me here and not them. I'm sure the night is young and all these guys will be looking for some action soon enough.

The drinks flow nicely, delivered by the freshmen members of the team—including my little brother—who grins at me when he passes me a fresh cup.

"Having fun?" he asks, not missing where Luca's hand is planted still on my thigh.

"Yeah, I'm not these guys little bitch tonight."

"Shut your face," he mutters, shooting me a cocky wink.

"Oh yeah, you fit right in with these assholes."

"You love me really, Sis." He nods before ducking back into the house. "Enjoying your new pets?" I ask Luca with a smirk.

"Nah, they love it. Makes them feel special."

"You're a dick. Aren't you supposed to be all fatherly and supportive of the new guys?"

"I am, I'm effectively teaching them how to respect their elders."

The rest of the team laugh, sharing a private joke and I can't help but wonder what else they've got their new freshman to do in the first week of the semester.

"Shame we can't get that other asshole freshman to kiss our fucking shoes," Colt barks, and Luca, Leon, and I all tense at the mention of Kane.

"That fuck is going to get what's coming to him. Don't worry."

"Luca," I warn. "You promised me you'd stay away."

"Don't worry, babe. Everything is under control."

A shiver races down my spine as he squeezes my thigh in an attempt to reassure me. It does nothing to make me feel better about the situation.

I take a sip of the drink Zayn brought me and force myself to trust that Luca knows what he's doing.

He's not starting quarterback for the Panthers for nothing and I have to believe he has his head screwed on when dealing with Kane.

"Guys, I'm out. I love you and all but I need some fucking pussy," Colt announces a few minutes later.

"Dude, girl present," someone barks.

"A girl who's more than used to Luca and Leon. I'm sure she can cope."

"I've heard worse. Any of you guys know Harrow Creek?"

A few shake their heads, but a couple of them nod.

"Isn't that where K—"

"Yeah, I'm a Creek girl. Trust me, nothing you can say

would shock me," I say in a rush before that name drops from Evan's lips.

He turns to the guys who have no idea about the Creek's reputation. "What she means is, don't mess with her. She's a badass."

A few look impressed, others couldn't care less.

"Come dance with me," Leon breathes in my ear, and I spin to take him in.

"Wouldn't you rather go *find some pussy*?" I drop the tone of my voice to mimic the guys.

A smile twitches at his lips.

"When I could dance with you instead? Never."

"Aw, you're too sweet."

Luca makes a gagging sound behind me.

"Anyone ever told you that you should have been born with a pussy?"

"So there wouldn't be anyone to make you look good on the field?" Leon shoots back before standing and tugging on my hand and pulling me from Luca's clutches.

"I don't need anyone to make me look good, bro."

"Of course, your ego already does the job just fine." Leon flips Luca off over his shoulder as he leads me inside.

He directs me to the bathroom first, and then we stop by the kitchen for more drinks. It must be almost an hour later before we actually find our way to the makeshift dance floor that someone's set up in, I guess what should be, the living room.

Leon spins me into his body and I look up into his eyes as I feel the burning hate stares of every girl in the room zero in on me.

Pressing the length of my body to his, I reach up to whisper in his ear.

"They all hate me." It's nothing new. It's how I lived my life in Rosewood. If anything, it's amusing that these college girls are as pathetic as the high school ones drooling after hooking up with a player.

"Nah, Cupcake. They're all just jealous that I get to dance with the most beautiful girl in the room."

My chest swells at his words. And, although Ella was right earlier, that what others tell me won't change my own opinion about myself, hearing those words come from Leon when he could literally have any girl in this room right now in his arms does make me feel special.

"You could have any single one of them. Don't you want to get laid tonight?"

He throws his head back and laughs. "I'm a guy, of course I want to get laid. But—" The amusement falls from his voice. "I'd much rather spend time with a friend who knows the real me, instead of a girl who only wants to bed me for bragging rights on social media immediately after."

My heart sinks for him. Is that really what it's like? That meaningless.

"I thought guys loved that shit."

"Guys might, I don't."

"You're one of a kind, Leon Dunn."

"Such a nice way to tell me I'm weird, Cupcake."

"Never," I gasp as the song changes and he moves his hips against me. "Have you learned some moves?"

"I guess you're about to find out."

We dance until our skin is damp with sweat and my face aches from the amount of smiling and laughing I've been doing. But I can't stop because right now, forgetting about everything, I feel on top of the world.

"Can I join the party?" Luca says, his hands landing on my waist and his front lining up with my back.

"I'm not one to turn down a Dunn sandwich," I slur before giggling like a schoolgirl.

I have definitely had too much vodka tonight.

"Whoa, girl," he grunts in my ear when I thrust my ass out into his crotch, his fingers grip my hips harder as he moves with me.

Leon steps in front of me, his hands on my waist, right above his brothers and we move together in tandem.

Dropping my head back, I rest it on Luca's shoulder and let myself just feel as their warmth and protectiveness surround me.

I don't care that everyone in the room is probably watching us, gossiping about us, making up stories about things that aren't going to happen between the three of us.

There might be wild rumors floating about what these two get up to behind closed doors, but despite how this might look, it's not what this is.

They're like my brothers. Okay, so I wouldn't dance with Zayn quite like this, but nonetheless, it's as far as it'll go.

"Oh hey," Luca says behind me, pulling away slightly when I assume another girl tries their hand at stealing one of them away. I lift my head from his shoulder and when I open my eyes, I immediately find Ella in the corner of the room watching me with hungry eyes.

"Will you do something for me?" I ask Leon.

"Anything."

"Dance with my girl. She's got a hella crush on the two of you. Don't tell her I told you that bit though."

He nods at me while laughing and I wave her over.

She shakes her head, and I get my first glimpse of shy Ella. It's pretty endearing to see.

"Come on," I mouth to her and finally she pushes from the wall she's leaning against and makes her way through the crowd.

"El, you know Leon, right?" Her cheeks turn beet red as she glances at him. "Dance with us," I say, pulling her into my side.

One song moves into another and another and finally, I manage to break away, making an excuse about needing the bathroom.

I back away watching Luca with his girl and Leon with Ella and I smile seeing them enjoying themselves.

I'm almost at the edge of the dance floor when a strong arm clamps around my waist and I'm hauled back into a hard body.

"I didn't think they were going to let you out of their clutches, Princess."

A violent shiver races down my spine as the deep, husky voice settles in my vodka influenced brain.

Oh fuck.

My body freezes as he tries to move to the music.

"What's wrong? You'll dance with them like a little slut but not me?"

"Get away from me, Kane." I fight to pull away from him, but his grip is too hard.

I should stamp on his foot with my heel, elbow him in the ribs, anything to cause him pain but I don't want to cause a scene.

If Luca and Leon learned that he was here... I shake my head, no. I can't let that happen.

"Fight me and I'll show everyone in this room exactly what you are, Princess," he warns in my ear. "I bet you're already wet for me and I haven't so much as touched you yet."

"Fuck you, Kane. You don't know a fucking thing about me."

"Oh, I know plenty, Princess. And what I don't know, you can be damn fucking sure that I'm going to get it out of you."

"Let me go."

I try to pull away again but he's having none of it.

"Move, Princess. Or I'll fuck you right here for everyone to see."

His free hand slides up the exposed skin of my thigh, only hesitating briefly as he meets the short hem of my dress.

"This dress is sinful, Princess. What do you say, dance or get fucked in public?"

Deciding to go with the lesser of the two evils, I roll my hips. His hand lifts but thankfully not under my dress, but instead, he wraps his fingers around my hip, his grip so hard that I've no doubt that he'll leave bruises. I wince, knowing just how boney I must feel since the last time he touched me, but I shove that concern down. I shouldn't give a shit what he thinks of me.

"That's it, Princess. Grind your ass against me just like you were against Dunn's cock."

I gasp. "I wasn't—"

"Don't try to play innocent. The entire room watched you with them. Did you want them to touch you? To fuck you?"

"No," I argue.

"So are you wet for them, or for me?"

"I'm not."

"Keep lying, Princess, and I'll just have to prove you wrong."

"Fuck you."

"You know what, that's not a bad idea."

He pushes me away from the mass of gyrating bodies and I have no choice but to stumble forward.

"What are you doing?" I squeal as we get closer to the stairs.

"I think it's probably better we do this in private, don't you?"

"I'm not going anywhere with you," I state.

"Oh no?"

Before I know what's happening the world spins around me and the next thing I know, I'm staring at Kane's ass as he marches me up the stairs.

"Ow," I scream when his palm lands on my bare ass cheek with a burning slap.

"That's for refusing my demands. You want more, you know how to act."

"Fuck yo—ow," I scream again as he hits the exact same spot.

"I know you're soaked for me, Princess. I can smell you."

My cheeks burn with mortification and I can only hope that he's lying.

We go up two flights of stairs while I slam my closed fists down on his ass, trying not to appreciate how solid it is while I continue to flail around, earning me more slaps than I can count after drinking just this much.

I knew coming tonight was a bad idea.

Why do I always believe people when they say he's not going to be there.

He's always fucking there.

I don't get a chance to register what room we've just barged into but seeing as no one screams at us to get out, I assume that it's empty.

My feet have barely touched the ground before my back slams against the door behind me.

All the air rushes from my lungs as his hand wraps around my throat.

When I finally lift my eyes to look at him, his dark gaze burns through me with the level of hate I expect from him and his teeth are bared as he snarls at me. His hood is pulled down low on his face, explaining how he got into the party that he was apparently banned from.

If Luca knew he was here...

My stomach erupts with a mix of nerves, fear, and goddammit, excitement.

"You don't want to do this," I say, ensuring that my voice doesn't waver one bit.

After everything I've been through, I shouldn't be scared of him. He should pale in comparison to the hell

I've lived through, but as I stare into his eyes, meeting his hate like for like, I can already feel myself crumbling.

He's only got one hand around my neck, yet that one touch scorches my skin in a way that neither Luca nor Leon's did downstairs.

Their touch felt nice, safe, but Kane's is downright dangerous and I can't stop my body from burning up, desperate for more.

It's wrong. Oh so fucking wrong.

He was the trigger that sent me spiraling last time, not that he has any idea of the fall out of that night, but he's also the only one who makes me feel this alive.

My chest heaves as he continues to hold me captive in his gaze, his warm whiskey scented breath fanning over my face.

"Do you know what, Princess?" he asks, sending my mind spinning until I remember that I issued him a warning not so long ago.

He leans closer, his nose and lips only a breath from mine and I'm flooded with the memory of what it was like to taste him.

My mouth waters, my breaths come out embarrassingly fast as I stand as still as a statue waiting for his next move, or his next vicious words.

"I really fucking want to."

I gulp loudly, my muscles tensing beneath his hand, and a smile tugs at his lips.

"Scared, Princess?"

"Of you? Never."

A growl rumbles up this throat as his fingers squeeze mine, momentarily cutting off my air supply.

"Do you know how easy it is to strangle someone?"

I shake my head, although my movement is so minimal it's almost impossible to see.

He leans in, his lips in my hair until they brush my ear.

"Really fucking easy," he breathes, sending a shiver racing through my entire body. "I could break you, Princess, with one quick move. You'd be gone and I could watch those fucking Dunn's cry over your grave while getting the fuck on with my life."

"Go on then," I taunt. "End it. Right here, right now. Put me out of my misery."

I don't mean it, and my heart slams against my chest as I force the words out. If I wanted to make it all go away then I'd have done it a year ago and not because this asshole thinks he can threaten me into wishing I were dead.

"And put an end to this little game? Lose my toy? I think I need to have some fun with her first."

Heat floods my core and I hate myself that little bit more that his barbed words and threats make me react this way.

I should have been burning from the inside out downstairs with the twins surrounding me while knowing what they're apparently capable of.

But I wasn't. Not like this.

His other hand lands on my waist, gripping hard and making me gasp before he slides it up toward my breast.

He cups me roughly and a whimper bubbles up my throat.

"Dirty. Little. Whore." His lips brush mine as he says the words but he doesn't kiss me.

"No," I cry, knowing just how far from the truth that statement is.

"You'd have let them do whatever they wanted, wouldn't you? I bet it's not the first time either."

My cheeks burn and he must read something in my eyes because a menacing smile appears on his face.

"Yeah, I thought so. But they're about to learn one very important thing."

"Oh yeah? Because to be honest, I don't think they give two shits what you have to say. They hate you because they love me."

His eyes widen and his nostrils flare. I have to fight to keep an accomplished smirk off my face. It seems I may have hit a sore spot there.

"You jealous, Kane?"

"Fuck you, Scarlett. I'm not jealous of those weak motherfuckers."

"Maybe not, but they've got me. And that is something you seem to want."

His chest swells as he sucks in a breath.

"They haven't got you, Princess. I think we all know who really owns you."

Fabric ripping hits my ears a second before coolness surrounds my breasts.

"You... you fucking ruined my—" A sharp gasp cuts off my words as he pinches my nipple between his thumb and forefinger and twists, hard. "Fuck."

His eyes hold mine as he leans in, pressing the entire length of his hard body against mine. I've never felt so tiny and helpless as I do in this moment and hell if it doesn't make me wetter.

"You like it, don't you?"

"I fucking hate you."

"Doesn't stop you from wanting to beg for me though, does it, Princess?"

"I'll never beg for anything from you."

"Want to fucking bet."

Before I know what's happening, his fingers are between my thighs, pushing my panties aside and spearing inside me.

"Oh, Princess. Just look how you've been lying to me."

Oh my God.

I close my eyes as the squelch of his fingers inside me fills the room.

I shouldn't like this. I should be shouting, screaming, getting anyone who might hear to come and rescue me.

But one touch and I'm fucking useless where Kane is concerned.

"Fuck, you're running down my hand already."

A moan rips from my throat as he pushes higher inside me. It's such an alien feeling after so long, but fuck. I need more.

"Look at me, Princess. You need to know who's doing this to you. We can't have two pussy fucking twins in your head while you come all over my hand."

My eyes fly open at his demand. I want to tell him that my thoughts are far from the guys I was dancing with right now, but I don't want to give him the satisfaction.

"Who owns you, Princess?"

I bite down on the inside of my lips in defiance.

"You're going to fucking regret that."

He rips his fingers from me, forcing me to cry out with loss. I was so close. So fucking close.

My core aches for him as he releases my neck.

For half a second, I consider running. But not only would it be pointless in these heels, even if he did let me go, he'd find me after and this whole thing will be ten times worse.

A thrill races through me.

Maybe I shou— "Argh," I cry in surprise when he places both of his hands on my shoulders and pushes until I've no choice but to drop to my knees.

He stares down at me with my ripped dress around my waist, exposing my bare breasts and my hands resting on my thighs with impatience filling his eyes.

"You fucking owe me, Princess. So what are you waiting for?"

I drop my eyes from his, run-down fitted black hoodie and then to the huge bulge in his dark jeans.

"I thought I repulsed you," I breathe, my mouth watering as I imagine what he might look like up close.

I barely got a chance to see anything last time.

"Even the evilest woman can suck cock, Princess. Now, time to show me if you're actually worth anything."

He lifts his hoodie to reveal his waistband and just waits.

But much to his irritation, I don't jump at his orders.

"I don't have all fucking night," he growls, his grip on reality slipping.

"Oh really. Shame because I do."

Lifting my hand, I trace my fingertip over the imprint of his cock.

"You—fuck."

Ripping open his pants, he lets the fabric drop to his thighs and pulls his cock out.

Holy fucking shit. He's pierced. No wonder he felt so good that night.

A fresh wave of heat floods my core as I stare at him wondering why the devil himself has to have such a perfect fucking cock.

"Open wide, Princess."

Before I've blinked, the crown is pressing against my closed lips.

I fight him because I can't not despite the fact I'm damn near desperate to taste him, to make him lose control.

He wants to be the one with the power, following me around, threatening me, scaring me. Yet right now, he's like putty in my fucking hands.

He growls in warning before I release my lips slightly allowing him to push inside my mouth.

He thrusts forward, hitting the back of my throat not a second later making me gag in shock.

"Don't disappoint me, Princess. Here I was thinking you were a dirty fucking slut. Or is it a different cock you want down your throat right now?"

I wouldn't reply, even if I could.

He pushes into me once again but I'm ready for him this time and I relax my muscles allowing him to go deeper without gagging.

"Fuck," he barks, resting one palm against the wall at my back as he watches me.

His length jerks in my mouth and I smirk, well as much as I can, wondering if he's that worked up by this that he's not going to last.

I suck him harder, deeper, give him everything I've got. If he's going to insist I'm nothing more than a dirty whore then I may as well live up to it.

My lungs burn as I continue, tears stream from my eyes from my lack of air and saliva drips from my chin but I don't give a fuck because every time he groans, each time his fingers tighten in my hair causing a sting of pain to shoot down my spine, I remember just how he's losing control because of me right now and a surge of power races through me.

He thinks he's so mighty with this scary little gang and his wicked threats but right now he's fucking nothing. I might be the one on my knees for him but I'm the one fucking owning him.

He says nothing other than his grunts of pleasure but I know the moment he reaches the point of no return because his length swells, his grip on my hair becomes impossibly tight and his eyes that are still boring down into me flicker with something I've never seen before.

Pride?

I push the thought aside because I'm not sure anything at the moment before he orgasms can ever be taken seriously. It's in those few seconds that people always do or say something that they later regret when the high has left their body.

His lips part as a roar rips past them as his cock jerks violently in my mouth spurting salty jets of cum down my throat.

I swallow it all, lifting my hand to wipe at my chin quickly before I'm hauled from the floor and thrown on the bed.

He flips me onto my back, presses his palms to my inner thighs, hooks my panties aside and dives for my pussy.

"Holy shit," I shout, bucking from the bed as he sucks on me.

My fingers find his hair as he continues his assault.

I've no idea if it's pleasure or torture as he keeps up his almost unbearable suction along with the teasing caress of his tongue.

"Kane," I scream as he slides two fingers deep inside.

"Fuck, you like sucking my cock, don't you, Princess. You're wet as fuck."

"Kane," I repeat as he finds my G-spot like a fucking pro and rubs at it while pinching my clit.

"I always knew you'd be so fucking sweet to ruin, Princess."

"Fuck you. You won't break me."

"Says the one with tears still on her cheeks." He reaches up and sweeps the wetness away that I didn't realize was still there before sucking his thumb into his mouth, tasting my tears.

It's weirdly erotic and intimate despite the fact he just had his head between my thighs.

"You taste like sin, trouble, and betrayal."

"And you taste like a special brand of cunt but did you hear me fucking complaining," I pant, the crest of my orgasm just within touching distance.

I'm moving once again, Kane's arm sweeps over all the items littering the desk before my bare chest is pressed against the cold wood.

I push to stand but his large palm presses down between my shoulder blades keeping me in place as he kicks my legs wider.

"What are you—" Stupid question, I know but the urge to say something gets the better of me. "Condom," I blurt in a panic but if he hears me, he totally ignores me.

"Shut the fuck up," he barks, thrusting inside me without warning.

"Oh my God," I scream as he begins pounding into me with abandon.

I can barely catch my breath as the desk crashes against the wall, my breast scratching against the rough surface but the bit of pain only adds to the pleasure surging through me.

He hits me deep, so fucking deep that I see stars. It's just like last time, only... it's more somehow.

His fingers dig harshly into my hips, bruises already beginning to form I swear.

"Don't you dare fucking come, Princess. I'll tell you when you can let go and not a fucking second sooner," he barks.

"Kane," I cry, my muscles ripple as he pulls out before quickly thrusting back inside. The tip of his cock, his piercing, hitting my cervix as he takes me.

Fuck, we shouldn't be doing this.

"Oh God, oh God," I whimper, balancing on the ledge and more than ready to crash.

Kane's hips thrust forward once more before he stills, his cock swelling once more before he rapidly pulls out and roars out a second release as hot jets of cum land on my bare ass.

His palm connects with my ass cheek again in the exact same place he hit before and the pain mixes with the pleasure of him thrusting his fingers inside me once more and I fall into mind-numbing bliss.

I'm unaware that I've even moved until long seconds later when I come back to myself and realize that I'm on the bed once more.

"Kane?" I ask, keeping my eyes closed, although I don't know why I bother, I already know he's not here. My skin isn't pricked with awareness and my heart isn't racing like it does whenever he's near me.

I give myself two more seconds before I rip my eyes open and take in the room around me.

"Oh fuck. Fuck, fuck, fuck." My eyes flick around the

room before landing on the one item that confirms all my worst fears.

Luca's framed Rosewood High jersey is hanging on the wall opposite me.

I drop my head into my hands as a sob erupts.

If I knew this was where he brought me to... I wouldn't have...

Who the fuck am I kidding? There was no way I had any chance of stopping that car crash.

"Fuuuuuck," I scream into my hands of images of what went down between us only minutes ago hits me over and fucking over.

All I can smell is him, all I can feel is his brutal touch but I'm in Luca's room.

Fucking asshole.

Pulling at my ruined dress, I try to figure out how to salvage the situation so that I can make my escape but I've got no chance.

Climbing from the bed, I find one of Luca's discarded shirts and pull it over my head, shimmying my dress over my hips and dropping it to the floor.

I make my way through to his bathroom and clean up, wishing that I could wash the memories from my head at the same time.

The booming music from two floors below filters up, telling me that the party is still in full flow despite the fact I left and made yet another fucking colossal mistake.

I stare at myself in the mirror above the basin. I've got dark makeup running down my cheeks, my lipstick smeared over my face. Lifting my fingertips to my lips, I realize that he never kissed me. Not once.

Asshole.

But I don't know why I'm surprised. There was nothing sweet or sentimental about that.

It was an exorcism.

One that I know for a fact isn't over yet. That wasn't the end of this thing between us. It was barely the beginning.

A shiver races through me knowing that there's more to come.

I came here to start over. Not to just fall back into this toxic thing with Kane. This was not part of the plan.

13

KANE

I drop into my car that I'd left on the other side of the street to where the party is still raging.

I can see both Luca and Leon through the large windows at the front of the house still enjoying themselves with their fan club.

They haven't even noticed that she's gone.

Fucking assholes.

So much for protecting her.

I walked straight in and took exactly what I wanted.

It was easy. Too fucking easy.

It barely took the edge off what I needed. I should have left with her. Thrown her in the back of my car and took her back to my room where I could have spent the entire night teaching her a lesson for all the mistakes she's made.

She'd have fucking loved that a little voice says in my head.

I rest my head back and close my eyes as the image of her on her knees with my cock between her red lips threatens to consume me.

I was not fucking expecting that.

I might have got off calling her a dirty whore, but I'm pretty sure the reality is very different.

Those fucking skills though, fuck.

I tug at my pants trying to make space for my rapidly swelling cock.

I should drive away, but I'm too intrigued to see what she's going to do.

Part of me hopes she comes running out clutching her dress to her chest and I'm able to pick her up and continue our night.

I must sit out here for almost an hour watching the party continue without me before I finally push the key into the engine and pull away, leaving her behind. Still in his bed? Maybe.

My fingers tighten around the wheel as I think about him finding her there in a few hours.

I had no idea it was his room, I just walked to the room the farthest away from the party but the second I pushed inside, I knew, and the smuggest fucking smile formed on my face.

But has that backfired?

If he finds her and she confesses to me being there, then he's going to be gunning for me even more than he is now.

He's spent all week trying to convince the AD that I shouldn't have a place on the team. I thought he'd succeeded when I got called in to see him after class this morning.

But thankfully, all he did was issue me with a warning about what Luca has been trying to do and welcome me to the team.

As it fucking well should be.

He has no idea how much I know, and truthfully, I don't know how deep his involvement is with Victor and the Hawks. It can't be much seeing as he continues to hold his position at Maddison, but I know for a fact that we've got enough dirt on him to wipe him from his position and ruin the reputation of every single sports team at MKU.

Or, and potentially worse, will Luca find her in his bed and continue with what they started out on the dance floor.

Watching her dance between the two of them turned my blood to lava.

Even now, hours later I can still feel the burning need to march over and rip her from their grasps.

She's too fucking good for a pair of pussies like them.

I pull up at the house only ten minutes later to find a similar situation to the Dunn's place. People fucking everywhere.

Only, where the Dunn party was full of serious athletes letting go for a few hours, this party is wild. And by wild, I mean the weed burns my lungs when I step through the already open front door and slip around a couple fucking against the wall before I make my way to the living room where Ezra is snorting snow off some girls fake tits and Devin is enjoying a lap dance. Ellis, as always, has his nose stuck in his cell. Fuck knows that he's reading with all this going on around him.

Someone moves toward me, and I have to give Reid, the oldest Harris brother, a double-take as he approaches.

"Dude, what the fuck are you doing here?"

He lifts his fist in greeting and I bump it before he scowls at a couple on the couch and they damn near shit themselves before scrambling up and running from the room.

He passes me a bottle of beer and we drop down.

"Brought the fucking party, didn't I? You don't think those pussy motherfuckers could have pulled this off."

I shrug, not telling him that this is college and the second word gets around about the kind of gear these brothers are going to be peddling then there will be a line around the block to attend.

"They not pulling their weight, Daddy had to send you in, eh?"

It's no secret in this house that the Harris brothers are here for only one reason. To lock up the drug supply in Maddison.

They've got Harrow Creek and Rosewood down tight and this is the next patch to claim.

"Nah, they're good. I just fancied being a college kid for the night. No responsibilities and all that." His eyes flick over to where Devin, his oldest little bother is now fingerfucking the girl on his lap.

"Oh yeah. How's that going for you?"

"How is it he's got a girl already and I don't?"

"Because you're talking to me," I suggest.

"Fucking right. I'll catch you later. I need some fucking college chick action."

"Don't do anything I wouldn't do," I shout as he walks away in search of a victim for the night.

I scan the room, half tempted to stay and watch the drama unfold but in the end, I find myself a bottle of vodka in the kitchen and make my way up to my room.

A few guys stop me for a chat as I make my way to the stairs but I don't hang around, especially when some of the drunken girls begin to get a little handsy. Usually, I'd return their attention without a second thought but tonight with the scent of Letty still in my nose, I push them away and jog up to my room to lock myself inside for the night.

Stripping out of my clothes, I throw them into the laundry pile in the corner before marching toward the bathroom. Part of me is desperate to shower and get her scent off me, but the other wants to fucking bottle it.

Turning the shower on as hot as it'll go, I step under and scrub my skin until I'm red.

I need her off my body and out of my fucking head.

It's wishful thinking, she's been deep inside both for more years than I want to admit.

She should have been yours all along the little voice in my head taunts me, but I shake it away.

She's never been mine.

I put someone else's happiness and desires before mine. And look where that got me.

With a dead best friend and a girl I can't forget who I'll forever hold responsible.

"Fuuuuck," I bellow, planting my fist into the tiles before me and watching as my blood begins to seep over the white porcelain.

I need to walk away from her.

To put her behind me.

But I can't.

The beast that lives inside me, the one that constantly seeks revenge for every fucked up thing that's happened to me, needs her. It needs to see her pay. To watch her crumble and shatter right before my eyes. And it doesn't matter that my heart beats to an entirely different tune because that motherfucker still thinks we're thirteen years old with a crush on a girl he can't stop thinking about.

My fist finds the tiles again and doesn't stop until two of them are cracked and the water beneath my feet runs red.

The pain helps, it always has but it's not enough.

The only thing that calms it is her. This is why I already know that I'm not going to be able to turn my back on her.

The house is a fucking disaster when I emerge the next morning. There are bodies in all states of undress as I make my way to the kitchen for a coffee.

The only sounds that can be heard are that of the passed out drunks snoring and someone heaving somewhere. I really fucking hope that's into a toilet, or at least in one of the guy's bedrooms.

"Thought you'd stay the night, eh?" I ask Reid as I join him in the kitchen.

"Shit in the Creek can wait for a bit."

I kick some guy in the stomach who's passed out in the middle of the kitchen.

"Out," I bark the second his eyes flicker open and he slowly climbs to his hands and knees and crawls from the room.

Slamming the door loudly behind him, I turn back to Reid.

"Why are you really here? You don't need college to get pussy," I mutter, knowing that he's got girls lined up in the Creek to get a piece of Victor Harris's firstborn son, the prodigy that's going to take over the empire one day.

"Maybe I wanted one who didn't know who the fuck I was."

"Really?" I ask suspiciously. It's no secret that Reid likes to flaunt his power to get whatever the fuck he wants, women included.

"What can I say? Change is good for the soul."

"You're full of shit."

Reaching for a mug, I start the coffee machine, feeling his eyes burning into my back.

"You got a question, just fucking ask it, bro."

He hesitates, giving me a chance for my mug to fill and I spin around, mimicking his stance leaning against the counter with a mug in my hands and wait for him to spill.

There's no fucking way he came here to party like a college kid. It's not his style.

"Do..." he starts before looking at his feet.

"Reid, say it. Ask it. Whatever the fuck it is. I've got your back, you know that."

He's a year older than Devin and me but we've grown up close as fuck. We've worked side by side for years for their cunt of a father. I know them better than my own family—not that I've got much of that left these days.

"Are things going okay around here, you know... with business?"

"It's only been a week," I say, my brows drawing together.

"I know but that's long enough to know if you've seen anything suspicious."

Devin and Ezra might think they own this place, that they're in charge of business, but the truth is that there's someone pulling their puppet strings, and that person is Reid. He might not have enrolled here, but there's no doubt about who's in charge of this little takeover mission.

The younger Harrises are just the ones on the inside making the connections.

"What exactly are you suggesting? That they're not pulling their weight," I say, tilting my chin toward the ceiling to indicate where his younger brothers are sleeping above our heads.

"I'm sure it's nothing. Vic's worried that they're not getting through shipments quick enough."

"Well, then he needs to slow down the fucking shipments. Three guys can only shift so much while studying and making it look legit."

"I know, I know. He just sent me to check things out."

I narrow my eyes on him, suspicious as fuck. Reid always has his finger on the pulse of this business. If he's suspicious then... something doesn't add up.

"You're hiding something."

He pins me with a hard stare. One that might make one of their weaker minions quake in their boots, but not me. I'm one of them. I might not be in the drug ring anymore—by fucking choice after the bullshit with my brother going down for possession for their stash but I'm as much one of them as they are. So fucking what my birth certificate doesn't say Harris. I've lived this life with them for as long as I can remember.

"If they fuck this up, then they won't initiate."

"They won't fuck it up," I mutter knowing just how vital this place is to their future. They'll wrap up Maddison in a nice little bow then Vic will complete their initiation and they can all join the senior chapter of the Hawks with Reid.

I should be heading in the same fucking direction but like fuck am I committing my life to that fucking asshole.

It's bad enough he's ruined my childhood with his bullshit.

Victor Harris and I have a deal. A fucking good one that he'd better not pussy out on. So far so good, but there's still a long fucking way to go yet.

"Go back to Daddy and tell him everything is fucking hunky-dory and get him off their backs."

"Alright, papa bear," he mocks. "How's things on your end?"

"Quiet, thank you. I don't have time for that bullshit."

"You know it's going to come to an end eventually."

"Yeah, when the season is over with some fucking luck."

"I still can't believe you managed it. A fucking Panther, man. It's pretty epic."

I nod at him, a smirk twitching at my lips. I might have sold my soul to the devil to get here but fuck, does it feel good.

14

LETTY

My head pounds as I come too. I try to swallow but my mouth is so dry that I've no chance.

What the hell happened last night?

I remember sitting out on the deck with Luca and Leon.

Drinking.

Drinking a lot.

Dancing. Their hands. Their bodies grinding against mine.

My cheeks burn at the memory. I bet I looked like a right...

"Dirty little whore."

I hear his voice as if he's actually here, and when someone groans beside me, I sit bolt upright with my heart in my throat.

Tell me I didn't. Please, for the love of Christ, tell me I didn't.

Sucking in a breath, I hesitantly look over my shoulder.

All the air rushes from my lungs when I find a mass of dark hair instead of dirty blond and perfectly clean skin instead of the inked-up arms someone else has.

"Thank fuck," I breathe.

Although I don't immediately lie back down knowing that it's safe. Instead, I have an internal war with myself as to whether I should attempt to sneak out.

I'm sure the last thing Luca wanted last night when he finally stumbled up here was to find me curled up in his bed.

Chances are, he'd brought a girl up here and I ruined his night.

"Stop overthinking it and lie the fuck back down, babe."

"I, um... I really should—"

"Lie the fuck back down?"

A laugh falls from my lips. "I was going to say go."

"I'll take you back later, don't worry. Right now, I'm too fucking hungover to deal. Now lie the fuck down and give me something to cuddle."

I snort but regret it when my head pounds.

"Y-yeah, okay," I cave, lying back down and curling up with my back to his chest.

He loops his arm around my waist and pulls me even tighter into him, so tight that his morning wood pokes me in the ass.

"Uh... Luc..."

"Shhh. Cuddles."

I open my mouth to respond but before I find any words, a soft snore falls from him.

Smiling, I relax back and tuck my hand under my cheek, closing my eyes and praying for a few more hours of sleep.

I must eventually drift off because when I come back to, the bed beside me is cold. Thankfully though, my head does feel a little better.

Turning over, I crack my eyes open and find Luca slumped back on his desk chair staring at me. He's only wearing a pair of gray sweatpants, and fuck, is it a sight to wake up to.

"Morning sleepyhead," he says, his voice still rough from sleep.

"You should have woke me."

"Nah, you looked too peaceful. There's water and pills if you need them." He nods toward the nightstand and I can't help but sigh at the welcome sight.

"Thank you."

I slide myself so I'm sitting in bed, more aware than ever that I'm just dressed in his shirt and a tiny pair of panties.

Memories from the night before threaten to surface but I force them down with the painkillers.

"So..." Luca starts, and my heart sinks. He wants answers and I'm not sure I'm prepared to give them to him. "How exactly did you end up in my shirt and in my bed last night?"

"Um..." My cheeks burn as I think about what actually happened in his bed last night. The image and sensations of Kane between my thighs hit me and my entire body flushes hot. "I... uh... had too much to drink."

"And you just happened to find my room?" I know what he's thinking. I've never been here before, the chances of me finding it in a drunken stupor are slim.

"Apparently so," I mutter, my face burning with embarrassment. "I hope I didn't ruin your chances with a girl when you found me here."

"Let," he sighs, his head tilting to the side like a cute puppy dog. "I'll always put you first if you need me. You know that."

Guilt rips through me because by the fact I'm here right now, it's clear that I wasn't putting him first last night. Not that I had a lot of chance to put much thought into anything.

I pull his sheets around me, needing to hide. My body aches and I already know that my skin is marred with marks and bruises from him. I can't let Luca see them. He will undoubtedly lose his shit if he thinks Kane has even laid a finger on me.

"I'll leave you to get sorted. You hungry? I make some mean pancakes."

I rip my eyes from him to the heap of fabric that is my dress behind him.

I can't put that on, it's ruined.

Fuck. I need to get out of here before anyone starts asking any more questions.

"Rain check? I really need to get back. I've got so much work to do."

His face drops and I hate myself that little bit more.

"Yeah of course. You want something to wear so you don't have to do the walk of shame in last night's dress?"

"That would be great, thank you."

He pulls out a pair of sweats he claims are too small for him and an MKU Panthers hoodie, drops them to the bed and with a kiss to my forehead, he leaves me alone in his room.

Dropping my head into my hands, I let out a groan of frustration.

My life is such a fucking mess.

Things were supposed to be getting simpler by starting here and being close to family.

I should have just gone home this weekend.

With a sigh, I throw the covers off me and make quick work of dragging on the freaking huge pair of sweats, pulling the tie cords so tight I could almost wrap them around my waist twice.

I'm a mess.

I splash my face with cold water and finger brush my teeth with Luca's toothpaste. I find my purse on his desk, and I cast my mind back trying to figure out if I put it there or if he found it sprawled across the floor when he discovered me here last night. Before mustering up every ounce of confidence I can find and pull open Luca's bedroom door.

Thankfully, the hallways are empty as I make my way through the house and when I get to the kitchen, I only find Luca standing, still shirtless, with a bowl of pancake mixture in his hands.

It's the thing dreams are made of.

"Aw, look at the Panthers all-star quarterback getting his bake on."

He looks up at me where I'm resting my hip against the doorframe and his face lights up.

"You sure I can't tempt you?" He tilts the bowl toward me and my stomach silently grumbles.

I'm just about to agree when movement above our heads reminds me exactly why I need to get out of this house.

I don't mind Luca and Leon being front and center to my disaster of a life, but I don't need half of the team and however many girls they hooked up with last night knowing.

"No, I really need—"

"Hey," a deep voice rumbles from behind me before arms snake around my waist. "I thought you'd ran away from us last night."

"She did. I found her passed out in my bed," Luca announces causing Leon to tense behind me. It's brief but I don't miss it.

Extracting myself from his hold, I turn to look at him but I can't help but laugh when I get a look at his face.

"Feeling rough?" I ask, taking in the dark circles under his bloodshot eyes.

"Someone—" He shoots a look at his brother. "Decided shots would be a fucking fabulous idea."

"Do not blame this on me. You are your own person and make your own decisions."

I laugh at the pair of them as they continue bickering.

"Just cook the pancakes and shut the fuck up," Leon mutters, ripping the refrigerator open and pulling out a can of energy drink.

"Okay, well I'm gonna..." I point toward the front of the house.

"Wait," Leon calls before I get a chance to escape, although I've no idea how seeing as my car is parked at the dorm. "How are you getting back?"

"I'll call an Uber."

I reach into my purse for my cell, but when I pull it out, I find it dead.

"I'll take you," Leon offers.

"It's okay, just—"

"I said, I'll take you," he repeats, leaving little room for argument.

"O-okay."

"I'll call you later," Luca calls as I follow a fully dressed Leon out of the kitchen.

"Thank you, Luc, for last night..." For not asking too many questions.

"Anytime." He winks at me before going back to his batter.

"Come on, Cupcake."

"Are you sure you're okay to drive?" I ask after dropping into Leon's BMW.

"Yeah, I'm fine." He reaches over and squeezes my thigh as he starts the car and pulls away from the curb. "So, slept in Luc's bed, huh?" He tries to make it sound like a casual question but I don't miss the tightness to his voice.

"Yeah, things got a little too much and I escaped."

"I was going to come to find you but then the shots happened and—"

"It's fine," I say, cutting him off. I wince as I think about what he might have seen had he have come looking for me.

Jesus.

No one needs to witness that.

How Kane treated me. It was degrading. It was rough. It was... *Everything you craved and you're getting wet just thinking about it.*

Shaking my head, I focus on the houses passing by out of the window.

"You want to talk about it?" he asks, clearly sensing that I'm holding things back.

"No, not really. Did you have a good night?" I ask, changing the subject.

"Yeah, it was okay. Missed you though."

"Did you pull?" I ask, ignoring his previous comment.

He chuckles and I look over at him.

He's pushed the sleeves of his hoodie up his forearms revealing the rippling muscles as he turns the corner.

I run my eyes up his arm until I find his face.

His profile is perfect. If football doesn't work out for him, he should really consider being a model because damn.

"I know I look like hell, you don't need to stare."

"You're hot and you know it."

"You think?"

"You know I do, and the majority of girls, and a good portion of guys at MKU." A smile twitches at his lips. "Don't let it go to your head though."

"I guess Dad's genes we're good for something, eh?"

"Your looks and your ball skills. Hell yeah."

"Let's be honest, no one wants any of his other... qualities."

"Oh I don't know, Luca got some of his ego."

Leon barks a laugh as he turns toward my dorm. "That he did, Cupcake. You want me to walk you up?"

I glance around. It's stupid, I know he's not here waiting for me but still my skin prickles as I think about it being a possibility.

"Nah, you get back and enjoy those pancakes."

"Okay. You know where I am."

I nod at him and climb from the car. I love them both dearly but I am more than ready to stand under the hottest shower I can bear and crawl into my own bed for a few hours to sleep off the rest of this hangover.

Stupidly, I opt for the stairs instead of the elevator, thinking that the exercise might wake me up a little.

Wrong. My thighs burn by the time I hit our floor. It's just a reminder of last night's mistake.

I'm still building up a wall to keep the memories out when I walk into our dorm to be met with a face I really don't need to see.

"Morning, Miss Scarlett. Nice little walk of shame on your first weekend at MKU," Brax announces from somewhere in the room but it's not him I'm focused on.

"Ellis?" His name falls from my lips before I've even realized I've said it.

"Hey, Let. How's it going?"

His eyes run down the length of me that's clad in Luca's clothes and I want the ground to swallow me up.

It's no secret that the Harris brothers have enrolled here. It's a fact that I'm sure every pill-popping, powder-snorting, acid-tripping student loves.

When we were kids, Victor Harris's reach didn't span out of Harrow Creek, but as his greed and need for power has grown and so has his patch.

He took over Rosewood while we were seniors, and now he's after Maddison. I get it, I guess. He's a businessman. If you can call a gangster one of those.

All I know is that he's terrifying, and he's single-handedly ruining the kids of Harrow Creek by convincing them that the best way to survive that hell hole is to become one of his boys.

Bullshit. All of it. And just another reason why I was so glad we left when we did.

Zayn was always a bright boy, and I'd have hated to see him fall into that trap.

The same one that we all know Kane and Kyle fell into, if Kyle's recent stint in juvie was anything to go by.

My eyes shift from Ellis to Micah who's sitting beside him on the couch, both of them with computers on their laps and looking equally as nerdy. It's almost endearing, or it would be if I didn't know that Ellis is as terrifying as his brothers, possibly more so because he's so fucking intelligent.

"It's g-good. You?"

"Can't complain. I was made for college. You know that."

"You two know each other?" Micah asks, looking between the two of us.

"Yeah, we go way back, right Scarlett?"

"We went to school together."

"You a fucking twin magnet or something?" Brax barks from his spot at the dining table. I don't look over though, I'm too intrigued by how Ellis tenses at the almost mention of the Dunn twins.

"Yeah, something. We were never really friends though, were we?"

Ellis's lips part as if he's going to respond but I put him out of his misery.

"If anyone needs me, I'm going to be in my room working." I march through the living area, aware of all sets of eyes in the room following me.

"Letty?" My spine straightens at Ellis's voice. I stop but I don't look back. "I know it wasn't your fault. It was just a tragic accident."

I nod, not wanting to get into the past with Brax and Micah listening to our exchange.

Without another word, I unlock my door and slip inside, quickly flipping the lock again to ensure my privacy.

After last night, I'm done with people for a few hours.

I'm halfway across the room when I feel it.

Something isn't right.

A shiver runs down my spine and I spin on my heels half expecting to find Kane hiding in the corner ready to pounce on me. But I'm the only one here.

My eyes flick around the room looking for something that is out of place. But as I find everything as I left it, I begin to feel ridiculous. I'm giving him exactly what he wants, I'm letting him get under my skin.

It's not until I lift my arm to place my purse on my desk that I see it.

Stuck to my laptop is a Post-It note.

Whose bed did you sleep in last night, Princess?

My entire body turns cold as I stare down at his words.

Taking a few steps back, my hand lifts to cover my racing heart as panic begins to consume me.

He was here. In my room.

I'm not going fucking insane.

I back up until I'm by the window. I've no idea what makes me look, a sixth sense or some shit, but when I turn to the left and stare down at the quad below, I find him standing down there and staring right back at me.

"Holy fuck," I gasp.

My head screams at me to move, to act like a normal person, and pretend that I haven't seen him staring up at my window like a creepy stalker.

I think back to the other night when I got this same feeling.

He was out there, wasn't he?

His eyes hold mine for another two seconds before he takes off running across the quad and finally out of sight.

It's not until he's gone that I'm able to breathe.

All the air rushes from my lungs as I stumble back to the bed.

This isn't ever going to be over is it?

I'm going to constantly be forced to remember everything I want to forget.

Maybe I should just try to talk to him. Have a rational conversation and get everything out.

But nothing about dealing with Kane is normal or rational. It's all anger, hate, vicious words and brutal touches.

I fall back, my purse landing on my stomach.

Reaching into it, I pull my cell out and blindly reach for the charger.

I plug it in and wait for it to power up.

I don't expect to have missed much. A message from Mom or Harley maybe. A few memes from Brax.

It buzzes after a few seconds but when I look at the screen to see who it is I find it's a number I don't recognize.

I open it, ready to immediately delete it but the words that stare back at me make me still.

Unknown: You're wet, aren't you? Give me one good reason why I shouldn't come straight up there and continue what we started.

My hand trembles as I stare at his words but my body betrays me as heat and lust wash through it. And fuck if he's not wrong because just reading that threat gets me going.

There's something very, very wrong with me.

I was in bed with the hot QB1 of the Panthers barely

an hour ago and I didn't feel like this but one message from that psycho and I'm practically panting for a repeat of last night.

Flipping over, I bury my face into my pillow and scream out my frustrations.

I need to reply. He's going to see that I've read it and I can't have him turning up here. I can't. No matter how much my body might think it's a good idea, my head knows better.

Sitting up, I stare down at his words once more, my head going straight back to last night.

I shouldn't have liked the pressure of his hand around my throat, but I did. I shouldn't have wanted his fingers to dig into my hips so they left bruises, but I did.

He wants to punish me for the past, and it seems that I'm more than willing to take it like I am in fact the guilty party.

Fuck. My. Life.

I tap out a message, lower my cell for a beat before picking it back up and deleting it.

Fuck.

Scarlett: Because I hate you.

It shows as read immediately as if he was waiting for it. I glance at the window and wonder if he's back. If he's waiting for my word and he's going to bolt up the stairs and storm inside to take what he wants.

My stomach flutters wildly at the thought.

Unknown: But doesn't that make it so much sweeter?

He adds a winky face emoji that stupidly makes my lips twitch into the beginnings of a smile.

Scarlett: No. It's bitter, toxic and dangerous.

Unknown: Exactly. Keep your door unlocked, Princess.

15

KANE

I smile down at our conversation before glancing up at her window. She's disappeared, but I know she's there. Thinking about me. About last night.

Reaching down, I rearrange myself.

Fuck, if I don't want a repeat. Although suspecting that she spent the night with a Dunn makes me question myself.

What happened after I left?

Whose bed did she sleep in? I might have left her in Luca's room, but Leon was the one to bring her back.

She probably won't believe a word of it, but I haven't actually been hanging around her dorm all morning waiting for her.

Yeah, so I broke into her room with Ellis's help, but I wasn't actually waiting for her, that was just good fucking timing.

I wait to see if she's going to reply to my demand, but after two minutes, I get nothing.

Part of me wants to go up and see if she's followed

orders, but I already know she hasn't. She makes a habit out of defying me and I don't expect her to change now.

I take off running, which was the reason for my trip around campus this morning, but not five minutes into it, my cell starts to ring.

Hoping it's her, I slow to a stop and pull it from my pocket.

I knew it was wishful thinking but disappointment floods me when I find the name of the person who's actually calling.

Victor fucking Harris.

"Yes," I bark. I would ignore it, but I know it's not worth it. If he wants me, he'll get to me one way or another.

"I've got a job for you."

"We're done, Vic. Or have you forgotten our deal?"

He laughs, and while it might make some of his boys cower, it does little to affect me.

They all might think he's God, but I know different. He's weak, hiding behind his money. But his power is nothing more than a reputation he's bought over the years.

The only person anyone needs to be scared of is Reid. And that motherfucker would take a bullet for me.

"No, I haven't."

"I've upheld my end, now it's time for you to do the same."

"All that can go away with one phone call from me, boy. Don't forget that."

"Don't fucking threat—"

"One job. It's Alana."

"I don't give a shit who it is."

"And I don't give a shit about what you think. I'll send you the details. You know the drill."

"But I've got—practice," I mutter the final word because he's already hung up. Cunt.

With one final look at Letty's dorm building, I take off in the opposite direction.

By the time I get back to the house, every muscle in my body aches.

"What the fuck is with the face?" Devin asks as I storm into the kitchen for a bottle of water.

I cut him a look and it seems to tell him everything he needs to know.

"Victor?"

"Yeah, fucking Victor."

"You knew this was going to happen."

"I know," I mutter before chugging the entire bottle. "I just hoped that maybe he wouldn't."

"He's not going to cut you free no matter what you do for him."

"He might not have a fucking choice when I kill him."

Devin stares at me with an emotionless expression on his face.

I'm sure most kids would look a little horrified if anyone threatened to kill their father but it's no secret that the Harris brothers hate their sperm donor as much as I do.

Unfortunately, they also know as well as I do that we can't just take him out.

There's no fucking way I'm going to spend my life rotting in fucking jail because I couldn't control myself and end up wiping him out.

We need to be smarter than that. Smarter than him.

Our time will come—or more so the brother's time will come. By then I can only hope that I've turned my back on this life completely, although I know it's wishful thinking.

"Want to go a few rounds?" he asks, understanding my need to purge this anger and frustration out of me.

"Yeah, let's fucking go. I'll drive."

The drive to the Creek is quick. Mostly because I'm on autopilot. I pull up into the parking lot at Paddy's not remembering any of the journey or the turnings I'd taken, but my knuckles are white against the wheel with the need to blow off some steam.

The second we enter the old boxing gym, all eyes turn on us.

"Good to see they haven't forgotten who we are," Devin mutters with amusement.

It's not likely they will any time soon seeing as we've beat most of their asses over the years.

We don't speak to anyone, not that any of our fan club try to talk to us, they just stare as we make our way to a suddenly empty ring.

Paddy sticks his head out of his office and nods in our direction before ducking back in. Probably to run and tell his boss that we're in town.

Fuck him. Fuck them.

I've had my every move dictated by that cunt this past year. He's owned my fucking ass. Yes, so far he's followed through on his end of the bargain. He made out that I had a stand-up job for the authorities when Kyle's time was up in juvie which ensured I'd get guardianship, even if it was only for a few weeks until he turned eighteen in the spring.

But in order for that to happen. I've had to do all his fucking dirty work. Most much less pleasurable than being forced to take care of the needs of Alana and whoever else he found who needed some company. Fuck knows what's wrong with their husbands. Maybe my rep is just that good.

A cocky smirk appears on my lips as I wrap my knuckles.

There was a time we'd have pulled the boxing gloves out. But Devin and I are well past that now.

We both need the pain as much as each other. We need to feel each and every hit.

I swear a silence falls over the entire gym as we step up to each other.

Lifting my hands, I crack my knuckles once more and stare Devin straight in the eyes.

I love him like a brother. But right now, and for as long we're in the ring, he's the enemy. He's his father.

And he's going fucking down.

I launch at him, hoping to catch him off guard. But he's ready for me and he blocks my first hit.

Asshole.

We've trained together for years. We know each other's moves, we almost know each other's thoughts as we dance around the ring but the second I manage to land a punch to his jaw—everything changes.

His eyes turn wild and the competition between us ramps up. As does the interest in our fight.

I've totally lost track of how long we've been in here by the time Devin makes one vital mistake. He drops his guard for the briefest moment and I manage to land a punch to his stomach that sends him stumbling backward and crashing to the floor.

We're both covered in sweat and blood but fuck, I've never felt better.

Actually, that's a lie. Last night, with her, everything

felt fucking better but it would be in my own interest to try to forget about that. Not that it's ever worked before of course.

"Okay, okay," Devin pants, holding his hand up and not even bothering to attempt to get back up and continue. "You can have it. This one is yours," he says with a smirk.

"Motherfucker," I mutter, the smile that pulls at my lips rips my split open once more, as I reach down to help pull him up.

He stands and shakes out his muscles.

"Fuck, I feel better now."

"Yeah? Well, you look a fucking mess."

"You too, bro. You've got a little..." He points at his lip to indicate the blood that's dripping down mine but the only response he gets from me is a slap across the head.

The locker room is empty when we get there, no huge surprise seeing as every member of the gym was crowded around our ring to see who'd win the showdown.

We shower, dress and head for the door.

"Breakfast?"

"Fuck yeah?"

"Hallie's?" I turn to look at him, my brow raised in question. "Okay, so stupid question."

We get stopped a couple of times on the way out. A few members of the Hawks junior chapter now decide that it's safe enough to talk to us without getting their heads caved in. They ask us the same bullshit questions everyone does.

How's college?

What's it like to get out of the Creek?

Are you all still members?

I've only been at MKU for a week and already this

shit is pissing me off.

Devin is a junior and has had this shit for two years already. I've no idea how he's put up with it.

"It's great, thanks," I say politely.

I can see by the creasing around their eyes as they stare at me that they don't understand how the fuck I got into MKU. And that's fine. I get it. Vic has never made me out to be anything more than his little bitch boy. A scary motherfucking bitch boy, but a bitch boy all the same.

I've let them think it. Think I'm all brawn, but it's so far from the truth.

Being one of Vic's minions has never been my calling in life. I want more, I crave more.

More than the Creek, more than the shitty trailer parks we were forced to grow up in, and more than the fucking Hawks.

"Yes, of course we're still members. Working on a Maddison Chapter as we speak." Devin winks, and the guys all nod excitedly.

"They're a bunch of fucking assholes," Devin mutters as we head for my car.

"They're just more than happy to live this life. Not their fault they grew up thinking that initiating into the Hawks is the best things are going to get for them."

"We're the weird ones because we don't want it."

I mutter an agreement.

"Be so much fucking easier if we could just fall into line though, right?"

I glance over at him, my brows in the air.

"Oh, fuck off," he grunts, knowing exactly what I'm getting at.

As far as anyone can see he is just falling into line. Doing his father's bidding.

I laugh at him as I start the engine and head to our favorite diner.

"We should call the others. They'll be pissed if we do this without them," I say when we pull up under the neon Hallie's Diner sign.

"You wanna wait for them to get their asses here?"

"Hell no, I was just saying the right thing. Let's go."

He barks out a laugh as I throw the door open and climb out.

We look a mess, but it's something Hallie is used to.

Her diner is right on the edge of town, in the middle of fucking nowhere. I've no idea how she keeps getting customers, but this place has been going for as long as I can remember yet it's always quiet.

It's about the only place in Harrow Creek the Hawks haven't taken over. It's been our safe haven for the past few years.

Hallie might be heading for her sixties but she's not naïve to the life we live or the things we do. Her old man was a Hawk. He died during a gang war about twenty years ago.

It was the only time Vic has nearly lost power. He certainly lost a lot of men that night.

I think Hallie feels somewhat guilty because although she lost her husband and the father to her girls, if her husband hadn't fought as hard as he did for that cunt then our lives—and those of the rest of the youth of Harrow Creek—might have turned out differently.

It's wishful thinking because, with the Hawks gone, another will only take over. I can't imagine much will have changed but I'd take anyone over Victor 'Vicious' Harris lording it over the town any fucking day of the week.

The second I push the door open, the scent of smoky bacon and sweet maple syrup hits me and my stomach growls loudly. Only a moment later, Hallie emerges from her kitchen wearing her standard pink and yellow flowery apron and the warmest smile.

She reminds me so much of my mom that it makes my chest tighten with the loss I still feel all these years on.

"My boys!" She holds her arms out wide as we walk toward her, allowing her to embrace us.

It's a welcome hug, one I know Devin appreciates as much as I do.

The only parent he has left is a cunt, and his stepmother. Well, the less said about her the better.

"Hey, Hallie," I say with a wide smile once again splitting my lip.

She scowls at both of us when she finally releases us.

"Has he been putting you to work again?" she damn near growls, her eyes taking in our injuries. "You're college boys now, he needs to—"

"Nah, Nanna H, we haven't been working, just... playing," Devin says making her wince. She hates that nickname.

"Doesn't look like it was much fun to me. You need patching up?"

"Nah, we're good. Just need a plate of your pancakes and we'll be good as new."

"Damn shame to cover those beautiful bodies in bruises if you ask me," she mutters, walking us over to our usual booth in the back.

"The ladies love it, Nanna."

"Speaking of the ladies. Anyone special for me to meet yet?"

Devin throws his head back and laughs. "You know

me, Nanna. I'm sowing my oats wide and far."

"Yeah, just make sure none of them grow into anything." She quirks a knowing brow at him.

"I wrap it, Nanna. Don't sweat it."

"And you?" she turns her eyes on me.

"Nah, sorry to disappoint."

"Still hanging out with the hoes, huh?"

Devin snorts at her words.

That's the thing about Hallie, she knows everything. Even the shit we don't tell her, and we tell her a lot.

"Yeah, something like that."

I think back to the night before and my need to tell her about Letty almost forces the words out of my mouth, but I can't, so I swallow them down and keep my mask firmly in place.

"You'll find her again," she whispers to me, squeezing my shoulder.

See. Knows fucking everything.

"You want the regular?"

"You got it, Nanna H." Devin rubs his belly, grinning up at her, making her cheeks blush.

She disappears off leaving us alone.

There are a few other customers, but none are paying us any attention as we sit in our dark corner.

"I missed her," Devin says after a few seconds. "Why couldn't she have been our nanna?"

"Because she's too nice? Anyone that sweet doesn't have Harris blood in them."

"Hey, I'm as fucking sweet as they come and you know it."

I stare at him with a blank expression thinking of all the less than sweet things I've witnessed him do over the years.

"Oh yeah. How about you ask those who are long dead and buried if they think you're sweet."

"Just my job, man. I'm a fucking teddy bear under all that. All the girls want to hug me."

"And then they come fuck me."

He flips me off as one of Hallie's servers brings us some coffee over.

The girl's young, probably a sophomore, maybe a junior at Harrow Creek High and the second we both look at her, she flushes from head to toe.

"Thank you," I say, accepting the mug before she all but runs from our table.

"Oh she really looked like she wanted to hug you."

"Bet she fucking would if I offered." He pushes his still damp hair from his head and stares at her ass as she scarpers away.

"She's too fucking young," I chastise him.

"I ain't touching."

I don't want to bring up what Reid said to me this morning. I really don't want to get involved with their business but after we've finished eating my need to find out if there is something up gets the better of me.

"How's... business?" I ask, sitting back in the bench seat and stretching out my legs.

"Fucking slow, man."

"Oh?" I ask, now even more intrigued.

"Something's going on with the shipments. Can't get the shit we need as fast as we fucking need it."

"What's Vic saying?"

He shrugs. "Ain't spoken to the fucker. Reid's sorting it."

I nod, although I'm suspicious as fuck.

"Gives me more time for actual college shit though, so

I guess I shouldn't complain."

"Can't believe you're a fucking junior, man."

"Tell me about it, I never thought I'd live this life. Shame I don't have a choice in what comes after."

"It's still two years away, anything can happen."

"You think I'm not already dreaming that someone's gonna be stupid enough to take him out and put an end to all this bullshit?"

"It might happen."

He grunts at my optimism. But it's just that.

The reality is that no one will touch Vic no matter what stunt he pulls.

"What about you? You survived a whole week at college. Was it all you thought it would be?"

I think about classes, but my thoughts don't linger there because they shift straight onto my interactions with Letty.

"Better."

"You wouldn't be fucking saying that if she weren't here," he mutters.

My lips part to argue, but I can't because he's right and he fucking knows it.

"You got a plan?"

"Yeah, fuck her over and get her out of my fucking system."

He shakes his head. I know he thinks that I need to let it go, to let her get on with her life. Like he has. But I can't. It runs deeper for me. He never wanted her. He never thought she was going to be his and have it thrown back in his face.

"We should move, I've got so much to fucking do."

"Same, man. Yo, Nanna H," he bellows across the diner before she emerges from the kitchen. "We're out."

16

LETTY

I remained sitting on the edge of my bed, waiting to see if he was going to storm up here for longer than I wanted to admit. I also don't want to admit quite how disappointed I was that he didn't show.

But finally, I realized that he was just playing me and I dragged my aching muscles to the shower.

The second I stripped and saw the bruises darkening my hips, I knew it was a mistake.

They were exactly the reminders I don't need about how his touch feels.

I hid in my room for hours studying, waiting until the coast might be clear and be able to emerge without bumping into Ellis again.

It's not him. It's who he's connected to.

His older brother Devin is Kane's best friend. I've no doubt that Ellis will know everything I need to know about Kane. Like where he lives.

I do not need to know that.

It's bad enough that he's found me.

I also have no idea how much any of them know

They were there the night of the party. Did Kane tell them what went down? Do they know he's out for revenge? Hell, was he only here because Kane told him to be. It's no secret that Kane holds power even over Harris blood.

In the end, I ventured out for snacks and luckily, Micah was alone, still with his tablet.

He watched me as I made myself some lunch but thankfully he never asked about Ellis, and I tried to tell myself it was because he didn't care. Not because Ellis told him everything he knew.

I slept like shit. Every bang, crash or slightly loud voice as the others returned from the parties they tried to drag me to had me on edge waiting to see if Kane was going to come barreling through the door.

But still. Nothing.

Was this his plan? To get me so worked up I'll do whatever he demands of me.

If it is, I fear that I'm playing right into his hands.

When a knock did come on my door, it was followed by a soft female voice inviting me to her morning yoga class.

And that's where I've spent my morning.

Trying to find my inner peace, or whatever it is I'm supposed to be channeling.

Mostly, I'm just trying not to fall on my ass or break my neck. So far so good.

"Okay, ladies. Tuck your elbows in and straighten your spines," the instructor says softly and I follow her move. "Deep, slow breaths."

I close my eyes and empty my mind, or at least I try to. But the image of him before me Friday night never leaves.

The instructor brings the class to an end and silently, everyone begins to stand and rolls their mats up.

I count to five and then open my eyes, hoping that when I do everything will be simpler.

I find Ella smiling down at me when I come back to myself.

"You're a natural," she whispers.

"I'm not sure I'd go that far."

"You feel better though, right?"

I pause for a few seconds. "Yeah, actually I do.

"Come on, I need coffee."

With our mats under our arms, we walk out side by side and head toward the coffee shop.

"Takeout? I've got to study."

"Sure."

"You going to tell me about Friday night yet?" She asks as we make our way across the quad.

"I drank too much and passed out in Luca's bed." It's not entirely a lie.

"What about you? Hook up with anyone after I disappeared?" I ask, taking the heat off of me.

When she doesn't answer straight away, I glance over to find her cheeks bright red.

"Who?"

She drops her head into her hands and groans.

"Oh my God was it Leon?" I left her dancing with him so it would make sense. But then why wouldn't he have said anything yesterday morning?

My stomach twists but I'm not sure if it's at the thought of him being with Ella or the fact he might have hidden it from me.

"It was Colt," she admits.

I don't really know enough about the guys yet to really

form an opinion but he seemed like a good guy. A total player, but in my eyes, if he's friends with Luca and Leon then he's got to be a decent guy.

"O-okay? Was it bad or something?"

"What? No, no. It was not bad in any way."

"So what's the issue?"

"He's been with half of Maddison."

"It was a party, it's college. I'm sure people have done worse."

"I know, I'm just... ugh. He was so good," she whines.

"Maybe he'll let you back for a second shot."

"Nah, that'll never happen. He's got a once only rule in place."

"Wow, he has rules. That's... yeah."

"Fucking shots," she mutters.

"Well, you said you wanted a player so..."

"Yeah, I never said I wanted the ultimate player though."

"Too late for regrets, Ella."

"I know. I need to put it behind me. Hell knows he's not thought about me since I left."

I look over at her in her yoga pants and crop top. I really hope he fucking has and he knows how fucking lucky he was.

"Ella," someone screams from the corner of the parking lot.

"Oh my God," she squeals next to me, bouncing on the ball of her feet in excitement for whoever she's just seen. "I won't be long," she promises before darting away.

"It's okay, I'll head back," I call to her, not wanting to stand around here like a loner.

She waves at me over my shoulder as she jogs toward where three people are watching her.

The second she's in front of them they pull her into a hug.

I lift my coffee to my lips and take a sip before taking off in the direction of our dorm and the assignment that's sitting on my desk waiting for me.

I walk along the edge of the parking lot, leaving Ella and her friends behind.

Cars come and go and the voices of students sitting at a couple of the benches filter down to me as I lose myself in my thoughts... or maybe regrets would be more accurate.

I round the corner and disappear behind a large black town car as our building comes in to view in the distance.

The door beside me opens and before I know what's happening a large hand clamps down over my mouth and I'm hauled back into the vehicle.

My heart thunders against my chest as I kick my legs and throw my arms behind me in the hope of making contact with my attacker.

"Calm the fuck down, Scarlett."

That voice.

That fucking voice.

I'm placed on the seat and I spin to look him in the eyes.

"What do you want?"

Victor Harris's mouth curls into a scowl as he stares at me. There's disgust in his eyes for a second before he drops his gaze down my body. Disgust rolls through me and I grab the sides of my zip-up hoodie to cover up.

He tsks, making my skin crawl.

"What. Do. You. Want?" If he thinks he's getting any respect out of me then he's shit out of luck. This isn't my first interaction with him. Although sitting here right now, I really wish the previous time was the last.

I don't care who he is. He can't just abduct me like this.

"I've got a job for you, although I'm wondering if you need teaching some fucking manners first."

I raise a brow at him.

"I thought Kane might have done the job by now."

If he wants me to react to his mention of Kane then he's going to be bitterly disappointed.

"I don't want your job. Get one of your minions to do it for you."

"No can do. I need someone... a little different for this job."

"I'm not interested, Victor." I spin away from him and reach for the door but before I have my fingers around the handle, Victor's fingertips dig into my upper arms and I'm dragged back toward him.

He pulls me so close his disgusting old cigarette and stale whiskey breath races over my face.

My stomach turns as he looks down at my lips.

"Get the hell off me," I bark, trying to tug my arm away, but all I achieve is for him to hold tighter.

"Now, now, Hunter. It's in your best interest to play nice."

"Fuck you," I spit in his face before the pain that blooms in my cheek and down my neck makes my eyes water.

But I don't take my eyes off him as I bare my teeth in anger.

"What do you want from me?"

"I told you, I have a job. Do it and you're free to go and continue on with your life."

"And if I don't?"

A maniacal laugh rips from his lips. "Let's just say that it's in your best interest that you do it."

"I'm not doing anything for you," I spit.

I know the kinds of things people who work for him end up doing, and I want no part of it or his stupid little gang.

"I have easy access to people you love, Scarlett," he warns. "You should never forget that."

A lump forms in my throat as I think of my family and he clearly notices my panic.

"Everyone has a weakness, Scarlett. And you have many. Now I need you to drop a few things off in my sons' house."

"Why me? You've got half the Creek on your payroll," I snap, sliding away from him after he finally releases me.

"They'll smell a rat if I send one of my boys in. I need this to be discreet."

"And you think me suddenly walking in will look fucking normal? You're deranged. Anyone ever told you that?"

He smiles as if my words actually please him.

Fucking psycho.

"I don't care how you go about it, Scarlett." I shudder, hating the way my name rolls off his tongue. "Get on your fucking knees if you have to." My lip curls at his suggestion.

"You want me to give your sons sexual favors to get into their house?"

"Pretty sure Kane will let you walk right in. That was where he was going last night, wasn't it? To see you?"

My gasp of shock answers his question.

Reaching forward, he lifts a small briefcase onto his lap and pops the clasps.

Inside are a series of small black squares.

"What the hell is that?"

"Cameras. I need to know what's happening in that house. You're going to plant these, get the intel I need and we're done."

"I can't control what they say."

"Well then, for your family's sake, you'd better fucking hope they do. I've already lost one son because of your family. I'd hate to have to return the favor."

My blood runs cold at the thought of what Gray, his youngest son, tried to do to Harley only a few months ago.

No one knows what happened to him. I don't even know if he's alive.

"They'll find them."

"Yes, they will. Ellis will detect them the second he cares to look. Hence my suggestion that you distract them for as long as you can to get me what I need."

"This is fucking insane."

"I'm losing money, and I think it's at the hands of my sons. Yes, there is a lot wrong with that."

"And if I do this?" I ask as he closes the lid on the case and passes it over.

"Your family will be safe and if I'm feeling generous, I might let your boy off a job or two. Hell knows he's shed enough blood for me this last year."

His words put images in my head I really don't need. I know Kane is tied up with this cunt, he always was. But to have killed for him? I really fucking hope not. Although, any of the other options to do with his business aren't exactly desirable. Drugs, weapons, dirty money, women. I shudder at the last one.

It's something that shouldn't be a part of anyone's normal life. But growing up in Harrow Creek. That's exactly what it is. Normal.

One of the many, many reasons I admire my mother so much for everything she did to get us out of there.

"He's not my boy. Do what you want with him."

His amused yet evil chuckle tells me that he doesn't believe a word of it.

"Can I go now?"

Victor nods to his driver and the locks disengage around me, allowing me to escape.

"It was good doing business with you, Scarlett."

"Bite me."

"I'd love to."

Swallowing down the bile that races up my throat, I jump from the car.

"I'll be in touch, *Princess*. You have a week."

A violent shiver rips through me as I slam the door closed and run away from the car.

I duck into a recess behind a building and lean back against the wall, sucking in deep lungfuls of air, making up for all the breaths I didn't take inside that car.

This cannot be happening.

I bang my head back against the wall a couple of times. Enough to convince myself that I am awake and that this isn't a bad dream but not enough to hurt myself.

Another car pulls out of the parking lot as I stand there with my hands trembling and my heart racing and I hear voices getting closer.

I need to get back. If Ella beats me and asks what happened... I shake my head.

I can't drag them into this mess.

It's bad enough Kane's unknowingly dragged me into it.

My fists curl at the thought of all this being because of him.

This kind of thing happens in his life. Not mine.

This is why we left Harrow Creek. Why I went to New York to start my own life.

Maybe it's true what they say.

The past is never very far behind and it always catches up with you.

"Fucking hell," I mutter, pushing from the wall and continuing with my quick walk home, glancing over my shoulder every few seconds as if another devil is going to jump out of the shadows.

I sit opposite Alana in some fancy restaurant in the center of Maddison. She looked impressed when she pulled up beside me in the parking lot.

She'd wanted me to pick her up, but I drew a line at dinner.

Vic wants me to entertain her for a few hours while he monopolizes her old man, fine—well not really, but here I am—but that's all this is. Dinner.

I spent all day studying, trying to get on top of things before practice and classes start again in the morning and take up almost every second of my time.

She talks about... fuck knows what as we wait for our desserts to be delivered.

I stare at her like I'm listening, but the truth is all I'm doing is picking out all the ways she's different to Scarlett.

Her skin is pale, too pale, almost to the point she looks ill. Her blue eyes are tired, missing the excitement for life that I once saw in them, the bags beneath complete the look despite the copious amount of makeup on her face.

Her lips are baby pink, in comparison to Let's bright

sexy red, and her almost white hair is too bright, too bleached.

She's just... wrong.

And I know that for some fucked-up reason all the effort she's put in has been for me. She wants to please me, I don't need to have spent as much time in the bedroom as I have with her to know that.

Everything she does, everything she says, it's like she's planned it to ensure I'll like her. Fuck knows why. She's married to a man who will never let her go despite their bizarre relationship. That's just not how things work.

She tugs at the high neckline of her dress and tilts her head at me.

"What do you think?"

"Uh..."

"Aw, hon. Is college taking it out of you already? I told you that it was going to be too much."

I quirk a brow. No she fucking didn't. Well... maybe she did. I'm getting good at tuning her voice out.

"It's fine, just a change of pace." No lie there. Vic had me working day and night in the lead up to be starting at MKU. Plus training on top of that to ensure I was in top form to join the team and I was fucking exhausted. I've come here for a rest.

"I was talking about the holidays."

"Okay, great."

"It'll be nice for you to have Kyle back this year. I'd love to spend the time with my family but—" She goes on, but I once again drift off.

Yeah, I might have Kyle back, but I'm not stupid enough to think that he's not going to be spending Christmas at the Hunter house with Harley. A place I certainly won't be invited to.

I sigh, contemplating spending another Christmas alone like I did last year.

My cell vibrating in my pants pocket drags me from my depressing thoughts.

Glancing at Alana, I find that she's still talking and I discreetly pull it out, hoping it's something I can use as a solid excuse to get out of this.

My eyes widen when I take in the name staring back at me. My heart jumps and my temperature spikes from her name alone.

Princess.

Unable to resist, I swipe my screen and open the message.

You never could keep promises. I'm disappointed.

My pulse thunders as I read and reread her words.

Is she... is she challenging me?

A smile curls at my lips as I think about her in her dorm room staring at the door, wondering if I'm going to come crashing through any moment.

My cock hardens as I consider doing just that.

Taking her against the window so everyone who's walking past knows who she belongs to. Understanding that she's my dirty little whore.

A slice of key lime pie being placed in front of me drags me from my wicked thoughts but suddenly, it's anything but appealing. The only thing I want for dessert is Scarlett.

I suck on my bottom lip as I remember how she tasted Friday night and my cock weeps. Although, one look up at the woman before me and it ruins my fantasy somewhat.

"Damn, I should have had that. It looks incredible," she complains, ignoring her own fruit salad and drooling over my dessert instead.

"Have it, I need to go," I say, shoving my cell back into my pocket and pulling out some cash to pay for the meal.

"What?" she screeches, making me wince. It's similar to the irritating sound she makes when she comes, and I rather never hear that again either. "You can't just leave me here."

"I'm really sorry," I lie. "It's an emergency."

Her face falls. "Oh no, is everything okay. Kyle?"

"You don't need to worry, but I really need to go."

Her lips part, I've no idea if it's to argue with me or what, but I don't care. I'm out of there before she has a chance to say a word.

I white-knuckle the wheel as I make my way back across town toward campus.

Impatience and frustration begins to get the better of me the closer I get.

I shouldn't have jumped quite so quickly, but it's not like I really needed convincing to get away from Alana.

If Vic finds out then he'll have my ass for this, but right now, with Letty waiting for me, I really don't give a shit.

I pull up into the parking lot behind her dorm building.

I can't see her window from here but I can picture her standing at it looking for me, waiting for me.

Pulling my cell from my pocket, I read her message again.

Kane: Didn't your momma ever warn you about playing with the devil?

I stare at the screen for two minutes, but the message never shows as read, and she doesn't attempt to reply.

If it weren't for the fact I could read her previous message above then I might start to think I'd imagined it.

I sit there a while longer, trying to convince myself that I should just go home.

But then, the main door to her building opens and a group of people emerge. I recognize them as her protectors. But she's not with them.

She really did plan this.

I wait for them to disappear before climbing from the car and making my way inside her building and up to her dorm.

The main door is open and after scanning the communal area, I make my way to her room.

Silently, I walk over.

She might be waiting for me, but that doesn't mean I'm going to announce my arrival early and give her the heads up.

Pressing my ear against the door, the low beats of her music sound out and every muscle in my body pulls tight.

She's right on the other side of the door.

My fists curl as I try to rein myself in.

A noise out in the hallway makes me jump into action and I wrap my hand around the door handle and twist in the hope that if she's waiting for me then it'll be unlocked.

And it is.

I suck in a breath and throw it wide open.

I scan the room quickly as I step inside, expecting to find her immediately. But I don't.

Her bed is made, the room is tidy and aside from the music, it's silent.

What the—

A closed door on the other side of the room taunts me and I walk over expecting to hear running water and for her to be in the shower.

Fucking perfect if she is.

But even before the door crashes back against the wall, I already know she's not here.

She's fucking playing me.

My teeth grind in frustration.

I knew I shouldn't have got out of the fucking car.

Turning my back on her bathroom, I come to a stop in the middle of her room.

Part of me is tempted to throw myself on her bed and wait her out, punish her the second she reappears for this little stunt.

But then my eyes fall on her desk and the campus map that's sitting there folded to reveal a small section of the vast college.

I glance down at my watch. It's nine p.m. on a Sunday night, it should be shut.

But that doesn't stop me swiping up the map and taking off.

Knowing it's not too far away, I leave my car where it is and take off on foot.

The campus is quiet as I pass building after building. The students who are about to disappear into dorm buildings for the night. Thankfully, no one stops me as I approach the building I want.

The Richard J. Armitage Library is by far the most ornate of the Maddison Kings University buildings. It's gothic architecture and stained-glass windows make it stand out from the rest. But I pay it little mind as I head toward the entrance.

The parking lot behind me is empty, bar one car. One that I recognize. One that stirs something within me. Because if my gut feeling is right then she's in there with them while trying to play me.

If that's true, it's really not going to end well. For her.

All the foyer lights are off but there are a few on deeper in the building. And it's seeing those that makes me push the door before me.

It opens, thankfully silently and I slip inside.

The entire place seems deserted as I scan the vast space. I recall seeing her here the other day, and I take a punt on the fact she might be on the same floor and head for the stairs.

I know I'm right because the moment I step on the third floor, I hear voices.

Deep male voices.

I move silently until I'm hidden behind a row of books and watch the three of them sitting around a table working.

They shouldn't be here this late. It should have been locked up hours ago, but then when you're the Kings of the college, I guess you can get away with anything.

I watch the three of them work, talk and joke together for the longest time as jealousy swirls around me like a hurricane waiting to touch down on land.

I'm still trying to convince myself that I should just leave when Letty stands, pushing her chair out behind her.

She lifts her arms over her head, stretching out her back and exposing a slither of golden skin between the waistband of her skin and her t-shirt.

Both Luca and Leon's eyes zero in on that bit of skin. Desire and naughty thoughts darkening their eyes.

You left her in his bed, a little voice pipes up in my head. If he's touched her, then it's all your fault.

I wanted to punish her and when I found we were in his room, I thought it was perfect. But my head was in the clouds, drunk on lust and her scent. Leaving her there with a ruined dress and drunk was probably the worst thing I could have done.

She speaks to them both briefly and when she takes a step away from the table, Luca rises too.

She shakes her head at him, and he immediately sits back down.

With a smile at both of them, she walks away from the table, past the aisle I'm hiding down and heads toward the very back of the library.

After a beat, I follow, watching her ass sway in her short denim skirt and her exposed legs all the way down to her red Chucks.

A smile curls at my lips as she turns down an aisle the farthest from the guys as possible. I couldn't have planned it better if I tried.

She comes to a stop in front of the books, her fingertip running over the spines as she searches for the one she came down here for.

Not finding it, she drops to the lower shelf, sticking her ass out in the process.

Her skirt is so short, I can see the curve of her ass.

Reaching down, I palm my quickly swelling dick.

She drops lower still and I make my move, walking up behind her but leaving an inch of space between our bodies.

She groans, clearly not finding what she came looking for and stands.

One of my hands wraps around her mouth, keeping her from screaming, and the other pins her body against mine.

"Nice try, Princess," I whisper. "But you can't outrun me."

Her body violently trembles against mine but I don't believe she's scared for a second. If she were, she wouldn't have set this up.

"Is this what you were hoping for by playing that little stunt?"

She shakes her head.

Liar.

"So you didn't tempt me to your dorm room and then leave the evidence lying around about where you'd be so I would come and find you?"

She tries to say something but fails due to the fact my hand is still clamped around her mouth.

"What was that, Princess? I can't quite hear you."

I slip my hand away, confident that she's not going to scream.

"Fuck you."

"Now we're talking."

Placing my hand between her shoulder blades, I force her to bend back over.

She goes without any argument and it tells me everything I need to know.

This is exactly what she wanted. Part of me wonders if I should refuse to give it to her. But now I'm here and she's pressed up against me, there's no way I could walk away without getting a taste.

Pushing her skirt up around her waist, I expose her bare ass and black thong.

My palm twitches to redden her cheek once more but I know the slap will ring out too loudly in the silent space around us forcing me to resist the urge.

Instead, I hook my finger under the lace of her panties and sweep it through her folds. She's fucking soaked.

"Have you been sitting here waiting for me, Princess?" I damn near growl.

"No," she argues, but we both know she's lying through her teeth.

"Liar. Your body tells me otherwise. Were you sitting there with them while imagining having my cock inside you?"

She thrashes her head back and forth in her denial as I plunge two fingers deep inside her.

She cries out and I fold over her, covering her mouth once again.

"You want this, Princess? Then you're going to need to be a good little whore for me, you got that?" I graze her G-spot as I talk ensuring that she's no choice but to do as I say.

"Kane," she whimpers and fuck if I don't nearly come on the spot at the desperation in her tone.

"You want my cock, Princess?"

Liquid gushes over my hand at my question giving me all the answers I need.

Dropping my free hand to my waist, I unsnap my belt and rip open my fly, freeing my aching cock.

"Oh God," she moans, her muscles beginning to tighten around my digits.

"I don't fucking think so," I grunt, ripping my fingers

from inside her. "If you come—and I mean *if*—then it's around my cock. Have you got that?"

"Yes," she whimpers.

"Good. Little. Whore." On the final word, I surge forward, filling her to the hilt and forcing her to fall forward.

I catch her around the waist before she flies headfirst into the bookshelf in front of her

"Fuck," I whisper as her heat engulfs me and her muscles ripple around my length.

When I finally got home after the fall out from our first night together, I thought it was my imagination playing tricks on me because there's no way this beautiful little liar was that good.

But then I sunk into her again on Friday night and I knew... it wasn't my imagination at all.

And that's how I know I'm totally fucking fucked when it comes to Scarlett Hunter.

Something tells me that I could seek revenge from her for the rest of my life and it would never be enough.

Nothing with her is ever enough.

Wrapping her mass of dark hair around my fist, I pull until she's no choice but to arch her back, forcing me deeper inside her until the tip of my cock grazes her cervix.

"Kane. Fuck," she groans, taking every brutal thrust I give her.

My hair falls down onto my face, sweat begins to cover my skin as my balls start to draw up.

I want this to last forever, but the longer I keep her down here the more chance we've got of being caught, and like fuck am I letting that happen.

I have every intention of sending her back to those

motherfuckers thoroughly fucked, walking on jelly legs with my cum dripping out of her.

"Fuck." My cock jerks at the thought alone.

My fingers tighten on her hips, I'm sure digging into the bruises I no doubt left behind on Friday night as my other hand skates up her stomach, lifting her until she's standing, her back to my front.

I squeeze her breasts hard enough for her to moan and writhe.

My hand continues up until it wraps around her throat.

"What did you do after I left Friday, Princess? Did you let one of them inside you as well?"

"No," she cries, her body stilling for a beat.

My fingers tighten in warning.

"Are you sure, or are you lying to me again? We both know how you love to betray me."

"I... I slept in Luca's bed. But he... he didn't touch me."

My chest constricts with the thoughts of him having his hands on what's mine.

"I hope you're telling me the truth. If I find out otherwise—"

"It's true," she breathes. "Luca has never—oh God," she moans, forgetting her words when I circle my hips.

"Now tell me," I whisper in her ear, loving the way she shudders as my breath hits her ear. "Did you plan for me to find you?"

Silence.

My fingers tighten once more.

"Scarlett," I warn. "This won't end well for you if you don't tell me the truth."

"Yes," she breathes.

"Have you been thinking about my cock since I left you Friday night?"

"Yes."

"Do you want to come?" I ask, my cock swelling with my own release.

"Yes," her cry is louder this time.

"Tough," I spit, pushing her away from me, spinning her around and forcing her to her knees. "Open," I demand, pushing my cock against her lips until she's no choice but to take me to the back of her throat.

She stares up at me with hate in her eyes. And if I didn't know she loved it so much, I'd think she was threatening to bite it off.

"Suck. Me."

Her eyes shutter and she tries to resist but after only a second her lips tighten around me and she sucks me hard.

"You look right at home on your knees for me, Princess. Bowing to your fucking king. Fuck," I bark as she takes me deeper.

My fingers thread into her hair, holding her in place as her tears begin to spill over.

So fucking beautiful.

I only last another two minutes before I reach the point of no return and my cock spurts hot ropes of cum down her throat.

So much for sending her back dripping with me I think as my cock slips from her lips. Seeing her tears and makeup streaming down her cheeks makes up for it somewhat.

"Remember this next time you want to play me," I warn, although we both know that it's not a warning at all.

She fucking loved it.

Tucking myself into my pants, I run my hand through my hair and smooth the front of my button-down.

"Wait are you—"

"Leaving. Enjoy the rest of your night."

I shoot her a cocky, satisfied smirk before turning my back and marching away from her.

Only one of us is going to win this game, Princess.

18

LETTY

I hold my breath as I walk back to the table where I left Luca and Leon, Christ knows how long ago. It could have been ten minutes or it could have been an hour. Time seems to stand still when Kane is anywhere near me.

My only positive thought is that if I were gone for too long then one of them would have come to find me.

"We were about to send out a search party," Leon jokes as I approach them but he doesn't look up from his computer screen.

Luca, however, lifts his head and looks right at me.

"Let, what's wrong?" Concern covers his features before the burning heat of Leon's gaze burns my cheeks.

"Oh, nothing," I say lightly. "I stubbed my toe on a bookcase. Thought I'd broken my entire foot for a few minutes."

They both stare at me for a beat. Assessing me.

Guilt threatens to drown me that I'm lying to them, but I can hardly tell them the truth, that I just allowed

Kane to fuck me in the darkest corner of the library while he called me a whore before coming down my throat.

My cheeks burn with my memories and my core aches for the release he refused to let me have.

Asshole.

It's my own fault. I poked the beast.

I may have known exactly what I was doing when I messaged him and then swiftly left my room. But I didn't consciously leave him evidence for where he could find me... did I?

"Do you want me to check it?" Luca offers. "Make sure you haven't broken it?"

The thought of him coming close enough that he might smell sex on me, or worse, Kane, has me backing away to the seat I vacated however long ago.

"No, it's fine. I was just being a girl," I say with a laugh, laughing at my ruined makeup.

Their eyes follow me as I lower myself to the chair and pull my laptop toward me.

"What happened to the book you went for?" Luca asks.

"Couldn't find it anywhere," I lie, keeping my eyes locked on my still asleep screen. "Someone must have taken it out."

"I thought it was a reference only book?"

I shrug. "Who knows, I'll try another day, ask a librarian if need be."

They both accept my words, but neither seem particularly convinced but I keep my eyes down and continue with what I can without the book I needed that I'm sure was right there on the shelf.

We spend another forty-five minutes in the silent

library before Luca follows the instructions he was given to lock the place up and we head out.

I guess that's just one of the perks of being the most popular guy in college. You can literally get anyone to do anything for you.

When he asks the girl who was working this evening if we could stay late she almost pissed her pants.

It was amusing but I felt for her. I know how intimidating the Dunns good looks and charisma can be.

"I need food," I mutter as Leon opens Luca's passenger door for me. "Thank you," I mouth to him and drop down before he shuts me in and takes the back seat.

"I know just the place," Luca says, starting the car and gunning it from the parking lot and then away from campus.

I breathe a sigh of relief as we leave that building behind. I've no idea if he's still there or even on campus, but I feel good getting away.

"Work up an appetite with all that studying?" Leon asks, poking his head between the two front seats after my stomach growls so loudly they both hear it over the low beats of Yungblud flowing through the speakers.

My cheeks flame once more.

"Yeah, that and I haven't eaten since lunch."

They both turn their eyes on me, Luca only for a beat as he needs to focus on driving.

"Don't start," I tell them. I've heard the lecture before that I know is on the tip of their tongues. I'm not great with food and routine, hence how I've lost so much weight but as athletes, it's one of the most vital things to them.

Thankfully, Leon sits back without saying anything and other than his slightly too-tight grip on the wheel, Luca keeps quiet too.

I'm more than aware I haven't been the best at looking after myself, I don't need to be told I look a mess as well.

"What's this place?" I ask as Luca drives toward a building covered in neon lights.

"Best burgers in the county."

My stomach growls once again as he pulls up to the takeout window and orders three of the same meals.

Leon doesn't say a word about his brother taking control so I sit back and let him do his thing.

The second the server hands three paper bags over and the scent of the food fills the car my mouth waters.

He passes them all over to me before driving over to a space to park.

"Trust me, you've never tasted anything like this."

He dives into his own bag, unwraps his burger and dives in.

I'm too fascinated by his enthusiasm to even open my bag.

"I thought you were hungry?" he mutters when he notices I haven't so much as moved.

"Uh... I am. You've got sauce," I say with a laugh, reaching out to wipe the blob from the corner of his mouth.

I gasp when he wraps his hand around my wrist and brings my thumb to his mouth. I'm totally enthralled as he wraps his lips around my thumb and swipes his tongue over my skin.

Tingles zero in on my still aching core as he stares at me, his green eyes darkening.

Holy shit.

A throat clearing behind me drags me from wherever I drifted off to and I tug my arm out of his grasp.

His eyes linger on me for a few seconds as I finally rip open my own bag and unwrap my burger.

"Let?" Luca whispers.

"Yeah?" I ask, refusing to look at him.

"Are you okay?" he asks, reaching out and tucking a lock of my hair behind my ear to stop me from hiding behind it.

"Of course," I force out before shoving my burger into my mouth.

Truth is, I'm not okay. Not by a fucking long stretch but there's shit all him or Leon can do about that right now.

I'm still trying to figure out how I'm supposed to complete my little task that's been set by the devil, let alone attempt to process what the hell happened with Kane tonight.

"You're right. This is insane," I say after swallowing my first bite.

Finally, Luca's eyes leave me in favor of finishing his food but I know this isn't the end of whatever this is. He wants me to talk, to open up. But as much as I know doing so will probably help, I know he's not the one I need to spill everything to.

He's not the one I've been lying to.

And telling him the truth is only going to anger him, and the last thing I want is to be the reason he fucks up the season before it's even started because of a rift with a teammate.

"We should get you back," Luca says once we've all finished eating.

I nod because what else can I do? Beg for him to take me with them?

I'm not scared of Kane turning up in my dorm room. I set myself up for that, after all.

But right now, I'm tired, frustrated and I really don't want to fall into bed alone.

The memory of sleeping with both of them in the previous week with their protective arms around me fills my mind.

But then my memories morph into my time with Kane tonight in the library and my entire body comes to life in a way it never has with Luca and Leon.

The danger. The hate. The punishment.

I shouldn't want any of it, but fuck if I'm not craving it right now.

I lift my hand to my hair and tug a little, mimicking the feeling of him pulling it earlier and the bite of pain I felt all the way down to where he was pounding into me.

My temperature soars and my pulse thunders beneath my skin, my clit begging for attention, to get the release I was so close to earlier.

Before I know it, Luca is pulling up in the parking lot behind my building and killing the engine.

"You want me to walk you up?"

I stare out around our dark and empty surroundings.

I got abducted in daylight, I'm not sure there can't be anything scarier hiding in the shadows than what I've already experienced today.

"No, I'm good. I'll message you once I'm safe." I wink at him before pushing the door open.

"You'd better," he warns, but there's no harshness to his voice.

"Thank you for this evening. It was just like old times."

They both smile at me.

"See you in the morning," Leon says.

I nod at them both before slamming the door and taking off toward my building. I keep my eyes focused on where I'm going but the need to look around, to look for him almost gets the better of me. If I didn't know that both Luca and Leon are watching my every move from the car then I might have because my tingles of awareness get stronger with every step I take.

Micah is at his laptop in the kitchen when I get up to our dorm.

"Evening," he says, glancing up for the briefest of seconds.

"Hey," I sigh lightly, grabbing a bottle of water from the refrigerator. "You been working all day?"

"Pretty much. Ellis had good things to say about you," he adds, lowering his screen so he can pay me some attention.

"Oh yeah? You been digging for intel?"

He chuckles. "Not at all. He just said you were cool."

"That was nice of him. He's a good guy," I say but immediately wince because I'm not actually sure how true that is. He's Victor Harris's son. Is it really possible for him to be a decent human being?

"I know who his family are, Let," he admits, clearly able to read my reaction.

"Good, that's good. Just... just be careful, yeah?"

"I know how to look after myself, Letty. But thanks for the concern."

"I'm sorry, I'm sure you can. It's just... the Harrises are a special brand of dangerous and I'd hate for you to get tangled up with them."

A cocky smirk tugs at his lips. It's one I'm more used

to seeing on Brax or West than I am on sweet Micah. "Who says I'm not already dangerous?"

He keeps his face emotionless for all of ten seconds before a wide smile breaks and he bursts out laughing.

"Were you even half-convinced?" he asks through his laughter.

"For a second," I lie. I know dangerous cruel bastards, and Micah Lewis isn't one of them.

"The worst I've ever done is bug my older sister's bedroom when we were kids so I could listen to her girl chat with her friends."

"You did not?" I gasp although it doesn't escape my attention that he could be useful to me right now.

"I did," he admits, a blush hitting his cheeks. "I had the biggest crush on one of her friends and I was convinced she liked me too."

"Did she?" I ask, pulling out a chair and sitting down to listen, already way too invested in this story than I should be.

He laughs but there's no humor there. "Nah, she'd spent the previous night blowing our high school's quarterback and spent way longer than necessary giving her friends—and me—the gory details."

"Oh my God," I snort. "You carried on listening?"

"Thought I could learn a thing or two."

"About blowjobs?" I ask, lifting a brow. As far as I know, he's straight but I could be way off the mark.

"No," he spits, a horrified expression appearing on his face.

Not gay then. Okay. Noted.

"About what girls want. About what might impress her."

"Did you ever get her?" I ask, although I already fear the answer.

I take a sip of my water.

"Yeah, gave her my virginity."

The water in my mouth comes flying out with my shock, soaking him and his laptop.

"Shit, I'm so sorry," I say in a panic, reaching for a towel to help dry him up—or more so his beloved laptop. "I'm so sorry."

"It's okay. I didn't expect that end either."

"So what happened next?"

He chuckles at me. "She kissed me on the cheek, told me that I was cute and that I was welcome before she left for college."

"Ouch. That's cold."

"Nah, I lived out my teenage fantasy. It was pretty sweet."

"You still want her?"

"No, she's married with two kids."

"How much older was she?"

"Only two years. She didn't last long at college."

"You don't say."

"Your turn. What's your forgettable first time story?"

I think back as a soft smile plays on my lips.

"It wasn't forgettable, actually. It was just like every girl dreams of."

"Oh?"

"My high school boyfriend. We'd been dating since we were fourteen. He had candles, soft music, the lot. It was really sweet."

"What happened?"

My chest pulls tight as I think about him and what

happened only months after we gave each other our virginities.

"H-he died."

"Oh fuck, Let. I'm sorry."

"It's okay. Well, it's not but you know."

Silence falls between us.

"Huh, guess I ruined the mood a little there, eh?"

"No, no not at all," he says, but I can see the awkwardness on his face as he does.

"I'm going to head to bed." I push from the chair and walk toward my room.

"Yeah, me too."

"Micah?" I ask before I push my door open.

"Yeah?"

"How'd you bug her room?"

He smiles. "I put hidden cameras in the best hiding places I could come up with."

"Did she ever find them?"

"Oh yeah. I've still got the scar to prove it."

I laugh because it's the normal thing to do when he points at a faint scar on his jawline but inside, every one of my muscles tenses because I fear that a cut and a lingering scar is going to be the least of my issues if I fuck this up.

"Night, Micah," I say, slipping into my room.

I rest back against the door, flip the lock and close my eyes. Sucking in a deep breath, I run through the events of the day quickly before a noise startles me.

My head flies up and I look around expecting him to emerge from the shadows.

But he's not here.

My heart thunders and then the sound hits my ears again, I realize that it came from the dorm upstairs.

"Calm the fuck down, Scarlett."

You've got this, you can play him at his own game and win.

I shake my arms out at my sides and suck in some confidence.

Just plant the cameras and get the hell out. The rest is up to fate.

If they don't talk about what they need to talk about then I guess I'll just have to deal with the outcome.

"Fucking hell."

Double checking that I locked the door, I march across my room, stripping out of my clothes as I go. By the time I step into my shower, I'm naked with my hair up in a messy bun.

I need to wash him from my body before I get into bed.

The cold blast of water does nothing to cool my burning skin.

Thinking back to our time in the library, I can almost feel his fingers digging into my hips, feeling him sliding in and out of me.

My clit throbs for the release it was denied and as I rub shower gel over my skin, I almost drop my fingers between my legs to fix the situation.

But then I have a better idea.

If I'm going to get myself into his house, then I need to up the ante.

Sure, I could ask someone in the know for the address. I'm sure Micah knows where Ellis lives. But I can hardly rock up and knock on the door. They'd smell a rat immediately.

There's no way I'd just turn up for a friendly visit.

If I want to get inside then I need him to take me. And I need him to think it's his idea.

Wrapping a towel around myself, I drop down on the edge of my bed and pull the drawer in my nightstand open.

I pull out the bag at the back and open the box.

My not so little pink vibrating friend isn't anywhere near a replacement for Kane's cock. I can admit that to myself right now, but it's the best I've got and he doesn't need to know that it pales in comparison to him.

Grabbing the panties I discarded on the floor, I drape them on the bed before laying the vibrator beside it.

Snapping a picture, I add a caption and hit send before I change my mind.

Letty: I don't need you for a good time.

Placing my cell face down on the bed, I tidy it all away, throw my dirty clothes into my laundry basket and pull on some pajamas.

I tell myself not to look but no sooner have I climbed into bed do I have my cell in my hand.

The second I see his name on my screen tingles shoot through my body.

Swiping the screen, I suck in a breath preparing for what he might have to say.

Kane: Dirty little whore.

I shudder. It's as if he breathes the words in my ear and before I know what I'm doing, my fingers slip inside my panties and I finish what he started. And when I finally come, it's with his name as a plea on my lips.

19

KANE

I sit at the back of the auditorium watching Letty sitting in a Dunn sandwich in our lit class. She might not be dancing with them and they might not be touching her, but I'm about as wound up by her closeness to them as I was watching the three of them move together on Friday night.

That message from her last night.

Fuck. That was unexpected.

The second I saw it, I was hard as fucking nails for her once again and it if weren't for the fact I'd had a few beers with Devin when I got back then I'd have got in my car and got my ass to her dorm room.

Also, something told me that was what she wanted. And I have no interest in playing into her hand.

I'm the one with the game plan here but she's trying to take control.

It pisses me the fuck off.

I clench my fists so hard the pencil in my hand splits in the middle with a loud snap. The timid, nerd girl next to me glances over, looking horrified by my actions.

I smile at her menacingly and she instantly cowers away.

When our lecture comes to an end, Letty's not as fast to run out as she has been in some of our other shared classes. Probably because she feels safe while surrounded by her protectors.

The second she scoops her books up from the table and heads toward the exit with the twins hot on her tails, I do the same thing.

"Scarlett," I call once we've all cleared the doorway.

She tenses at the sound of my voice but she doesn't stop or turn around.

"Scarlett, Princess," I say, jogging up to her and placing my hand on her shoulder to stop her and turn her.

"Get your fucking hand off of her," Luca growls, taking a step toward me with his chest puffed out.

"Careful, QB1. Don't blow a vessel."

His lips thin as a low rumble vibrates up his throat in warning.

"Anyway, she seemed to like me touching her last n–"

"What do you want, Kane?"

I turn my eyes on her, she's wearing a pair of leggings and an oversized sweater, nothing overly sexy but damn, with her wavy hair hanging around her shoulders and her natural makeup, she's fucking banging.

"Our sociology assignment," I start.

"What about it?" Leon asks.

"I need a little help with it. Wondered if you wanted to do it together. Thought we could meet in the library. I hear it's open late in the week."

"Why the fuck would she want to do anything with

you, asshole?" Luca steps closer but I don't so much as look at him.

I don't give a fuck about either of them. It's Scarlett I want.

"So what do you say?"

"Nah, you're alright. Find yourself a tutor or something if you're struggling."

I stare at her, drilling my eyes into hers. Her dark eyes sparkle with the gold that appears when she's horny.

"Okay, fine. I'll message you later, see if I can change your mind."

I drop my eyes down her body once more before walking away from them.

I feel her eyes following me and when I turn around, I find exactly what I was expecting. Her heated stare boring holes in my back while Luca and Leon look from me and down to her with confusion written all over their faces.

"What the fuck was that?" one of them barks when they think I'm out of earshot.

"He's just trying to wind me up. Ignore him."

Oh, I'm trying to wind her up alright.

———

The second I walk into the locker room for our afternoon practice session I can almost predict what's going to happen.

And I'm right.

I haven't even got my bag off my shoulder before Luca backs me against the wall with his forearm against my throat.

"What the fuck was that?" he growls in my face, his nose only a breath from mine.

I don't react. I just stare at him with a smirk on my face.

"Threatened that she might want me and not you?"

"You?" He spits. "Why the fuck would she want you?"

My smile grows wider. "Because, Captain, I can give her what she needs."

"Fuck you." He steps closer, pressing against my neck harder but nowhere near cutting off my air supply. If I wanted to, I could have him on the ground in a heartbeat.

One day I will.

But that day isn't today.

"Nah, I think I'll save that for her. Something tells me you won't like it if I pulled your hair."

His chest puffs out.

"You're lying."

"Am I?"

"Dunn," one of the coaching staff barks and he's no choice but to release his hold on me. His eyes remain on mine as Leon steps up beside him.

"You stay the fuck away from her. And if I find out you've so much as touched her—" His words are cut off as Leon drags him away.

"Leave it, Luc," he demands before shoving him to the other side of the locker room to get changed.

Luca is in my face any chance he gets during practice and I'm amazed that I leave the building that he's not at least attempted to throw a punch.

I'm almost at my car when someone calls my name.

Knowing it's not one of the Dunns, I slow and wait for him to catch up with me.

"What do you want, Hunter?" I ask without looking at Letty's little brother.

"Luca's right. You need to stay away from her."

"What the fuck has it got to do with any of you?"

"Dude, she's my sister. Luca's best friend. You hurt her, you fucking hurt us too."

"Scarlett and her fucking army," I mutter, rolling my eyes.

I stop at my car and Zayn's palms collide with my chest, the shock of the move ensuring I bump up against it.

"What the fuck?" I growl.

"Stay the fuck away from her, Kane."

"Why, don't you want both your sisters fucking a Legend?" I smirk.

"Leave Harley and Kyle out of this." Of course he'd jump to my little brother's defense, the two of them were always tight. And I'm always the fucking bad guy. I mean, I probably deserve that title but still. His attitude pisses me the fuck off.

"You do know he's fucking her right? I've heard them on the other side of the wall." I know I shouldn't bait him but it's too fucking easy.

His shoulders harden with tension and his jaw pops.

"As long as he treats her right, I'm happy."

"And what if I treat Letty right?" I lean into him. "She sure seems to think I am when she's screaming my name."

He cocks his arm back and swings at me but I'm faster than him, more experienced and I catch it long before it makes contact with me.

"Nice try. I think it's probably best if you continue playing with Kyle like a good little boy and stay the fuck out of my business."

"My sister is my business. She's been through hell because of yo—" He slams his lips shut.

"Because of what?"

"Nothing. Just leave her the fuck alone to get on with her life. If she knew you were going to be here this semester, I can assure you, she wouldn't have been."

"Whatever. Are you done?" I push him away from me and open my car door.

I'm desperate to ask more, to find out what he's hiding but I don't want to look like I care.

Instead, I drop down into my driver's seat, start the engine, throw it into drive, and wheelspin out of the fucking parking lot like I don't have a care in the world.

My cell rings in my pocket as I pull up at the house and I groan when I pull it out.

"What?" I bark, really not in the fucking mood for his bullshit right now.

"You bailed on Alana."

"Had an emergency. She had a great meal, what else did you want?"

"It's not my needs I'm worried about, boy."

"I'm sure she got by just fine. Maybe if her husband got her off once in a—"

"Enough. I don't pay you to question me." *You don't pay me anymore, asshole. We're supposed to be done.*

I blow out a breath, trying to find the strength for this conversation. I'm exhausted, I'm hungry and I've got a shit ton of work to do.

"I've got a job for you. I need you in the Creek within the hour."

"I've just finished practice."

He doesn't say anything. But I hear his warning loud and clear.

"Fine. I'll be thirty minutes."

I swing by a takeout place on the way to the Creek and I'm pulling up at the Hawks clubhouse less than forty minutes later.

I ignore all the eyes that turn on me as I march through the communal areas where there are guys shooting pool, drinking and watching a couple of girls that are dancing around the makeshift pole.

This is what all the schoolboys think gang life is going to be like. It's what they see in the movies. The hanging out with your brothers and banging every whore who wants a piece. But it's fucking bullshit. Sadly, nothing anyone can say or do will stop them though and they'll give Vic their left testicle if they could be a fucking part of it.

I take the stairs two at a time and storm toward his office, not bothering to knock as I throw the door open.

Inside I find Reid and Devin waiting for me.

"What the fuck do you want?" I ask, ignoring my boys and turning my frustration on the boss.

He slides two photographs across his desk.

"Know these two?"

"No. Should I?"

He shrugs as the three of us stare at the images.

"I need them gone. Tonight. This is where they will be. You know the rules, don't be seen and make it painful."

"Fucking hell," I mutter. "I'm supposed to be done with this shit."

"Yeah, well. I need my best boys. And you, son, are one of them."

"I'm not your fucking son."

Anger swirls around in his dead, evil eyes and the

fingers of his right-hand clench as if he's imagining wrapping them around a gun.

Fucking try it asshole and we'll see who ends up dead first.

I know for a fact that the boys on either side of me have my back over their father.

"Fine," Reid barks, swiping the paperwork from his father's desk. "Consider it done by sunrise."

"I'll expect a debrief first thing."

Reid doesn't respond. He knows how this works by now and I know from experience the less conversation he has with his sperm donor the better.

"This is fucking bullshit," I spit once we're in the parking lot and inside Reid's SUV.

"I told him we'd take someone else but he was adamant you had to be here."

"Why?"

"Fuck if I know."

"Who are those guys?"

"Assholes who tried to intercept our shipment."

"Just two of them?"

"They're junior members of the Ravens. Thought it would impress their Prez if they could fuck us over."

"Have they got a death wish?"

"Apparently so. You ready for this?"

He glances at me before looking at his brother in the rearview mirror.

"Always. Let's go fuck them up so I can get to bed before practice, eh?"

"Sure thing." He cracks his knuckles before putting his car in reverse and heading across town to the bar these pricks are apparently going to be at.

I get two hours of sleep before I have to get up again for training.

My knuckles are busted, I've got a fucking black eye and I did such a shit job of showering when I finally got back last night that I've still got blood splattered up my arm.

I drag my ass through the entrance of the training center at six a.m. barely able to open my right eye.

Coach is going to lose his fucking shit, but what choice do I have.

I get more than a few curious glances as I stumble into the locker room.

I throw my shit into my locker and head straight out to the field house.

"Legend," is growled the moment I attempt to pass Coach's office.

"Yes, sir?"

"You look like shit."

"I'm aware. It won't happen again." It's a promise I already know I can't keep. Vic is a law unto himself. I fucking knew he'd make me pay for everything he helped me with past our original agreement.

"If I find out you've been involved in anything you shouldn't be, I won't have a choice but to reconsider your position here."

"Understood, sir." I nod, itching to get out and away from a lecture I don't need.

"Good. There's only so much I can do if you're going to continue with that... shit."

"I got jumped on my way home last night. It was nothing," I lie.

"Be more careful. Now get the fuck out there. I won't have anyone thinking you're not earning your place here."

"You got it, Coach."

I take off jogging, my muscles screaming at me as I join the others and start warming up.

By some miracle, I make it out of practice without any more threats from either Luca or Zayn, but they don't need to say the words out loud. I can read them in their hard stares. They don't want me here. I get that. They want me to fuck up. The chances are that I will at some point. But like fuck am I going to let them intimidate me into thinking I don't deserve this place on the team because I fucking well do. Hell knows I've worked fucking harder—and dirtier—than them to get here.

I'm early to class even with stopping at the coffee shop for a double espresso and a breakfast wrap.

I dump my bag on the chair next to me and that, along with the state of my face ensures that no one attempts to sit next to me as the auditorium starts filling up.

That is until one person slows to a stop beside me.

I know who it is without looking up. My temperature spikes and my fists curl, cracking my knuckles once more.

"Tell me that wasn't Luca and Leon," she demands. Her need to protect the two of them from me pisses me off.

Dragging my bag from the chair, I dump it on the floor with a loud bang.

"Sit."

She refuses to move and when I finally glance over, she's got one hip jutted out, her arms crossed over her chest, pushing her tits up in her tank and an irritated expression on her face.

"I'm not a fucking dog."

"Did I say you were, Princess? Now sit down... *please*." I force politeness into my tone and smile up at her. It's insincere and she knows it.

"Only because you asked so politely." She rolls her eyes before dropping her bag to the desk and turns around.

It's only then I notice her friend behind her.

"What the hell are you doing?" her friend hisses, shooting me daggers over Letty's shoulder.

"It's fine," she assures her friend, who still refuses to look away.

She's cute. A petite blonde and she's staring at me as if I should be scared of her. It's amusing.

I blow her a kiss and flash her my winning panty-melting smile but instead of the usual reaction it gets, her face twists in anger.

"If he tries anything, I'll sic the boys on him."

I roll my eyes at her, just about managing to hold in my snort of laughter.

Letty whispers something else to her before our professor joins us and she's forced to find a seat, thankfully, at the other side of the auditorium.

"Is she for real?" I whisper as Professor Nelson begins our class.

"She's just worried and doesn't trust you."

"She doesn't even know me," I argue, feigning offense.

"She knows enough," Letty mutters as she arranges her books and grabs a handful of colorful pens.

I can't help but laugh. Some things never change.

Her school books used to be full of multi-colored writing and doodles.

I study her as she copies the title from the board and adds the date.

A chuckle rumbles up my throat.

"What?"

"It's like sixth grade all over again."

"You should probably pay attention seeing as you need help with your assignment," she says, referencing my bullshit excuse to get her attention yesterday.

I laugh and shake my head. She really believed that shit?

"Yeah, I guess I should."

Flipping open my notebook, I slouch down in my seat, widening my knees enough to ensure my thigh bumps against hers.

Her entire body jolts with the contact and she sucks in a little gasp.

Leaning over, I lower the tone of my voice and whisper in her ear.

"Still desperate for my cock, Princess?"

A barely-there whimper falls from her lips but I hear it, and I feel the waves of heat coming from her.

"Maybe if you're a good girl, you'll get a reward."

"Fuck you," she breathes.

"Oh, that's right. You're not a good girl, are you?"

Brushing her hair aside with my nose, I bite down on her earlobe hard enough to make it burn.

"How wet are you right now?"

"Kane," she growls, but her warning is weak at best.

"I really should have sat at the back. You could have sucked me off and no one would know."

Reaching down, I shift myself behind the fabric of my pants, ensuring that Letty sees everything.

"Nothing gets me harder than imagining you bending to my every whim."

"Keep dreaming, Legend. You've taken what you wanted, it's not happening again."

"Is that right?" I ask with a knowing smirk.

She's fucking soaked for me right now and I know for a fact it wouldn't take much for me to get inside her.

"I hate you."

"The feeling's mutual, Princess. But I really love it when you take it out on my cock."

She growls and shifts away from me, trying to look like she's focused on what Nelson is talking about but I know her head is in the clouds and full of dirty thoughts.

She sits tensely for the rest of the class and the second the lecture comes to an end she starts packing up. I expect her to hop up and run but she doesn't, she spins to me and pins me with a look that turns me the fuck on.

"Stay away from me, Kane. Stay away from Luca and Leon. If you ruin this season for them and their chance at being first draft picks next year then I'll never forgive you."

"Huh, a bit like I'll never forgive you for—"

"Enough," she snaps. "You've taken what you wanted from me. We're done."

She stands, tugs her bag up higher on her shoulder and storms away.

If she believes the words that just came out of her mouth then she really needs to think again because we are so far from being done.

I don't get a chance to talk to her again for the rest of the day because come statistics, her personal bodyguards are in place.

The second Luca catches my eye, his narrow in warning. He's itching to continue what he started in the locker room yesterday. I can only imagine he's pissed right now that someone else got to me first.

I smile at him before moving my eyes over to Letty, ensuring my eyes linger on her long enough that she's no choice but to feel my heated stare.

She doesn't look up, but I know she's aware of me.

I can see it in the hard set of her shoulders.

Just to piss me off, Luca spends the entire class with his arm over the back of Letty's chair. His thumb intermittently stroking her shoulder as if she's his.

Asshole.

The second class is over, I blow out of there like the place is on fire without looking at anyone.

I'm fucking wiped but I've still got a two-hour training session with his highness to get through.

I knew joining the team, becoming part of Luca's offense would be a fucking challenge but shit. At this rate, we're going to kill each other before our first game next week.

The thought sure is tempting but as much as I might hate him, he's a fucking killer quarterback. And I hate to admit it, but there's a part of me that's looking forward to playing with him, not against him like we always have in the past. Not that I'd ever admit that to anyone though.

I forgo dinner after practice and studying doesn't even enter my head as I fall face-first into my bed and almost immediately pass out.

She manages to avoid me all day Wednesday despite the fact I try to search her out just to rile her up.

By the time I get back to the house, I've almost decided that I'm going to head to her dorm to see if I can sneak in and prove to her just how wrong she was after class on Tuesday by telling me that we're done.

Only, it turns out that I don't need to make that much effort because no sooner have I finished my statistics assignment for the next day does my cell buzz on the nightstand.

I smile when I see her name. Has she been missing me?

Princess: Is there any chance you could come and help me with something?

Flipping the blade closed, I slip it inside the zip pocket of my purse before pulling out my compact mirror and my lip gloss.

My cell pings and I lift it up and smile.

Kane: Leaving now.

I glance over at my quickly deflating tire and smile.

Got you, you sonofabitch.

I saw him today, hiding in the shadows searching for me. Stalking me as if I were his prey.

It shouldn't have excited me as much as it did knowing that I could see him but he had no idea where I was.

I wasn't hiding. I was in the campus coffee shop with Ella, Violet, and Micah. But the one-way glass between us meant that I could watch his every move and he had no idea that I was watching as he impatiently searched me

It was the tense look on his face that assured me that he'd fall for this little stunt.

I'd dreamed it up in the middle of the night when thoughts of him and the things he whispered in my ear during our sociology class played on repeat in my head turning my body into a raging inferno.

I tried to put as much conviction as possible into my parting words to him because I knew that he would see them as a challenge. There's no way he's going to let me walk away from whatever this is.

He clearly wants something from me. And right now, I need something from him, so I'm more than willing to play him at his own game.

I apply a new layer of gloss, before wiping up any stray makeup from under my eyes and smoothing my hair down.

Thanks to Micah, I managed to find out where the Harrises lived, and as far as I know, Kane lives with them so I headed to their side of town before pulling into a dark layby and setting up my little damsel in distress act.

My heart thunders in my chest as a set of headlights approach.

There's a chance some other creep will pull over and try to help me and I pray to God that there are no good Samaritans out tonight who decide to help me out before Kane arrives.

Thankfully, the car sails straight past and I breathe a sigh of relief.

It's another five minutes before another car appears at the end of the street. Something feels different about his set of lights and I shamelessly tug my skirt a little higher and lower the neckline of my tank.

The car slows as my heart thunders so fast that I wonder if I'm about to pass out.

It's not until I catch the make of the car that I relax a little.

He might be the devil, but it's better the devil you know, right?

The gravel of the layby crunches as his old Skyline rumbles to a stop behind my car.

I suck in a breath when he throws his door open and climbs out.

He's dressed all in black with his hood up over his head. He looks like every woman's worst nightmare when she's alone on a quiet, dark street with no way to escape.

I should be terrified. So why is it that my panties get wetter the closer he gets?

"You must be desperate if you called me to help you," he says, marching right up to me. The light from his headlights illuminating my body and his eyes run the length of me, making my skin burn.

"Dangerous," he mutters. "Maybe I should have left you to be found by some other guy to make use of you."

"You'd let that happen, would you? You'd let someone else touch me?"

He's on me in a flash. He pushes me back against the hood of my car, taking my chin between his fingers.

His cold, hard eyes hold mine. I can almost hear the chemistry crackling between us.

The moment I pull my bottom lip into my mouth, his eyes fall to them and his tongue sneaks out to wet his.

"So?" I taunt, just about able to get the word out with the hardness of his grip.

"What the fuck do you think?"

He releases me a little, allowing me to answer.

"I think that you hate how much you want me," I sass. "You say you want to hurt me, but really deep down in here." I tap against where his black little heart is. "You just want to prove me wrong."

"How's that?"

"You want to show me that I should have chosen you all those years ago."

"Well you were fucking wrong, don't you think? You set all this in motion, Princess."

"I said yes to a boy, Kane. I didn't sign up for all this bullshit."

"You killed him."

My lips curl and I laugh at him.

"You still trying to sell that story. I did not kill him, Kane. I am not responsible for the actions of him or anyone."

His fingers tighten until the inside of my cheeks are between my teeth, stopping me from saying another word.

"Did you want my help or not, Princess?"

I nod as best I can.

"Why me?" he asks, his brows drawing together. "Of all the people you could have called tonight, why me?"

Panic twists my stomach that he can see right through my actions.

I fight to swallow as saliva fills my mouth faster than I can control.

He releases me, but he doesn't let me go. Instead, he plants both his hands on the hood of my car on either side of me, pinning me in.

"B-because everyone else is busy."

"Everyone?" he asks, his brow quirking.

I nod. "L-Luca, Leon, Zayn, and the guys are at some team thing."

He jolts at my words and I know they hit where I intended but he recovers quickly.

"How unlucky." He smirks. "For you."

His hands land on my waist and I'm lifted onto the hood of my car.

"What the—oh God," I gasp as he rips down the neck of my tank, taking my bralette with it and exposing my breasts.

His lips wrap around my nipple and he sucks so hard it hurts, it sends a bolt of liquid lust straight to my already soaked core.

He bites down, making me cry out in pleasure. My legs wrap around his waist and I tighten them, sliding down the hood a little until my core presses against his length.

"Dirty little whore," he murmurs against my sensitive peak as I rub against him, needing everything he can give me.

Taking both my breasts in his hands, he looks up at me. His hair is falling down into his dark eyes as he looks through his lashes at me.

"This what you had in mind when you called me?"

I shake my head, but his smirk tells me that he doesn't believe a word of it.

"Is everyone else really busy tonight or did you just want to play out one of your wicked fantasies, Princess?"

"They're really busy," I lie. Well, they probably are busy with studying and stuff but I didn't actually ask any of them what their plans were.

"So you didn't just want to get fucked on the hood of your car?"

"No, I want my tire fixed," I gasp as he skims his huge hands down my body and pushes my skirt up around my waist.

"So pretty," he whispers, running a fingertip along the edge of my pink lace panties. "But such a waste."

Before I get a chance to ask what he means, he tucks his fingers under the fabric and tugs until the sound of ripping hits my ears.

"Hey," I cry. "They're my favorites."

"They're mine now."

He scrunches them into a ball in the palm of his hand.

"Fuck, Princess. They're soaked." He lifts them to his nose and I swear my body is about a second away from combusting.

"Kane," I whimper, and he stuffs the ruined bit of fabric into his back pocket.

I rock my hips again and a growl rips from his throat.

"Fuck, Princess."

He pushes his sweats down just enough to release his length. He pumps a couple of times and I stare, fascinated once again by how fucking big it is.

Asshole's like Kane should not be graced with that girth. It's not fucking fair.

My thoughts are soon forgotten when he pushes me up the hood a little before lining his cock up at my entrance and dragging me back down.

"Oh fuck." He stretches me wide and steals my breath, not giving me a chance to recover before he pulls out and slams back in. "Oh God. Oh God."

"Not God, Princess. Just a fucking Legend."

I laugh in disbelief at his words but I soon forget

when his piercing brushes my G-spot and I cry out once again.

The release that he denied me in the library surges forward. It doesn't matter that I've got myself off more times than I want to admit to that memory, none of them hit the spot like I know he can.

He fucks me without touching me and my body screams for more. I need him everywhere. I need to lose myself in the burning sensation of his mouth, of his lips, his teeth.

Reaching forward, I capture his hand and drag him forward, arching my back and thrusting my tits in his face.

"Who's calling the shots around here, Princess?"

"You," I cry as he grinds his hips against mine because I know it's what he wants to hear.

"Correct. It'll do you good to remember that."

His hands wrap around my hips, his fingertips digging into the healing bruises from the other day.

"Your biggest concern should be whether I'm going to let you come this time."

"I'll fucking kill you," I warn, much to his amusement.

"Oh, Princess. That I would pay to see."

One of his hands releases me and skims up my body, gripping on to my breast and squeezing until I cry out in pain. He pinches my nipples making my pussy clench around him before his hand settles around my throat.

I swallow harshly and he smiles knowing that I'd never admit it, but I fucking love this right now. I love that he doesn't treat me like I'm made of glass and about to shatter, no matter how likely I am to do just that once this is all over.

"Fuck, Princess," he grunts, his hips piston in and out

of me. "Fucking sinful."

"I could say the same."

Lifting my hands, I cup my own breasts. His eyes widen as he takes in my move.

"Pinch them until it hurts," he demands, watching my every move.

And like the good little whore that I am, I immediately follow orders. Heat surging to my core as the pain shoots straight toward my clit.

The first splash of cool water on my chest makes me still but then another hits and another before the sound of rain hitting the ground around us ruins the silence.

"Oh God, oh God," I chant when my release begins to build, the sensations in my body mixing with memories of another night of us out in the rain.

His hot fingers drag my hands away from my body and pinning them above my head against the windshield.

He drops his head beside mine, his rough jaw rubbing against my cheek as his hot breath coats my ear.

"Don't come."

"W-what?"

"Don't come and I promise to make it worth your while."

"W-what?" I repeat.

"Just do as you're fucking told, Princess."

His thrusts get more violent as his cock begins to swell.

"No condom," I whisper right before I sense he's going to explode.

A stream of curses falls from his lips before he stands tall, pulls out and takes himself in hand. Not two seconds later does he growl his release into the silent dark night and jets of hot cum hit my clit.

Squeezing my eyes closed, I try to force the feelings down and do as he said. Fuck knows why I chose this moment to do as the fuck I'm told. If I had to guess, I'd say it was the promise of more to come.

Jesus. I'm so fucked up.

The rain continues to lash at us, cooling my overheated body and soaking my clothes.

Kane's chest heaves as he stands before me, his eyes locked on my pussy that's dripping with his cum.

Reaching out, he runs one finger through my folds, rubbing his seed into my clit.

"Mine," he growls. "This is fucking mine. And tonight, I'm going to fucking ruin it."

I swallow down the desire that surges through my body at his words.

My body begs for me to demand he does it right now, but my head knows this is the worst idea in the world.

It's a shame that whenever I'm around Kane Legend that my brain doesn't stand a chance. Because when he releases me and allows me to slide to my feet and right my clothing, I don't argue with him or demand he just fixes my tire and leaves.

Instead, I stand there in the downpour and watch as he pulls open my driver's side door, rips the keys from the ignition and swipes my purse from the passenger seat.

"Let's go," he barks, throwing my purse at me, which I only just manage to catch before he marches toward his car.

He's almost inside before my body gets the message and I take off behind him.

I fold myself into his passenger seat, aware that I'm soaking wet—from the rain—and I'm wearing no panties— equally as wet.

I tug the fabric as far down my thighs as possible as Kane throws his car into reverse and wheelspins onto the street before flooring it in drive in the direction of his house.

My lips twitch at the corners at his desperation to get back.

"What about my car?" I ask, although right now with the steady throb in my core and the scent of Kane surrounding me, my car is the last thing I care about.

"We'll sort it tomorrow. I've got other things on my mind right now."

"Oh?" I ask, desperate to hear his dirty words.

"Like wondering why you keep trying to pull your skirt down." He reaches over, nudges my knees apart and drags his fingers up my thighs.

"Kane," I warn.

"What? Don't you think you'll be able to hold it?"

"You're a cunt."

His fingers still at my words and I suck in a breath, wondering if that was a bit harsh.

But after the longest second of my life, he turns to me, his eyes burning the side of my face.

"Say that again," he demands.

"What? You're a cunt."

"You can knock off the beginning bit."

"Okay. Cunt."

"Fuuuck, Princess. If we weren't so close, you'd be sucking my cock right now."

A weird noise of disbelief falls from my lips.

"Don't even pretend that you wouldn't."

My lips part to argue but he shoots me a look that says "don't even bother," and I close them again.

"Wow," I say when he pulls up in front of an

impressive modern townhouse.

I'm not sure what I was expecting really but this wasn't it.

"Vic sure knows how to treat his boys," Kane deadpans.

"Oh yeah, he's well on his way to winning father of the year," I mutter, climbing from the car, gripping my purse tight.

This is it. This is my in. I can wait for Kane to pass out, throw some cameras around the place and get the hell out.

I've only just closed his car door when he's suddenly behind me and pushing me toward the front door.

"Are the others here?" Stupid question really, seeing as there are multiple cars parked out the front.

"Why, did you want me to share you?"

"What?" I squeak. "N-no."

"Good, because it's not happening. Plus, I'd rather they don't even know you're here."

His words cut more than they should even if I do understand them.

Our mutual hate for each other isn't a secret and if they see him ushering me into the house then they're likely to have questions. Questions I really have no interest in answering.

I've got a job to do and I fully intend on seeing it through and putting this whole disaster behind me.

But that all comes crashing down the second we step into the house because we walk straight into Devin. My eyes land on him immediately and note the cut on his lip and the dark shadow marring his cheek. I guess that explains Kane's black eye. They were on a job together.

Fucking Victor.

He looks to Kane and opens his mouth to say something but then he realizes that Kane isn't alone and his chin drops when his eyes find me.

"S-Scarlett?" he stutters, his eyes narrowing on Kane in question. His shoulders tensing as if he's preparing for a fight and his lips twisting in frustration.

"Excuse us, we're just going upstairs."

"Kane?" he barks, reaching out to grab his arm and stopping us from walking farther into the house.

"Princess?" I turn to look at him. "Top floor, second door on the right. Be ready," he winks at me and I flush from head to toe when Devin turns to look at me once more.

I bolt for the stairs, not wanting to be the object of their attention and needing to get away in case Ezra and Ellis want to join the party.

My stomach flips as I remember his suggestion about him sharing me.

Hell no. I might be up for his wicked touch and evil words but I draw the line at him bringing a friend in to help torture me.

Only, it's not really torture when Kane touches you, is it?

I shake the thought from my head.

I know I should hate the brutal way he touches me, throws me around like a rag doll and the belittling things he says to me, the way he calls me a whore. But I can't find it in me to hate it when all I do is crave more.

The rumble of their booming voices echoes up to me but I don't stop to try to eavesdrop. Something tells me that I wouldn't like what they're discussing. Devin clearly wasn't happy about me being here—if only he knew the truth.

I push through the door Kane directed me to and fall back against it.

My body trembles with nerves. This whole scheme didn't seem so scary before. But now I'm here.

"Fuck," I breathe. "Fuck. Fuck."

My head bangs against the door.

What the hell am I doing?

If they catch me, what will they do to me?

I might be terrified of Victor and what he's capable of, but he's trained every pair of hands under this roof and I know for a fact that they are more than capable of taking out any threats.

And if Victor is right and they're playing him and I expose them.

A violent shiver wracks my body.

They'll kill me if this goes wrong.

I pause for a moment. Does it matter? Do I have anything left to lose?

Images of my family flash through my mind and I talk myself down.

I can do this. Choose the right hiding places and everything will be fine. Come the weekend they'll surely have a party and it could have been any one of the guests who planted the cameras.

It's not until heavy footfalls from the stairs sound out that I push from the door and walk into the room. It's the first time I really see it as well.

The sheets are black—like his soul—the walls are a dark gray and the furniture black, the corners chipped, and the drawers scratched.

I jump a mile when the door opens even though I knew it was coming.

I suck in a deep breath willing my heart to stop racing.

Her scent fills my nose the second I push the door open and my hard-on returns.

I might have only had her less than thirty minutes ago, but it's not enough. Even Devin's attempt to rip me a new one for going anywhere near her isn't enough to make me reconsider what's going to happen next.

I don't really give a shit about his opinion. I don't need him to tell me that this is a bad idea, I already know that it is.

My fascination with Scarlett has only got worse as the years have gone on. And now, she's right here, apparently getting off on this weird hate vibe we've got between us as much as I am and like fuck am I about to pass up the chance to indulge a little.

It won't be long until she's had her fill and turns her back on me because we all know that she's too fucking good for a fuck up like me.

She might have screwed me at every turn over the years. But Scarlett Hunter deserves better than a trailer park boy whose puppet strings are controlled by Victor Harris.

I shake my head, trying to make the thoughts fall away.

None of that matters right now.

What does matter is the fact she's standing in the middle of my room looking like a rabbit caught in headlights and she's... Not. Fucking. Naked.

Reaching my hand behind my head, I drag my sopping wet hoodie from my body and throw it at the laundry basket in the corner. It misses and lands on the floor with a wet thud.

Letty gasps and when I turn back to her, her eyes are locked on my chest.

A smirk curls at my lips as I realize that this is the first time she's seen me without clothes for a lot of years, and I am certainly not the boy she probably remembers.

"You're wearing too many clothes. I told you to be ready." I take a step toward her and she immediately takes one back.

Excitement explodes inside me.

Okay, Princess. Game on.

I drop my eyes to her chest, her nipples are hard and begging for me behind the wet fabric of her tank and bra.

"Off," I demand, nodding at her top.

"Uh..." She hesitates.

"Too fucking late to be shy, Princess. I've already seen it all, remember?"

I take another step toward her, tugging at the ties on my sweats and kicking my sneakers off.

She once again backs away.

"You can't run from me in my own bedroom," I mutter, looking at her from under my lashes. "If you didn't want to be here, you should have tried escaping before now."

"You'd have let me?"

"Hell no, but it would have been fun to see you try."

"Why are you doing this?"

"You know why." I close some more of the space between us and her chest begins to rise and fall faster, her pupils dilating as I step into her personal space.

"But what will it achieve?"

"Oh, it will make me feel so much better."

"Will it though?" she asks, cocking her head to the side like she's really curious about this.

"Yeah. I want to hurt you like you hurt me."

"By fucking me?"

She takes the final step back and bumps up against the wall.

I don't stop until my body is pressed up against the length of her and I lean down to whisper in her ear.

"By using you, Princess. By fucking you until you're raw and ensuring that no matter whoever else you let touch you in the future, it'll never compare to how thoroughly I fucked you." I pull back and look into her eyes as I lift my hand and tap my finger to her temple. "I want to be inside here... forever."

Her breaths come out as short sharp pants.

"You're nothing to me, Kane. I will always forget you." Her eyes bounce between mine, her nostrils flaring slightly with the lie.

"Well then, I'd better make sure that's not possible."

Grasping her wrists, I force her arms above her head, taking them both in one of my hands.

I run my tongue up the length of her neck, not

stopping until I get to her ear. Her shudder is so violent that I feel it at her wrists.

"Get ready to beg, Princess, because I'm going to push you to the very edge."

"Oh fuck," she breathes, her nipples only getting harder beneath her shirt.

Sucking on the soft skin of her neck, my free hand teases her breasts, circles her nipples and trails down her stomach.

Her hips roll at my touch as she tries to find the friction she needs to get off.

She should be so fucking lucky.

Finding the hem of her skirt, I hike it up, kicking her feet wider with my own.

"You still wet for me, Princess?" I ask after releasing her neck with a loud pop. I study my handiwork.

By the time she stumbles out of this room later, everyone on campus is going to know she's owned.

She doesn't answer me.

"If you don't give me what I ask for here, then you won't get what you need," I warn.

"Yes," she cries. "Please, Kane."

"Good start, Princess, but this is only the beginning."

"Shit," she gasps as I part her folds and dip my fingers inside her.

She's dripping still and my mouth waters for a taste of her.

"Kane," she warns as I set a punishing pace rubbing at her walls, curling my fingers so I hit the spot that will have her seeing stars, if I'd let her fall that is.

Dragging my fingers from her pussy, I move them farther back and she stills as I rub her juices around her puckered hole.

"Anyone ever taken you here, Princess?"

She shakes her head as I push gently.

"Oh God."

"Good, this is mine too. Every fucking inch of you is mine. You understand that?"

"Y-yes."

"Who do you belong to, Scarlett?"

"You, Kane. Only you."

"Good girl."

I release her and take a step back. Her body sags against the wall but she only gets a second of reprieve because I reach out, wrap my fingers around her shirt and drag it up her body. It lands on the floor somewhere behind me as I go for her bra. Her skirt follows before I drop to my knees before her and tug her shoes off so she's standing before me totally naked.

She's so fucking beautiful she makes my breathing falter, but I don't tell her that.

Instead, I throw one of her legs over my shoulder and dive for her pussy.

Her taste explodes on my tongue as I lick at her.

"Fuck, fuck, fuck," she shouts as I spear my tongue inside her, lapping up her juices.

I don't stop until she's on the edge of release, then I pull away, lift her into my arms and throw her on my bed.

She bounces as I make my way over, pushing my sweats down over my hips and kick them off as I go.

"Holy shit," she gasps when she looks up at me looming over with my cock in my hand. "Kane." She scrambles up the bed a little but I'm quicker.

Wrapping my fingers around her ankle, I drag her down the bed until she's sitting before me.

"Suck me. I want to come in your dirty little mouth, Princess."

She stares up at me, anger, frustration, and desire shining bright in her dark depths, the gold within them brighter than I've ever seen.

"I fucking hate you."

"I love it when you talk dirty to me," I reply. "Now suck my fucking cock."

I don't give her a chance to respond, instead, I make the most of her parted lips and thrust the tip of my cock past them.

She sucks me like a fucking popsicle. But as good as it might feel, I need more.

I know what she's capable of and I need it all right fucking now.

Fisting her hair, I hold her still as I fuck her mouth.

She takes everything I give her, gagging on my length as it hits the back of her throat.

Tears spill from her eyes as she fights to suck in the air she needs as her nails dig into my ass so hard that I won't be surprised to find she's broken the skin when I care to look.

I don't let up until she's swallowed everything I have, and only then do I pull her away from me.

"Fuck, you're a little bit too good at that."

With my hands around her waist, I throw her further up the bed. Her head collides with the headboard but she doesn't complain as I crawl onto her and drag my teeth down the length of her leg until I latch onto the soft skin of her thigh and suck and bite until I break the skin, tasting the copper of her blood.

Her nails scratch at my shoulders, her fingers pull at my hair to try to get me to release her but I don't.

My need to mark her, to make her mine consumes me.

When I finally release her, she's got an angry red mark on her thigh and my chest swells with pride and ownership.

Mine.

I trace it with my finger, collecting up the small amount of blood from where I broke the skin.

Her fingers tighten in my hair once more until she's tugs with such force I've no choice but to fall over her and take her lips.

Our kiss is brutal as we fight for dominance.

I can taste myself on her lips and I've no doubt she can taste herself on me.

Our tongues duel and our teeth collide as we devour each other, our chests heaving for oxygen but we both refuse to let up. Finally, after she sinks her teeth into my bottom lip, I pull back.

"Fuck, you're everything." I don't mean for the words to spill from my lips.

Her eyes widen in shock as she registers what I just said.

In my need to distract her, I wrap her legs around my waist and rub my cock through her folds.

"Kane, please," she begs as I push the tip in. "I need—"

"I know," I bark, forcing myself to hold back, to tease her some more but finding it increasingly hard to fight my need for her.

"Fuck," I growl before thrusting forward and filling her completely.

"C-condom, Kane."

I look up from where we're connected.

"I'm clean."

"And I don't fucking believe you."

"Don't you think it's a bit late. I've already taken you once tonight."

"Don't care."

The panic written all over her face is enough to have me pulling out of her and reaching for the top drawer of my nightstand.

In record time, I have the rubber down my length and am guiding myself back into her velvet heat.

"Better?"

She nods as her eyes roll back in pleasure.

I know she's close, I can read it on every inch of her but she's following my orders for once and not letting herself fall.

Part of me wants to know why she's not defying me like usual, but the other part really doesn't give a fuck while I'm deep inside her pussy.

I fuck her like a man possessed and she matches me move for move.

Her nails scratch while my teeth nip. Our chests heave, our skin red with each other's brutal touch and flushed with sweat.

"Fuck, Princess. Fuck," I bark, flipping her over and slamming my palm down on her ass cheek.

She screams so loud that there's no doubt to everyone in this house, and possibly the house on either side has to know what's going on right now.

Lifting her up on her knees, I take her from behind, slamming into her over and over.

With her hair wrapped around my fist, I tug harshly, forcing her to arch her back so I can hit her deeper.

"Kane, Kane, Kane," she cries, her pussy squeezing me impossibly tight.

Reaching around her, I pinch her clit hard and she detonates.

Her entire body convulses with her release as she milks my own from me.

"Fuuuuuck," I groan as my cock jerks and my body collapses on top of hers.

I pin her to the bed beneath me as I try to catch my breath.

"Fuck, Princess."

"I guess I should leave now," she says, shocking the shit out of me.

"No fucking chance."

I lift back up, flip her over and straddling her body so she can't hide from me.

Taking my weight on one hand, I wrap my other around her throat. Her muscles ripple as she swallows and I let my gaze drift down her body.

She's covered in bite marks, hickeys, and scratches. A smile curls at my lips knowing that I put them all there. My cock swells for more.

When I get back up to her face, my eyes lock on her swollen lips.

"We're not fucking done yet," I warn before diving for them.

We're not done until she has no choice but to think of me every time she moves, every time she looks at any inch of her body.

I am going to fucking own her.

22

LETTY

My body aches but it's soon forgotten when Kane's fingers pinch my clit and I tumble over the edge once again.

For someone who started the night refusing to let me fall, he now seems obsessed with how many times he can make me come.

His cock jerks inside me, once again in a condom. His hand tightens on the tender flesh of my throat and his arm around my waist holds me against his chest, allowing me to feel his heaving breaths.

"Fuck," he pants, pulling out of me and throwing the condom out of the shower.

The water rains down on both of us, washing away the sweat of the past few hours.

When he said he wanted to ruin me, he wasn't fucking joking.

I can barely feel my legs. I've no idea how I'm holding myself up right now, and I really have no clue as to how I'm supposed to walk back to his bed.

I can honestly say that I've never been so totally fucked.

Figuratively and literally, because something tells me that no one else is ever going to be able to give me what he just did.

I'm becoming addicted to every single one of his vicious touches and his brutal words.

I'm like a fucking junkie waiting for their next hit, craving the unknown, a part of me is about to sing with a delicious mix of pain and pleasure, what barbed, dirty words he's going to say to me next.

Part of me wonders if I'm allowing this because deep down I know I deserve it.

I've kept something huge from him and I deserve his wrath even if he still has no clue about what happened.

Guilt swamps me as the coolness of his shower gel coats my breasts.

"Kane," I whimper as he plucks at my sore nipples before running his hands over my stomach and down to my pussy.

It's swollen and so tender but as he touches me, my stomach still clenches and liquid lust fills my core, ready for more.

"I could fuck you all night long," he groans in my ear.

"Careful, you sound like you're beginning to enjoy it a little too much," I whisper back.

"You've no idea how much I enjoy fucking you over, Princess. It's been a long time coming."

Once he's happy we're clean enough, he flips off the shower and steps out, passing me a towel only a few seconds later.

We're on weird territory here.

It's been a lot of years since we were able to be in a

room together without throwing insults at each other. It's why I expected him to ruin my plans and send me away the second he'd finished with me.

Yet, I'm still here. And he just washed me as if he... as if he actually... cares?

No. He's just proving that deep down under it all there is actually a hint at a decent human being.

"You want a drink?" he asks when I manage to finally get back to his bedroom on shaky, weak legs.

"Um... yeah. Water would be great."

He nods once before disappearing through the door, his body still bare bar the towel around his waist.

The second the door closes behind him, I feel cold.

The room is pretty bare, just a couple of pieces of furniture and a pile of clothes ready for laundry. It doesn't look like he's really moved in yet.

It makes me wonder if he's actually planning on sticking around.

Him being here, getting into college and being accepted onto the team is... surprising.

Is it actually all for real or just a scheme on Victor's part to get something he wants?

The thought makes me shudder.

I really want to think that this really is Kane trying to make something of his life, but while he's connected to that asshole, I guess anything is possible.

He's certainly the only reason Devin is here. No offense to Devin, he's a half-decent guy—family connections aside—but he's not exactly college material.

Walking over to the dresser, I stop and look at the one personal thing in this room. It's a framed photo of Kane, Kyle, and their parents. They're all in the yard at their trailer in Harrow Creek. Looking at how old they both are, I'd say it wasn't taken too long before they both died.

My heart aches for them both. No child should lose one parent, but both at the same time in the same fatal collision. Devastating.

I run my fingertip over a young teenage Kane, wondering if this was the turning point in him changing. The catalyst from where his anger and hate grew. Hell knows that he was pretty easygoing prior to this.

Footsteps heading my way, force me to back up from the image. There might be a part of me that enjoys the angry side of him, but I'm exhausted. I'm not sure I can handle any more of him. Plus, I'm quickly growing quite fond of the softer side of him.

"Here," he says, passing a bottle to me.

The air turns awkward. I should have got up and left before he dragged me into the shower. This right now, this isn't what we do.

He places his own bottle on the nightstand, drops the towel around his waist, giving me a shot at his toned ass before he jumps into bed.

I need to leave, I should leave, but as I glance at my purse that's got the cameras from Victor inside, I know that I can't. I need to stay until I get a shot at planting them.

Nerves race through me.

"What's wrong?" he asks and I'm powerless but to look at him.

He's lying on his side, elbow on the pillow and his head resting on his palm. The sheets are pooled low on his waist, barely covering him and I wonder if he did that on purpose.

He knows I like his body. Hell, after the past few hours there's no way he can't know.

His skin is covered in deep gouges and scratches from my nails along with bite marks and hickeys.

My cheeks burn as I think about the animal he turns me into.

I didn't look at myself in the mirror in the bathroom, I was too scared to face what was going to look back at me, but I know I look like I've been locked in a cage with a lion, I feel it.

"W-why haven't you kicked me out?" I don't mean to ask the question but it falls from my lips without instruction from my brain.

He shrugs as if it's no big deal.

I stand there in the middle of his bedroom with the bottle of water in my hand and only wearing a towel feeling more awkward than I have in my entire life.

"Walk out if you want, but I'm not giving you a lift back to the dorms now."

"Uh..."

"Or just get the fuck in bed and go to sleep."

"Y-you want me to sleep in your bed?" I ask, my eyes as wide as saucers.

"Stop overthinking, Princess. I still hate you."

"G-good. Me too. Hate you, I mean."

"Wouldn't expect anything less."

"C-can I wear one of your—"

"No," he interrupts.

"N-no?"

"Naked or nothing."

I consider my options but in the end, the decision is taken out of my hands.

The towel is ripped from my body, the bottle in my hand crashes to the floor and I'm dragged into bed.

"Sleep," he demands. "Or I'll fuck you again."

The latter is certainly tempting but I know it's time I shut this shit down and start closing the lid on the little box I've shoved Kane and all this bullshit inside.

I just need to wait for him to fall asleep, do what I need to do and then get the hell out.

I awake with a start, my heart thundering in my chest as I look around the dark room trying to figure out where I am.

Memories hit me one after another.

The hood of my car. His bed. The shower.

Fuck.

None of that should have happened, but I know I'm the reason it did.

I set this up.

His muscular arm pins me to him.

He's holding me.

Kane fucking Legend is holding me in his sleep.

Even though I know it's true. That I can feel his hard body against mine. I find it hard to believe.

What I do know is that I need to get the fuck out of here.

Twisting my head, I glance up at his alarm clock.

Three a.m.

The house sounds like it's in silence.

It's now or never.

Lifting his arm slowly, I slip out from beneath him.

The second I'm gone, he pulls the pillow I was laying on into his body.

The sight has a lump crawling up my throat.

He doesn't look like the angry, hate-filled Creek boy in his sleep. He looks softer, vulnerable, and it makes me wonder who Kane really is underneath the bad boy image.

But I don't have time to stand here and figure it out, instead, I quickly gather up my clothes and purse before slipping from the room and praying that the hallway is empty and I'm not about to flash any of the Harris brothers.

I tug my still slightly damp clothes on in record time before rushing down the stairs.

Pulling the small cameras from my purse, I use the flashlight on my cell to look around the room for ideal places to hide them. He said he wanted to hear what they are up to, not that he wanted to see, so I use that to my advantage and start placing them around the living area.

Behind the TV. Under the wireless speaker. On the coffee machine.

I make quick work of securing them in places I really hope won't be spotted too easily and before I have a chance to overthink it, I rush from the house, silently closing the door behind me and all but jogging down the street as I call for an Uber.

My muscles burn as I move to remind me of what went down last night.

Did I expect that?

Yeah, I guess I did. Might have had something to do with why I was wearing one of my shortest skirts and tiny panties.

By the time I get back to my dorm, I can barely keep

my eyes open. But I don't crawl into bed until I've had another shower. A shower that will wash him off of me and out of my head.

Still, I refuse to look in the mirror. I can't deal with that right now.

I'll worry about it in a few hours when I need to head to class.

With my hair still dripping wet, I pull on a tank and pair of boy shorts and all but crawl into bed.

Every single inch of me aches. The bite marks on my thighs and chest sting from my shower gel but I can't help getting hot just thinking about them.

Fucking Kane.

He told me he wanted to ruin me. I didn't think it was possible seeing as he already had a hand in shattering me before, but I fear he might just have accomplished what he set out to because there's no chance of me forgetting tonight.

It's like he knows exactly what I need, what my perverted mind craves and he gives it all to me and more.

I think of Luca and Leon.

Why couldn't it have been one of them to stir whatever this is inside me? To sate the twisted needs I have.

Why'd it have to be Kane fucking Legend?

The boy who wants to ruin me for everyone else.

The boy who hates me more than anyone else.

The boy I've been lying to for well over a year.

A single tear slips from my eyes as I think about everything he lost but has no idea he was ever going to have.

When my alarm goes off the next morning, I can barely move.

With a groan, I let my arm hang off the bed in the hope I can reach my purse and silence my cell.

I can't.

"Fucking hell," I mutter, rolling out of bed to find it on the floor by the door where I abandoned it when I finally got in last night.

I turn the alarm off and crawl back into bed, telling myself that I'll have ten minutes.

When I wake again, it's to the sound of Ella knocking and calling out my name.

Scrambling to grab my cell, I find that an hour and a half has passed and that I really need to leave for class.

"Fuck. Fuck," I bark.

"Letty, are you ready?"

"No," I call back. "Go without me."

"Is everything okay?"

"Uh..." I hesitate, trying to come up with an excuse. I can hardly tell her the truth. She'll want to have me committed. "I'm not feeling great. I'm not sure I'm going to make it in."

"Is there anything I can do?" she asks, not even questioning my lie.

I smile to myself. I've really landed on my feet here with these guys.

"No, I'm just going to sleep it off."

"Okay. If you want me to pick you anything up or whatever just call me, yeah?"

"I will, thank you."

"Feel better soon," she says softly before her footsteps disappear and the dorm falls quiet.

Rolling onto my back, I blow out a long breath.

He'll have woken up and found me gone by now. Will he have cared that I crept out in the night? Will he have been relieved that we didn't need to do the awkward morning after when he remembered just how much he hates me and kicked me out on my ass? Or worse, have they found the cameras yet?

Victor said that Ellis has the equipment to trace them. How often does he do that? Is them getting bugged such a threat that he does it every morning?

My hands tremble and my heart races as I consider all the options. None of which end well for me. Either Victor will get me for failing this job and follow through with his threats to my family, or the brothers will give him the intel he wants and they'll figure out I was the one who allowed it to happen.

Either way, I'm fucked and I'm pretty sure Victor knew that.

Asshole.

I lie there contemplating life for the longest time. I don't need to look at the clock to know that class has started because my cell starts pinging.

Lifting it from the bed, I find Luca's name staring back at me.

Luca: Ella said you're not well? Are you okay?

I smile at this concern. It's sure more than I've got from the man who put me in this state.

Letty: Yeah, just not feeling great. Spending the day in bed. Take notes for me later?

Luca: Always. Feel better soon. You feel like a visitor later, let me know.

Letty: Thank you x

It would be so easy to ask him to come and make me feel better but I know I can't. I can't drag him any farther into this than he already is.

This is my mess and it's time to put an end to it once and for all.

These stolen moments with Kane might be fun but I already know that I'm going to be the one hurting at the end of it.

He's playing a game and the more time we spend together, the more I'm starting to feel things I shouldn't.

I'm starting to need him, crave him, and that really, really needs to not happen.

It's long past lunch by the time I drag my ass out of bed, preferring to hide from reality under my covers, but I know I can't disappear from life forever.

Although the second I turn toward my sink to brush my teeth and I glance at myself in the mirror I wish I could.

"Fucking hell."

I look like I've been mauled by a wild animal. I guess I was.

Lifting my hand, I run my fingers over the red angry bruises that cover my throat. If I didn't know better, I'd think he was trying to kill me.

I drop lower to the hickeys that cover my chest and all the way down to an actual bite mark hiding just below the neckline of my tank.

I bend slightly, looking at my thighs. Bruised

fingerprints darken the skin before I find my Kane Legend brand.

Well, if he was intending to stop me from being with anyone else then I think he's probably achieved it. Fucking caveman.

I stare back at myself. My eyes are dark and swollen from lack of sleep and my lips still swollen from his kiss.

I made the right move not going to class.

If Luca or Leon saw me like this, well... I dread to think what would happen next.

"**G**et the fuck out of my way," I bark, shoving against Luca's chest when he lingers in the locker room doorway, stopping me from escaping after our morning training session.

I'm pissed. Really fucking pissed. And he's staring at me like he's ready to go a round or two.

Bring it fucking on, QB1.

I'd love nothing more than to fuck up your arm and screw up your fucking season.

I knew suggesting she stayed was a fucking mistake but the sex and the sheer number of orgasms affected my brain and for some reason, I thought it was a good idea.

Then I woke up this morning with a raging hard-on and craving another round before training to find I was alone.

She fucking bolted in the middle of the night while I was passed out next to her.

That is not fucking cool.

I fucking rescued her when no one else could come to her aid and she just fucks off the second I close my eyes.

I have no idea if she even fell asleep or just bolted the second I started snoring.

I shouldn't care.

I fucking hate her.

But fuck. I want inside her again.

"For someone who clearly got laid last night, you're in a bitch of a mood, Legend," Luca mocks, his eyes dropping to the scratch marks down my cheek and neck.

I don't even remember at what point she clawed at me like a fucking cat but hell if it didn't make me hard looking at the marks she left on my body this morning.

I can only imagine how she looks.

A smirk curls at my lips.

I can't fucking wait to look in her eyes and demand to know why she left.

It certainly wasn't because she didn't fucking enjoy herself.

"Jealous, Dunn?" I ask with a smirk.

"Fuck you, I don't want your cheap little whores."

"You sure about that?" I take a step forward, getting right in his face. "She was fucking wild, man. I guess you wouldn't be able to handle her."

"Fuck you," he spits, getting so close his chest almost brushes mine.

"Dunn, stand down," the quarterback coach calls when he spots us about to get into it.

Luca holds my eyes for two more seconds before he shakes his head and takes a step back.

"You're fucking lucky I need you."

I laugh at him.

"You're a fucking pussy, Dunn."

He flips me off and trails after the coach, leaving me

to shower and dress without the threat of taking him down.

I crack my knuckles as I head for the shower.

"You need to stop baiting him," a voice says from behind me.

"Oh yeah. Why am I not surprised you think that?" I ask, turning on the other Dunn twin.

"He's your fucking captain. I don't give a shit what the fuck is going on off of the field. But here, practice, training, games. You need to keep yourself in fucking line."

"Whatever." I wave him off, dragging my shirt over my head and stuffing it into my bag.

"No, not what—fucking—ever, Legend. You're here because you want to play. You want to win. You want a fucking championship just like the rest of us, so start fucking acting like it."

"Fucking hell, you sucking off Coach or something?" I mutter, marching toward the shower.

"What the fuck did you just say?"

My back collides with the tiles before Leon's fist connects with my jaw.

"Motherfucker." I launch back at him but hands wrap around my upper arms the second I leave the wall.

"Enough," someone barks, but I don't look back, my eyes are locked on Leon's.

"You want to keep your place on this team, your scholarship? You need to get in fucking line."

Grabbing his bag, he stalks out of the locker room.

"Get the fuck off me."

When I spin around, I find Zayn and the two guys who live with Letty.

I level them all with a look and not one of them says

anything, although I can practically hear Zayn's warning that I'm sure is on the tip of his tongue.

Marching past them, I continue toward the shower. There's no fucking way I'm going to be late to class and miss watching her walk in.

As planned, there are only a few nerds already in the auditorium when I get there with my takeout coffee.

I make my way up to one of the seats in the shadows at the back and wait.

But as the room begins to fill and she doesn't show, I start to get the feeling that something's wrong.

The two guys from the locker room appear without her, and when the professor appears, I start to think that she's not going to show.

Is it because of me?

I slouch down in my chair, trying to imagine what her body looks like this morning.

I bet it's fucking beautiful with all the marks and bruises I left on her.

Letty doesn't show her face all day and my cell remains quiet.

Part of me is itching to message her and demand to know why she left in the middle of the night and why she's not in class, but there's a bigger part that wants to leave her on edge.

She's going to be waiting for me to turn up to demand answers and I'm more than happy to leave her stewing.

Luca is surprisingly calm as we run plays during our afternoon sessions and I wonder exactly what the quarterback coach threatened him with earlier to put him in line.

I know he's still pissed, I see it in his eyes whenever he pins me with a look to silently make demands.

I might accept that on the field. Leon was right, he is our captain and our starting quarterback, but he needs to think again if I'll follow his fucking orders the second we step off this field.

I've no idea if he suspects the scratches he pointed out earlier and Letty's absence today are linked or not, but the fact he's not said anything about it makes me think he's either not put two and two together or that he's trying to convince himself it can't be true.

Either is fine by me.

But the time is coming when the truth is going to come out and I'm not entirely sure where that's going to leave us.

He's meant to be in charge. The one ensuring our team works effectively and all that shit, and he's going to find himself right in the middle of the tension. Leon too.

If it comes down to it, I know Coach will back them over me. But he won't do it easily. Leon and I are by far the best wide receivers this team has. Everyone knows they'd be leaving too much up to chance if they go into the season with someone else on the offense.

My need to see her finally gets the better of me when I drop down into my car after practice.

I'm fucking starving, but that's going to have to wait.

I'm not missing a chance at seeing her while I'm still on campus.

I start my car and just about to throw it in drive when my cell starts ringing.

Pulling it from my pocket, I find Devin's name staring back at me.

"Yeah?" I bark, preparing to hear that we've got another fucking job despite the fact I'm supposed to be done.

"You need to come back to the house. Now."

"Why? What's going on?"

"Just get your ass here now."

"Right. Fine. I'm just leaving."

Throwing my cell down in the center console, I spin my tires out of the parking lot right as Luca and Leon emerge from the entrance. Flipping them the bird as I pass, I head home to find out what the fuck is going on.

All three of their cars are parked out the front of the house, which is unusual for this time of day.

"What's going on?" I ask as I walk into the living area to find Ezra and Ellis on the couch with concerned expressions on their faces while Devin paces back and forth.

"Look," Devin spits, pointing at something on the coffee table.

"What's that?"

"Hidden cameras?"

"What? Who would do that? Victor?"

"Funny, we were going to ask you the same thing."

"Me? I didn't fucking plant them. If I wanna know some shit, I'll ask you."

"We didn't mean you, asshole," Ezra spits.

"Okay so—"

"Your girl," Devin mutters.

"Scarlett? Nah, she wouldn't..."

"Was she still here when you woke this morning?"

"Uh..."

"And why was she even here, Kane? You fucking hate her."

Realization dawns and my body tenses in anger as it begins to burn up.

No, no she wouldn't.

I really try to convince myself that those words are true, but I already know they're not.

Last night was a fucking stunt. She fucking played me.

"She's going to fucking pay for this," I promise the others as I swipe a few of the cameras from the table and retrace my steps from only minutes ago.

By the time I pull up in the parking lot behind Letty's, I'm more than ready to unleash hell on her.

What the fuck was she thinking?

I'm out of the car and halfway up the stairs before I've even taken a breath.

I don't stop to think about her roommates, I wrench the main door open and storm through.

"What the—"

There is a guy and girl I don't recognize at the dining table. Both stare at me with their mouths gawping as I march through their space.

"Do you mind?" the girl snaps but I don't so much as look her way.

"Shut the fuck up and mind your own business."

I'm pretty sure she's more stunned than following orders but she doesn't say anything else as I come to a stop outside Letty's door.

"Princess, open this fucking door."

My fists rain down on the chipped blue paint, the entire thing rattling under my force.

Nothing.

"Open this fucking door, Scarlett, or I'll kick it the fuck in."

"You need to leave," a weak voice says from behind me.

When I look over my shoulder, I notice that the guy has grown a pair of balls and is attempting to stand up to me.

"Fuck off."

Ignoring him, I go back to Letty's door until I hear the unmistakable click of a lock.

Not a second later does the door open.

My palm slams down on it, forcing it to swing wide open, Letty just about manages to jump out of the way in time to save her from going flying across the room.

"Shall we call Luca?" the girl screams as I barge inside Letty's room.

"No, everything is fine," Letty calls back. "Just leave it, yeah?"

Fuck knows what the pair of them think but I don't give a shit. I'm not here for them.

"You left," I state, stalking toward her, wrapping my hand around her throat and continuing until her back collides with the wall with a thud, the air rushing from her lungs in shock. "I woke up and you were fucking gone. Why?" I get right in her face, my increased breaths mixing with hers.

Her eyes are wide as she stares at me. She looks terrified and it makes my cock hard.

"Why, Princess?"

"I-I just thought it would be b-better not to do the awkward morning."

"Bullshit. Fucking bullshit. You're such a fucking liar,

Hunter. Has anything that's ever come out of your mouth been the truth?"

"I haven't lied to you, Kane." But as she says the words, something flashes in her eyes.

"Lies," I spit. "Fucking lies."

"What did I ever do to you, Letty? I fucking wanted you. Just fucking you and you chose him," I hiss, my fingers tightening on her throat, but at no point does she try to stop me.

Because she knows she's guilty, a little voice says in the back of my head, but even still I pray that I'm wrong. That she's not the deceitful liar she's turning out to be.

"You chose him and then you fucking killed him."

My hands tremble and there's no way she misses the reaction.

Releasing her before I squeeze even fucking harder and do something that I'll forever regret, I take a massive step back.

Lifting my hands to my hair, I sweep it back from my brow and pull at the lengths until it hurts.

"I didn't kill Riley, Kane, and you fucking know it. What he did... it was an accident."

"You broke his heart. It's your fault," I seethe, turning back to her and pinning her to the spot with my death stare.

"It's not my fault he got in his car drunk, Kane. He was his own person with his own mind."

"You should have stopped him."

"How?" She throws her arms up in despair. "He wasn't drunk when he left me. How the hell was I supposed to know what was going to happen. I'm not fucking psychic."

My chest heaves as I stare at her. I know she's right.

I've always known that, but it's easier to pin his death on her and hate her for it than to accept the truth.

"He fucking loved you," I bellow.

Her shoulders slump in acceptance.

"He always loved you, why do you think I let him have you?"

"You let him? How fucking big of you."

A growl rips up my throat. "It should have been me," I bellow.

"But you fucked up and I chose him. What the fuck are you going to do about it now? You going to hurt me, punish me. Get your sweet fucking revenge so you can sleep at night. Well, newsflash, asshole." She lifts her shorts and exposes her upper thighs to me. "You're too fucking late. You've already done all of that. So what's next?"

Tension crackles between us as I stand immobile, staring at the bruises I caused.

For the briefest moment, I feel bad for hurting her, for marking her. But then I remember why I'm really here and I forget all about being a decent human being.

"'Tell me the fucking truth, Princess?" I calm my voice and drop my tone. "Why did you run this morning? And think very carefully about your answer."

She stares at me, her eyes narrowed trying to read me.

"You already know," she states, calmer than I want her to.

I want her to fight, to scream, to tell me that I'm wrong. But she's not. Because she's fucking guilty.

A roar rips from my throat before my fist collides with the wall beside her head.

She lets out a squeal of shock but she doesn't move as

I stand, staring down at her, waiting to hear the words from her lips.

"Why? Why the fuck would you do that?" I ask quietly, searching her eyes for the truth.

"You ruined my life, Kane." Her voice is so calm, void of the anger from a few moments ago. Her mood change damn near gives me whiplash. "Why wouldn't I?"

"You left. You fucked off to Columbia. How the hell did I have any effect on your life? You turned your back on all of us, walked away from Riley's memory and got on with your life."

A laugh falls from her lips but she's anything but amused.

"You want to know what happened? You really want to know?"

"Yes, I fucking want to know. What went so wrong that you had to leave your beloved Columbia and slum it here with us."

"You happened, Kane," she seethes, her anger resurfacing.

Resting my forearms on either side of her head, I stare down at her waiting for her to fill in all the fucking gaps.

"That night at the party..." She sucks in a breath as if she needs to find the strength to say the words. "You fucking got me pregnant, you asshole."

It takes three long seconds for her words to settle in my brain and when they do, I back up.

"W-what?" I stutter, still not believing those words just fell from her lips.

"You. Got. Me. Fucking. Pregnant," she spits like she's talking to an idiot.

I rip my eyes from hers and look down at her belly.

"B-but—"

My mind races as I try to put everything together. The party was... the party was like... eighteen months ago.

A year and a half.

Pregnant.

Baby.

"Where's my baby, Letty?" The words sound wrong coming out of my mouth.

A sob erupts from her as her hand lifts to cover her mouth, her eyes filling with tears.

"Scarlett, where is my fucking baby?"

I take a step back toward her, my fists curled and my muscles tight.

"G-gone," she whispers, her tears finally dropping as she says the word.

"Gone?"

"I'm sorry. I'm so sorry."

A red haze descends as I stare at her, refusing to hear the words she's saying as fury spreads through my veins like poison.

"You killed my fucking kid?"

"What?"

I take a step back and then another, knowing that if I don't put some fucking space between us right now, then I'll squeeze the fucking life out of her.

"You killed my best friend. You left me. Then you killed my fucking kid?" I roar.

Blood rushes past my ears at such speed that I can't hear my own voice.

Everything is a blur. Nothing makes sense.

I'm vaguely aware of my name being screamed as I take off. I run through her dorm and fly down the stairs in my need to escape.

My entire body trembles as I stumble from the

building, colliding with some other students as I run around the corner toward my car.

I hear her voice but I've no idea if it's in my head or if she's actually following me. All I know is that I must leave. I need to get away from her, from the truth, from the pain, from the betrayal, the lies, the deception.

The second I'm in my car, I start the engine and floor the accelerator.

I don't see my surroundings, I don't register the stoplights or the intersections or the other cars.

I just drive.

I know where I'm heading without even thinking about it.

But as I turn the corner before the entrance to Hallie's, I take the corner too wide and end up nose to nose with a truck.

Horns blast and tires squeal before the sound of crumbling metal surrounds me and everything goes black.

Letty and Kane's story continues in
The Deception You Weave

ABOUT THE AUTHOR

Tracy Lorraine is a *USA Today* and *Wall Street Journal* bestselling new adult and contemporary romance author. Tracy has recently turned thirty and lives in a cute Cotswold village in England with her husband, baby girl and lovable but slightly crazy dog. Having always been a bookaholic with her head stuck in her Kindle, Tracy decided to try her hand at a story idea she dreamt up and hasn't looked back since.

Be the first to find out about new releases and offers. Sign up to my newsletter here.

If you want to know what I'm up to and see teasers and snippets of what I'm working on, then you need to be in my Facebook group. Join Tracy's Angels here.

Keep up to date with Tracy's books at
www.tracylorraine.com

ALSO BY TRACY LORRAINE

Falling Series

Falling for Ryan: Part One #1

Falling for Ryan: Part Two #2

Falling for Jax #3

Falling for Daniel (A Falling Series Novella)

Falling for Ruben #4

Falling for Fin #5

Falling for Lucas #6

Falling for Caleb #7

Falling for Declan #8

Falling For Liam #9

Forbidden Series

Falling for the Forbidden #1

Losing the Forbidden #2

Fighting for the Forbidden #3

Craving Redemption #4

Demanding Redemption #5

Avoiding Temptation #6

Chasing Temptation #7

Rebel Ink Series

Hate You #1

Trick You #2

Defy You #3

Play You #4

Inked (A Rebel Ink/Driven Crossover)

Rosewood High Series

Thorn #1

Paine #2

Savage #3

Fierce #4

Hunter #5

Faze (#6 Prequel)

Fury #6

Legend #7

Maddison Kings University Series

TMYM: Prequel

TRYS #1

TDYW #2

TBYS #3

TVYC #4

TDYD #5

TDYR #6

TRYD #7

Knight's Ridge Empire Series

Wicked Summer Knight: Prequel (Stella & Seb)

Wicked Knight #1 (Stella & Seb)

Wicked Princess #2 (Stella & Seb)

Wicked Empire #3 (Stella & Seb)

Deviant Knight #4 (Emmie & Theo)

Deviant Knight #5 (Emmie & Theo)

Deviant Reign #6 (Emmie & Theo)

Ruined Series

Ruined Plans #1

Ruined by Lies #2

Ruined Promises #3

Never Forget Series

Never Forget Him #1

Never Forget Us #2

Everywhere & Nowhere #3

Chasing Series

Chasing Logan

The Cocktail Girls

His Manhattan

Her Kensington

THORN

SNEAK PEEK

CHAPTER ONE
Amalie

"I think you'll really enjoy your time here," Principal Hartmann says. He tries to sound cheerful about it, but he's got sympathy oozing from his wrinkled, tired eyes.

This shouldn't have been part of my life. I should be in London starting university, yet here I am at the beginning of what is apparently my junior year at an American high school I have no idea about aside from its name and the fact my mum attended many years ago. A lump climbs up my throat as thoughts of my parents hit me without warning.

"I know things are going to be different and you might feel that you're going backward, but I can assure you it's the right thing to do. It will give you the time you need to... adjust and to put some serious thought into what you want to do once you graduate."

Time to adjust. I'm not sure any amount of time will be enough to learn to live without my parents and being shipped across the Pacific to start a new life in America.

"I'm sure it'll be great." Plastering a fake smile on my face, I take the timetable from the principal's hand and stare down at it. The butterflies that were already fluttering around in my stomach erupt to the point I might just throw up over his chipped Formica desk.

Math, English lit, biology, gym, my hands tremble until I see something that instantly relaxes me, *art and film studies.* At least I got my own way with something.

"I've arranged for someone to show you around. Chelsea is the captain of the cheer squad, what she doesn't know about the school isn't worth knowing. If you need anything, Amalie, my door is always open."

Nodding at him, I rise from my chair just as a soft knock sounds out and a cheery brunette bounces into the room. My knowledge of American high schools comes courtesy of the hours of films I used to spend my evenings watching, and she fits the stereotype of captain to a tee.

"You wanted something, Mr. Hartmann?" she sings so sweetly it makes even my teeth shiver.

"Chelsea, this is Amalie. It's her first day starting junior year. I trust you'll be able to show her around. Here's a copy of her schedule."

"Consider it done, sir."

"I assured Amalie that she's in safe hands."

I want to say it's my imagination but when she turns her big chocolate eyes on me, the light in them diminishes a little.

"Lead the way." My voice is lacking any kind of

enthusiasm and from the narrowing of her eyes, I don't think she misses it.

I follow her out of the room with a little less bounce in my step. Once we're in the hallway, she turns her eyes on me. She's really quite pretty with thick brown hair, large eyes, and full lips. She's shorter than me, but then at five foot eight, you'll be hard pushed to find many other teenage girls who can look me in the eye.

Tilting her head so she can look at me, I fight my smile. "Let's make this quick. It's my first day of senior year and I've got shit to be doing."

Spinning on her heels, she takes off and I rush to catch up with her. "Cafeteria, library." She points then looks down at her copy of my timetable. "Looks like your locker is down there." She waves her hand down a hallway full of students who are all staring our way, before gesturing in the general direction of my different subjects.

"Okay, that should do it. Have a great day." Her smile is faker than mine's been all morning, which really is saying something. She goes to walk away, but at the last minute turns back to me. "Oh, I forgot. That over there." I follow her finger as she points to a large group of people outside the open double doors sitting around a bunch of tables. "That's *my* group. I should probably warn you now that you won't fit in there."

I hear her warning loud and clear, but it didn't really need saying. I've no intention of befriending the cheerleaders, that kind of thing's not really my scene. I'm much happier hiding behind my camera and slinking into the background.

Chelsea flounces off and I can't help my eyes from following her out toward *her* group. I can see from here that it consists of her squad and the football team. I can also see the longing in other student's eyes as they walk past them. They either want to be them or want to be part of their stupid little gang.

Jesus, this place is even more stereotypical than I was expecting.

Unfortunately, my first class of the day is in the direction Chelsea just went. I pull my bag up higher on my shoulder and hold the couple of books I have tighter to my chest as I walk out of the doors.

I've not taken two steps out of the building when my skin tingles with awareness. I tell myself to keep my head down. I've no interest in being their entertainment but my eyes defy me, and I find myself looking up as Chelsea points at me and laughs. I knew my sudden arrival in the town wasn't a secret. My mum's legacy is still strong, so when they heard the news, I'm sure it was hot gossip.

Heat spreads from my cheeks and down my neck. I go to look away when a pair of blue eyes catch my attention. While everyone else's look intrigued, like they've got a new pet to play with, his are haunted and angry. Our stare holds, his eyes narrow as if he's trying to warn me of something before he menacingly shakes his head.

Confused by his actions, I manage to rip my eyes from his and turn toward where I think I should be going.

I only manage three steps at the most before I crash into something—or somebody.

"Shit, I'm sorry. Are you okay?" a deep voice asks. When I look into the kind green eyes of the guy in front of me, I almost sigh with relief. I was starting to wonder if I'd find anyone who wasn't just going to glare at me. I know I'm the new girl but shit. They must experience new kids on a weekly basis, I can't be that unusual.

"I'm fine, thank you."

"You're the new British girl. Emily, right?"

"It's Amalie, and yeah... that's me."

"I'm so sorry about your parents. Mom said she was friends with yours." Tears burn my eyes. Today is hard enough without the constant reminder of everything I've lost. "Shit, I'm sorry. I shouldn't have—"

"It's fine," I lie.

"What's your first class?"

Handing over my timetable, he quickly runs his eyes over it. "English lit, I'm heading that way. Can I walk you?"

"Yes." His smile grows at my eagerness and for the first time today my returning one is almost sincere.

"I'm Shane, by the way." I look over and smile at him, thankfully the hallway is too noisy for us to continue any kind of conversation.

He seems like a sweet guy but my head's spinning and just the thought of trying to hold a serious conversation right now is exhausting.

Student's stares follow my every move. My skin prickles as more and more notice me as I walk beside Shane. Some give me smiles but most just nod in my direction, pointing me out to their friends. Some are just downright rude and physically point at me like I'm some fucking zoo animal awoken from its slumber.

In reality, I'm just an eighteen-year-old girl who's starting somewhere new, and desperate to blend into the crowd. I know that with who I am—or more who my parents were—that it's not going to be all that easy, but I'd at least like a chance to try to be normal. Although I fear I might have lost that the day I lost my parents.

"This is you." Shane's voice breaks through my

thoughts and when I drag my head up from avoiding everyone else around me, I see he's holding the door open.

Thankfully the classroom's only half full, but still, every single set of eyes turn to me.

Ignoring their attention, I keep my head down and find an empty desk toward the back of the room.

Once I'm settled, I risk looking up. My breath catches when I find Shane still standing in the doorway, forcing the students entering to squeeze past him. He nods his head. I know it's his way of asking if I'm okay. Forcing a smile onto my lips, I nod in return and after a few seconds, he turns to leave.

THORN and the rest of the ROSEWOOD series are now LIVE.

DOWNLOAD TO CONTINUE READING